The Last Emperor

Peter Monaghan

First Published by New Generation Publishing in 2023

Text Copyright © 2023 Peter E. Monaghan

Cover Design © 2023 Peter E. Monaghan and Mark Lloyd

First Edition

The author asserts the moral right under the
Copyright, Designs and Patents Act 1988
to be identified as the author of this work.
A CIP catalogue record for this book is available from the British Library.

ISBN 978-1-80369-974-5

All Rights Reserved. This work is subject to copyright. No part of this publication may be reproduced, stored in a retrieval system or transmitted, in any form or by any means without the prior consent of the author, nor be otherwise circulated in any form of binding or cover other than that which it is published and without a similar condition being imposed on the subsequent purchaser.

Exempted from this legal reservation are brief excerpts in connection with reviews or scholarly analysis or material supplied specifically by the author for the purpose of being entered and executed on a computer system, for exclusive use by the purchaser of the work.

While the information in this book is believed to be true and accurate at the date of publication, neither the author nor the editors nor the publisher can accept any legal responsibility for any errors or omissions that may be made. The publisher makes no warranty, express or implied, with respect to the material contained herein.

The Last Emperor

Contents.

Introduction

Chapter 1:   Rumours of War

Chapter 2:   Winter Quarters

Chapter 3:   The March

Chapter 4:   The Medway

Chapter 5:   Securing Londinium

Chapter 6:   The Sword in the Stone

Chapter 7:   Securing the Roads

Chapter 8:   The Council of Britannia

Chapter 9:   The New Army

Chapter 10: Icel

Chapter 11: Winnifhoere

Chapter 12: The Gathering Storm

Chapter 13: Badon

Chapter 14: An Emperor

Chapter 15: The Fellow Countrymen

Chapter 16: Theoderic

Chapter 17: The Demetia Campaign

Chapter 18: Glevum and the Settlement of the North

Chapter 19: Dumnonia

Chapter 20: The Government of Britain

Chapter 21: The Years of Peace

Chapter 22: Camlann

Chapter 23: The Aftermath

Glossary and Notes

Acknowledgements

Introduction

There have been very many books purporting to tell the story of King Arthur. In almost all he is depicted as a mediaeval King, the son of a King, surrounded by a court made up of knights and barons. Intrigue and infidelity, love triangles, rebellions and murders figure large in the story. Magic plays a huge part in the tale in which wizards and sorceresses cast spells and make prophecies. Arthur is made King by taking a magic sword from a stone. The story is set in a sort of limbo between Christianity and paganism.

It is a legend of immense power. It has held the imagination of countless generations of people. It is rightly seen as a myth concerning the early days between the passing of the Romans and the coming of the English. Like all myths it deserves study because myths are almost always vehicles of historical truths.

Most historians will admit that King Arthur, or someone very like him, was a real person. He must have been of immense influence or his story would not have been remembered and passed on to be embroidered and made fantastical by much later writers who no longer knew its context nor the history of which his life was an important part.

Much of the traditional tale, as it has come down to us, is the romancing of the troubadours of the twelfth and thirteenth centuries who added many other, later tales, to build a corpus of legends, yet the story stems from the late fifth and early sixth centuries. It is in that context that it must be set and the myth has to be stripped of the accretions of later ages.

Many modern historians opine that Arthur was merely one of many leaders and that his myth is a conflation of all the different tales under one romantic heading. This flies in the face of what we know of the late Roman Empire. The Roman Empire was a centralised and almost totalitarian State. Its people were used to centralised authority and to the layers of Imperial bureaucracy. When the Emperor Honorius told the British cities to organise their own government, in 410, they would have had to put in place something very like the Imperial system - they knew no other.

They faced a very real problem. They had backed the usurper, Constantine

III, who had been acclaimed Emperor by the army of Britain. He was most likely the Comes Britanniarum, the commander of the British field army, and had immediately left for Gaul, almost certainly taking most of his army with him. He may well have taken the troops who garrisoned the south east coastal forts as well. That left only the static border forces of the north in Britain under the Dux Britanniarum. The south was undefended. It was this fact that may have led the British to return their allegiance to the real Emperor, Honorius, hoping for his help. It was not forthcoming; that same year Rome was sacked by the Visigoths.

In this book I have tried to write what might have been. I have tried to put the story in its proper context using what we know of late Roman Britain and late Roman institutions. Although based on History, this is not written as such. Artorius starts out as a cavalry officer. The legends stress his mounted 'knights' and the only mounted warriors in late Roman Britain were the remnants of the cavalry of the Field Army. The only cavalry near to the region of Saxon raids was a detachment of Sarmatian horsemen - heavy cavalry used for shock tactics in battle - stationed at Ribchester or, possibly at Chester after the Irish colonisation of the Lleyn Peninsula in north Wales.

Artorius rises fast in a time of emergency and comes to rule by the acclamation of the army he has led to signal victories. That was nothing unusual in his time. Something of what he did as ruler is remembered. The moving of Marianus from the Lothians to what became Merioneth is a fact that can only be explained by its being the policy of a strong central government in Britain, else he and his tribe would never have been allowed passage by the army at York.

The other characters in the story are also real enough. Vortipor's tombstone proclaims him as 'Protector', a late Roman rank signifying an officer in the Imperial bodyguard. He could hardly have gained such a specific title if there had been no Emperor to protect. Cato of Dumnonia became the Sir Kay of legend. Bedwyr is Sir Bedevere stripped of its French form and put back into a British one. Agricola was the first 'king' in a reconquered Demetia and was father to Vortipor. Marcellus named several places in Wales along the route from Hay on Wye to Porth Mawr and eventually gained a short-lived kingship in Brittany. Gawain has a specifically British name. The mix of Roman and British names locates the tale in the very late Roman Empire.

The majority of the people of fifth century Britannia continued to speak the British Celtic language. Latin was the language of Law and Religion and was the only written language. It was the language of commerce in the Western Empire and the language in urban centres. Many people would have been bilingual but the majority would have used the Celtic tongue in conversation. Names were a hotchpotch of Roman and Celtic names.

There is no Sir Lancelot in this tale. He was almost certainly a late French interpolation into the story. If he lived at all it was in France, possibly in Brittany, and probably much later. Equally there is no tale of Tristram and Yseult. Tristram was the grandson of Cato, Drustan, and plays no part in the story of Arthur.

There is no Merlin either. Merlin, the name meaning 'song thrush', if he existed at all, was no wizard but a bard. His wizardry was with words. Arthur may or may not have employed a bard, but the custom only became a norm after his time and it is likely that, like Lancelot, Merlin is an interpolation into the tale.

We know nothing of Arthur's father. He was likely a cavalryman too, but the surname 'Pendragon' is easily explained. Late Roman heavy cavalry used a standard in the form of a dragon's head with a gaping mouth. To this was attached a long tube of cloth that would stream behind in a charge and make a loud humming noise. These standards probably came with the Sarmatian cavalry in the early third century. The pre-fix 'pen' means 'son of'". If Arthur's father was the 'son of the dragon', it was because he was 'born in the camp', the son of a cavalryman. He might have been the descendant of a standard bearer.

We know nothing of Arthur's place of birth. It was certainly not at Tintagel where archaeology has shown that the earliest settlement was a monastery that was most likely founded after Arthur's time. Recent archaeology has found traces of an even earlier complex that might have been a residence of a local chief with trading links to the Mediterranean but the site lies within the area of Irish colonisation and cannot have been an Arthurian site until after the reconquest of the area which was led by

Cato of Dumnonia.

The Empire into which Arthur was born was in terminal decline. Its permanent division into two halves, East and West, in the fourth century had fatally weakened the West economically at a time when the whole economy was in almost permanent crisis. Barbarian raids and invasions were common in both halves but the East could afford to pay the invaders to go elsewhere, most often to the West. Insecurity was a fact of life.

The only part of the Western Empire that had come through the fourth century intact and relatively undamaged was Britain but civil war and troubles in Gaul had led to Britain being stripped of most of its garrison. Its military establishment was pathetically small at a time when external threats were growing. From having a basic establishment of three legions of six thousand men each, Britain was now left with but one legion of about one thousand men. The rest were small detachments of auxiliaries, most of whom were permanently stationed in the forts along Hadrian's Wall. They probably numbered only a few thousand and were difficult to move.

It is a fundamental error to assume that when the Emperor Honorius told the British cities to organise their own defence, in the year 410, all Roman troops had been immediately withdrawn. All that could have been taken to Gaul had gone long before. The remnants were still trained and professional but too few to give their commander-in-chief any flexibility in their deployment.

It is in this context that the story of Arthur begins. It is the story of a junior officer thrown into a desperate war of survival in which he rises, through sheer ability, to become the great hero who alone is seen as able to secure his people. It is the story of a man who fights to save and restore an age-old civilisation which had actually died by the time he won his final battle.

At the beginning of his rise to power Britain was still wealthy and literate. Within a century after his death it was impoverished and almost totally without literature. Most of the educated men had fled to Brittany, many after Arthur's death, where writing continued but Britain was silent except for the monks in the new monasteries who had gone there to escape the filthy and violent politics of their times. They were more concerned to write the lives of Saints than to record the doings of Kings whom they despised. Most of what we know of these times was written by foreign visitors and some by later Saxon historians, such as St. Bede. Some precious poetry, composed by royal bards, survived in Welsh record but this tells of the fall of the later British kingdoms and says nothing of their origins nor of their debt to King Arthur. The written record of his life is blank. Thus we can only tell his story by inference from what facts we have and by stripping away the obvious additions to his legend which was preserved among the British in Armorica and then embroidered by later troubadours.

It should be noted that most of what is called Welsh mythology is in fact derived from Irish sources and Breton record. Wales had been long absorbed into the Roman Empire and had lost its folk memory. Later Welsh Kings had to fabricate their genealogies using Irish King lists and linking themselves to whichever mythical heroes might add lustre to their dynasties. In Glamorgan the kings named their sons after Arthur. Very little of ancient Welsh record can be taken as factual and thus cannot be relied upon for historical accuracy.

Arthur is often seen as being from Wales or the south west: this is possible but not definite. His memory was perpetuated there after it had been superseded by the Saxon conquest of the rest of what later became England where his memory might have been just as strong or even stronger. He is often used to illustrate lives of Saints who lived well after his death and to substantiate claims to Church lands and exemptions from taxes by monasteries that were not founded while he was alive. His most likely centre of activity was in the lowlands and east and his capital, Camelot, was almost certainly Camulodunum (Colchester).

Wherever possible I have used the Roman names for cities and towns, giving their modern names in parentheses after their first use. I have called Wales by its modern name for the sake of clarity. A glossary and notes are appended.

Chapter 1: Rumours of War

The fort at Deva (Chester) was much as it had always been. The high circuit of walls still stood above the double ditches that defined the military area even though the occupied part of the fort was less than one third of the original. There was still a principium with the images of the Emperor of the West and the standards but the altar at its front was now dedicated to the Christian God. There were the usual rows of neat wooden barrack blocks, five stable blocks and three huge granaries. Men and horses had to be fed. This was the base of the Sarmatian Cavalry, originally posted to Britain during the visit of the Emperor Septimius Severus in the early third century to put down the first major barbarian incursion. They had been moved from their original base at Bremetenacum (Ribchester) so as to be nearer the threat from the Irish who had colonised the Lleyn Peninsula in Wales.

The army was much as it had always been except that, by the fifth century, each unit was smaller. The lack of revenue to Rome had enforced huge cuts in spending and, since the army was by far the largest expense borne by the Government, the axe had fallen most heavily on the military. A Legion was now just over one thousand men instead of the six thousand established by the first Emperor, Augustus. All but one Legion had been withdrawn from Britannia to help prop up usurping Emperors in Gaul or to fight the barbarians who were intent on overrunning that Diocese. All of the other troops in Britannia were auxiliaries and were based in the north along Hadrian's Wall to guard against incursions from the Picts and the Irish. Their Commander-in-chief was the Dux Britanniarum at Eboracum (York). He had the responsibility of holding the line of the great wall built by Hadrian and defending the north-eastern coasts against the Picts who had begun to outflank the wall by sea.

The threat from the Irish to the west was met by small garrisons in the refurbished forts in what would later become Wales and along the Lancastrian and Cumbrian coasts, the Roman Province of Valentia. The Sarmatian Cavalry at Deva were a mobile field reserve for these garrisons. They were comparatively few in numbers and were commanded by a Tribune.

Ever since the beginning of the third century Britannia had been subject to barbarian raids. The worst of these had hit the north. Twice the great barrier of Hadrian's Wall had been overrun by Picts and Irish. Once the Dux Britanniarum had himself been ambushed and killed. Twice Roman Emperors had had to send powerful armies into Britannia to restore order and evict the raiders. The threat remained constant even after the Romans had imposed Roman Prefects to govern the tribes immediately north of the Wall.

The Dux had his hands full and had few men to spare to help guard the south. When the Emperor Honorius told the British cities to look to their own defence against Saxon and Irish raiders the Dux had refused to move his troops and the south had had to raise volunteer forces. The Saxon raiders had soon gone home but many of the Irish had settled in the Lleyn peninsula and in Demetia (modern Pembrokeshire) and also in Dumnonia (modern Devon and Cornwall) where they had established tiny kingdoms.

The new Government of Britannia, formed by the council of the cities, had met this threat by political and military means. With the consent of the Dux at Eboracum it had called Cunedda, the Chief of the Votadini, north of the Wall, to come into Britannia with half his tribe to confront the Irish in north Wales: modern Gwynedd takes its name from him. The Cornovian Cohort of auxiliary infantry was moved from its homeland around Viroconium (Wroxeter) to confront the Irish in Dumnonia and a British bishop named Patricius was allowed to go to Ireland in the hope that, if he could convert the High King, Irish support for the fledgling Irish Kingdoms in Britannia would be withdrawn. There remained the threat of renewed Saxon and Pictish raids into the east.

This was met by the age-old Roman policy of setting one pirate against another. Three ships full of Saxons had come to Britannia (in about 428) seeking employment. Since the Roman fleet had been withdrawn to Gaul, they were allowed to have a base on the Isle of Thanet in return for patrolling the coast to prevent other Saxons and Picts raiding. Their leaders, the brothers Hengest and Horsa, became federates of the Roman Diocese of Britannia. They made themselves useful and with the permission of the Governor, Vortigern, increased their numbers, establishing more bases on the coast of East Anglia and as far north as modern day Northumberland.

Romans in Gaul, surrounded by armed barbarian immigrants and with a broken economy, marvelled at how the British had secured their Diocese almost intact.

It was, however, fragile. The great landowners, those who held the palatial villas in the west country, had paid up to protect their property during the emergency but were unwilling to pay once it was over. Vortigern had to extort taxes from them to pay his federates. When refusal led to civil war in 437, Hengest brought more Saxons to aid Vortigern against Ambrosius the Elder whom the landowners who dominated the Council of Britannia had proclaimed Governor in his place. Hengest gave his own daughter as wife to Vortigern to prove his loyalty. Vortigern won but still found he could not pay Hengest and his now much larger forces. He gave him the whole of Cantium, modern Kent, and ceded what would become Essex and Sussex but this did not satisfy Hengest who rebelled in 441 and advanced on Londinium (London). Seven years of war followed in which Horsa died and which proved that while the Saxons could be beaten in battle they could not be evicted.

A truce was declared and a peace treaty proposed. To conclude it, Vortigern and a hundred of the leading Roman landowners went to Cantium. Hengest entertained them in his great hall and during the banquet had his men kill all but Vortigern. The political leadership of Roman Britannia had perished. Vortigern was no more than Hengest's puppet and the Saxons flooded westwards on a rampage. Villas burned. Thousands of the wealthy fled to Armorica (Brittany) taking many of their tenants and servants with them. The towns held behind their walls but the economy was wrecked.

News of this renewed assault soon reached Deva. At first it was just rumour. The richest men were leaving Britannia and going to Armorica. Londinium (London) was under siege. Saxons had taken most of the land around Lindum (Lincoln). No-one seemed to be doing anything to stop them. More and more Saxons were coming from across the sea to set up new settlements across the midlands.

The first hard news was a letter sent by Ambrosius Aurelianus, newly declared Governor of Britannia, asking for military aid to halt and reverse the Saxon advances. He had requested aid from the Dux, who had declined, saying he needed all his troops to hold the north. All he might spare was the mobile reserve at Deva since Irish raids had virtually ceased. If they were willing to help, Ambrosius could ask them to move further south.

The letter detailed the need for trained cavalry. The Sarmatians were the only trained force available and would be invaluable in training new forces. Ambrosius had the support of the Cornovii but they were infantry and could not move fast enough and were too few to stem the Saxon advances let alone push them back. Cavalry would be invaluable in gaining intelligence: they could be the eyes and ears of the army. Ambrosius was recruiting men as fast as he could but needed professionals to train them. Ambrosius wrote in the first year of his office, 460.

The letter was delivered to the young Tribune, Artorius, who commanded at Deva. He was a youngster of some eighteen years old, tall and athletic. He had already led his men in skirmishes against the Irish and had garnered experience in fighting barbarians. He had the usual scarred thighs of a cavalryman. He read the letter with care and weighed up the consequences of agreeing. He was conscious of his unit's lack of numbers and resources. If he acceded to Ambrosius' request, Deva would be undefended and the forts in the west would lack support. Although very young, he had learned caution. His unit was too small to risk heavy casualties since recruits would be hard to find to replace any losses and it would take much time to train men to equal his experienced troopers.

He wondered what his father would have decided in his place. His father had been a tribune too but had died in a skirmish with Irish raiders when Artorius was just fourteen years old. His mother had been able to finance Artorius' promotion to the Tribunate (in the late Empire promotions were usually bought) and thus he had come to command the Sarmatians. His father had always counselled caution and duty as the best attributes of an officer. He also advised listening to the advice of senior decurions before committing men in action.

Artorius called all the decurions to the praetorium and showed them the letter. "What would you have me do?" he asked. "We are only three hundred men at full strength. We usually have about thirty unfit for duty. We will be facing thousands. If we take many casualties, they will be very difficult to replace and the replacements will be ill-trained and less effective. If we lose horses, and that is very likely, we will find it difficult to get more. I am saying all this so that you know the possible consequences of any hasty decisions. What do you think?"

There was a murmur among the dozen or so men. Then Bedwyr, the senior decurion, spoke. "We could stay here and carry on our normal duties. Ambrosius might stop the Saxons without us. If he should fail and the south and west are overrun, we will be on our own and without our normal supplies. We could not survive very long. If he should succeed, he will not take our refusal to help kindly and might cut off our supplies anyway. The Dux has none to spare for us. I say we should go to Ambrosius to help train his new forces. I say we should help him but on our terms. He must not throw us away in foolhardy attacks. We must retain the right to refuse to fight battles we know we cannot win."

There was a murmur of assent. These were professional soldiers who had a distrust of amateur generals like Ambrosius. He might believe they could work miracles. They knew they could not. They believed, like all soldiers, that theirs was the best unit in the field. They knew their traditions and were unafraid of enemies. What they feared was the incompetence of inexperienced commanders demanding that they attempt the impossible.

"So be it," said Artorius. "We go south. We take everything with us, supplies, spare horses, weapons, armour, forges and tools, the whole hospital - everything. We march to Glevum (Gloucester) and then to wherever Ambrosius has made his base. You have three days to get all ready for the move. If you can manage it in two, we move then."

He trusted Bedwyr. He was a good, solid officer who would never order any of his men to do what he would not. He had a wealth of common sense and was a good thinker. It was not by luck that he had risen to be the senior decurion. The other officers trusted him too. He rarely spoke much but when he did others listened because his words were measured and wise.

The officers left. They were fired up with the prospect of action. The fort became a hive of activity. Wagons were commandeered with oxen to pull them. The armoury was emptied, with suits of mail wrapped in cloth and stowed on wagons alongside swords, bows, arrows, spears and javelins. The granaries were emptied too, their contents going into sacks that were piled high on yet more wagons. Four covered wagons were obtained to transport the sick from the hospital and a fifth for the surgeon and his specialised tools and medicines. Weapons were checked and sharpened and oiled against rust. It took just two days to prepare the move and on the morning of the third Artorius called a full parade of his men. They formed up in their nine turmae of thirty two men each plus their decurions and standard bearers, each standing by his horse.

Artorius stood on the steps of the principium to address them. "We are going to war. We will have to fight an enemy who vastly outnumbers us. We will need to use all our cunning and all our training to have any chance of success. Many of you will be detailed to train new recruits. You will have little time to get them up to standard. We are the only cavalry left in southern Britannia. We must grow our numbers and show the Saxons what we can do. They have no cavalry. They have no horses. We can move faster and further than they can. That is how we will win this war."

He stepped down and mounted his horse. "Mount!" he ordered and the troopers leapt onto their horses and formed a column of march. In front went one turma to act as scouts. Behind came three more with Artorius at their head. Next behind followed the grain wagons and the spare horses and another turma and then the wagons of weapons and tools and those of the hospital. Three turmae brought up the rear. The remaining turma provided a flanking screen to the column. It was an impressive sight. The men were all in full armour, their mail suits glittering in the morning light, their narrow oval shields at their sides and their spears and standards held aloft. Their horses too glittered in the sun. The Sarmatians were heavy cavalry and used armoured horses. They went at a walk. Oxen are slow and the troopers had to adopt their pace. It was going to be a long march.

Artorius watched the first turma trot on ahead and felt quite alone at the head of the column. He had committed his men to war. How many would survive it? Some were married and had children back at Deva. His mother would stay in the care of the nuns. Would they ever see wives and children again? The responsibility weighed heavy. He knew too little. Where were the Saxons? How many were they? Who was this Ambrosius who now governed Britannia? The name, Aurelianus, spoke of a good lineage. He might be a descendant of the Emperor Aurelian, one of the better Roman Emperors. Would he be open to advice? Command was a lonely business.

They passed through open country, the huge fields empty except for stubble and the trees showing the first golden signs of Autumn. It had been a good harvest and all the granaries were full. Men had already begun to burn off the stubble in readiness for ploughing and blue smoke drifted across the fields. Corn-drying ovens were in use, adding their own smoke in pale columns rising into the cool clear air. One tenth of the produce should come to the State as tax but Artorius knew that much would be hidden away by the rich villa owners to avoid paying their proper due. They passed many large villas, each having some four or five thousand acres of land tilled by indentured labourers who lived in the great barns alongside the livestock. In the past these men and women would have been slaves but the advent of Christianity as the official religion had freed them. Even so, they were little better off than their ancestors.

They marched for the best part of a week to reach Glevum, camping at the side of the road each night, with sentries posted all around. Artorius was taking no chances: Saxon raiders could be anywhere and their new settlements had reached as far as the River Avon in the midlands. Caution was the best policy when intelligence was uncertain.

Glevum was a great town sprawled on the bank of the Severn. It had once been the fortress of the Twentieth Legion (long since withdrawn to Gaul) until the frontier moved north and west. Now it was a wealthy city with rich senators and many craftsmen and merchants. It had its own port on the river with quays, warehouses and workshops. The old fortress was at the heart of the city and contained the major public buildings, the basilica, Senate House and Church but it had spread beyond the fort and was ringed by strong walls and bastions. When they arrived they found the gates closed against them. The City Watch were taking no chances. When Artorius demanded passage into the city he was told to wait.

He waited fully two hours before a deputation of senators came out to meet him. They were not keen to have armed men inside the city they said. Artorius and his senior officers were welcome but the troops would have to camp outside the walls. Artorius mentioned that he was there to support Ambrosius Aurelianus, at Ambrosius' request. This cut no ice. His men were not welcome. Ambrosius was not there. He should march east to Sorbiodunum (Old Sarum by Salisbury) where Ambrosius was gathering his army. When Artorius asked for supplies for his men he was refused: the city needed all it had for its own people in case of siege. Artorius was furious but held his anger in check. He thanked the senators for the information, telling them he would report their 'help' to Ambrosius and ordered his column to resume its march.

Artorius could not comprehend the attitude of the senators of Glevum. This was a time of emergency yet they sought only their own safety and were unwilling to support the war effort. He had passed great villas with huge estates, their barns stuffed with grain. Glevum had more than enough and plenty to spare yet would not give a couple of wagon loads of grain for his men and horses. The senators were keen enough that his men should fight the Saxons but would not give anything of their wealth to maintain the army that would fight for them.

It took three more days to reach Sorbiodunum, a small settlement on top of an isolated hill. It had once been a Celtic hill fort and still had its ring of ramparts and its deep ditches. Outside, on the flat land below the hill, were hundreds of tents set in neat lines. Men were marching and counter-marching while others practised with wooden weapons. A larger tent, near the middle of the huge camp, was clearly the headquarters. By its entrance a standard had been set up, a red banner emblazoned with a white boar, the badge of Ambrosius. Artorius ordered his men to pitch camp alongside the rest and went to the big tent with Bedwyr. Two sentries guarded the entrance but allowed Artorius and Bedwyr to pass. They recognised cavalry armour and equipment. Inside, the tent was divided by a screen. In the half near the entrance was a table and sat at it was a clerk. He looked up as they entered.

"What is your business?" he asked.

"We are the Sarmatian cavalry from Deva. We have come in response to an appeal by Ambrosius. We need to see him." Artorius was in no mood to be told to wait or come back tomorrow. The clerk sensed this and rose to open a flap in the screen. He ushered them through.

The other half of the tent was furnished with a camp bed, a large table covered in parchment scrolls with stools set along either side and a single chair at its head in which a middle-aged man sat reading. He was slight of build with piercing eyes and hair greying at the temples. He looked up questioningly as they came in.

"I am the Tribune, Artorius, commanding the Sarmatian cavalry. I have brought my whole command here. They are pitching camp beside your recruits right now. We need to talk."

"Thank God you are here!" said Ambrosius. "All I have here are raw recruits and no cavalry. The Cornovii are on their way from Dumnonia, so I shall have some battle-hardened infantry who can help train more but I have no experienced cavalry. Cavalry I shall need most of all to give me news of where the Saxons are and what they are up to."

Artorius immediately warmed to Ambrosius. This was no jumped-up amateur general but a man who sensed the enormity of the task he faced and had already thought long and hard as to what he needed. "So you want us to act as scouts to keep an eye on the enemy," said Artorius.

"Yes. And also to harass them so that they cannot concentrate forces easily."

"A good strategy. We can do that. What about your new troops here?"

"They need training. When Gerontius and his Cornovii arrive, they will train the infantry. I need someone to train more cavalry. There are many men here who claim they can ride but managing a horse in battle must be a different matter."

Artorius agreed. He knew full well that being able to ride was only the very first step to being a cavalryman. A trooper had to be able to ride in formation. He had to be able to control his horse with his legs alone so as to have both hands free for fighting, one for his shield and one for his weapon. He had to have the confidence to lean sideways from his saddle to strike at enemy infantry with his sword. He had to be disciplined so as to obey trumpet calls instantly and instinctively. He needed to be thoroughly skilled in handling his spear and the long cavalry sword. In addition he needed to be trained in caring for his horse and its equipment - a faulty girth could cost him his life and a sickening horse might founder on a march.

"I have nine turmae of cavalry," he said. "If three are sent out as scouts, the rest can help in the training. I doubt the Saxons will advance any further now that winter is coming. They have few wagons for supplies and there will be nothing for them to forage. They will be busy making themselves homesteads and ploughing for sowing crops. My men can harass their new settlements and vanish. The Saxons have no horses, so we will always be able to outrun and outdistance any pursuit. A few mounted men can do them a lot of mischief and remain safe."

"That is what I was thinking," said Ambrosius. "Meanwhile we must establish a proper base here. You will need stables for your horses and for the remounts I am getting. We need proper granaries and barrack blocks and defences. The Saxons are not good at attacking defended places. A deep ditch and a rampart will be all we need and good, strong gates."

"My men will build the stables," said Artorius. "Yours can dig the ditch and raise the rampart. That will be the start of their training. An infantryman wins wars by digging. Tents will suffice for now. Barrack blocks can be built later. What do your men have in the way of weapons and armour?"

Ambrosius explained that he had blacksmiths who could make spear heads and arrow heads. Some were sufficiently skilled to fashion swords too. He lacked proper armourers. Chain mail could not be got, so he was equipping his men with hardened leather cuirasses doubled over the shoulders. It would take time to equip all the men. Artorius emphasised that helmets were of the greatest importance. The Saxons fought with long swords, spears and axes. An axe could reach over the top of a shield and strike down at the head or shoulders. Leather armour would be too little protection. "If your blacksmiths can turn out small metal disks, you could wire them to the leather and make scale armour. If the disks are overlapped they will be strong enough to block a sword slash and arrows.

My standard bearers wear scale armour. One of their suits could serve as a model."

It had been a good meeting. Ambrosius had deferred to the professional knowledge of the young Tribune and had demonstrated much common sense. Artorius had proved himself co-operative with no hint of arrogance towards a commander who lacked any military experience. A good working relationship was possible. After promising to commence eastward patrols immediately, Artorius left the headquarters tent and returned to his men. Three turmae were detailed to set out as scouts. They were to seek out the nearest Saxons and harass them while sending back regular reports. They were to stay in the field for four weeks and then return to be replaced by another three turmae. They would take spare horses and as much food and fodder as possible without slowing them down. They were to capture what supplies they could from any new Saxon settlements and were to buy from any villas they found that were still occupied.

Ambrosius had given written orders addressed to the Senates and Councils of any towns they visited to grant them shelter and supplies. He had also written a stiff letter to the Senate of Glevum pointing out that, in time of war, the military had prior claim on supplies and in future they would not deny entrance or supplies to his army. If they failed to obey, he could dismiss the Senate and appoint a military Governor in its place. He was not going to be trifled with by a bunch of complacent, over-rich and arrogant Senators.

Three days later the Cornovii arrived. Five hundred infantrymen marched six abreast behind their chief and commander, Gerontius. They were in full armour, their mail chinking and chiming as they marched in perfect step into the camp. They formed in three ranks outside the headquarters tent for Ambrosius' inspection. Gerontius was proud of his cohort. All were Cornovian Britons, and uniquely in the Roman army, they had always served in their home Diocese. Technically they were auxiliaries but the distinction between auxiliaries and legionaries in terms of equipment, training and capability had long disappeared. Beside Gerontius was his son, Cato, a young man in his late teens, whom Gerontius was schooling as the next to command the cohort.

In terms of the late Roman army, this cohort was large. While the army had shrunk over the last two hundred years, the Cornovii had fought to maintain their numbers. It was a tribal tradition for eldest sons to serve in the army and they had maintained their strength. Even the command had become semi-hereditary. Gerontius had followed his father and was now training his son. By the look of the cohort, Gerontius was a good commander.

After the inspection, Ambrosius and Artorius met with Gerontius in the great tent. Gerontius was a short, thickset man with the round head of a Celt. He had piercing blue eyes. "I saw your recruits as I came in," he said. "They are very raw."

"We need time to train them," said Ambrosius. "That is why I need you and your men so much."

"We'll do what we can. You'll need good centurions and optios to make anything of them."

"I have a couple of retired centurions training them at the moment but two are not enough. What do you suggest?" asked Ambrosius.

"Borrow some of my optios and make them centurions in your new army. They'll soon lick your men into shape. They'll not like being transferred out of the Cornovii but there is little else we can do if your men are going to be any good in battle."

"You'll allow that? Won't that weaken your cohort?"

"I can promote replacements. We've time. There will be no battles this winter. Let's spend it getting ourselves an army that can fight."

Thus it was agreed. The Cornovii would provide centurions to the new army and train their men. Artorius and the Sarmatians would train new cavalry. Together they would forge a mobile field army capable of meeting the Saxons and defeating them. Both Gerontius and Artorius knew the difficulties they would face. It was one thing drilling men and practising them in formation and in the use of weapons. It was another throwing them into their first battle and making them kill enemies. Killing for the first time in hand-to-hand fighting is traumatic. That was when discipline might break down.

Despite lack of numbers, the Roman armies of the fifth century were competent and efficient. They were better trained, better equipped and better disciplined than any of their barbarian enemies in the western provinces and their method of fighting, in close order and always with half the men as a reserve, gave them advantage in battle even when faced with much larger enemy forces. They rarely lost major battles. Each man was armoured and had a large oval shield made of strong ply-wood. Their armour and equipment was vastly superior to the padded leather and heavy weapons of their enemies. More importantly, when they fought, they kept their casualties to a minimum while maximising those among their enemies.

Ambrosius decided that both Gerontius and Artorius should have rank commensurate with their responsibilities. Gerontius should be Magister Militum, commander of infantry, and Artorius, Magister Equitum, commander of cavalry, both with the rank of Prefect. "This will rank you equal to any jumped-up senator," he said. "You'll have to deal with them. They are an arrogant lot. Most of them have riches salted away on which they will not pay tax. Most claim to be educated but cannot see how their meanness cripples the Government. All want protection but don't want to pay for it." Ambrosius was himself a senator and knew his class well.

It was the age-old problem. The rich evaded taxes and passed the burden to their tenants. They lived opulent and luxurious lives while their tenants became ever poorer. Any disasters were blamed on the Government that the rich refused to finance. In Armorica the tenants had risen in rebellion and the discontent still simmered with outbreaks of violence even while Gaul was being partitioned by barbarians. In Rome there were still senators who had an annual income of four thousand pounds weight of gold and who paid almost nothing to the State. Rome was a perfect example of the fundamental injustice of unregulated capitalism. It was the super-rich with their ability to evade taxes who had forced the Emperors to debase the coinage, using copper blanks washed in silver or gold, and this had caused galloping inflation. By the fifth century, the poor had abandoned cash in favour of barter. Soldiers were no longer paid in money but received corn, salt and oil instead.

The word 'salary' comes from 'salarium" - a payment of salt.

Chapter 2: Winter Quarters.

The fine weather of late Autumn soon gave way to rain and fog. Life in camp became wet, cold and miserable. The tents were islands in a sea of almost liquid mud and it was difficult to find or keep dry kindling for fires. Training had to halt while wooden barrack blocks were hastily built to keep men healthy and dry. As always, the troops did the work themselves under the direction of any carpenters and builders who had enlisted. Granaries were constructed to keep food supplies dry and safe. These were built on stilts to keep out rats and mice.

By now the base was ringed by a deep ditch and a rampart with four gates built into tall wooden towers. It was like a small town. The new barracks were laid out in straight lines well inside the rampart so as to be out of range of any fire arrows an enemy might shoot into the camp. Duck boards were laid along the roads between the barracks. On top of the rampart was a wooden palisade with a walkway behind for defenders. On the roads that led to the camp picquets were stationed to give advance warning of approaching enemies. The Sarmatians patrolled further afield for the same purpose.

Within two months of their arrival, their numbers had swelled. The new recruits were now capable, if inexperienced, cavalrymen. Three extra turmae had been formed and the new recruits were spread throughout the force so as to gain from serving alongside more experienced men. Drills were constant.

Much the same was true of the infantry. Cato was now Tribune in command of infantry training and was determined to make his force competent. Each day was spent in marching and in weapons practice. The blacksmiths worked overtime to provide swords and spears, particularly the pila, the throwing spears with their long soft iron shafts and tiny pyramidal points that would pierce an enemy's shield and then bend making the shield useless. The Saxons used large, heavy, round shields made of solid wood and a pilum was the best weapon to use against them. The short heavy darts that clipped into the back of the Roman shield and were standard infantry equipment were less useful, so Gerontius had opted for the old-fashioned pilum instead.

Cato had talked with Artorius about fighting barbarians. Artorius had battled the Irish raiders who fought very much the same as the Saxons. The Saxons fought as individual warriors, each using his favourite weapons. Some favoured the long, heavy spear of some two and a half metres length which they would thrust over-arm at the faces of their opponents over the top of their shields. Others liked the battleaxe which would also be wielded from on high to smash down onto a man's head or be swung horizontally at the neck. Only the richest Saxons had swords. These were long, with blades of about a metre length some six or seven centimetres wide. They had short, rounded points that limited their use for thrusting. Instead they were swung as slashing weapons and were heavy enough to crack a Roman shield or to slice through mail armour.

Cato told his men what they could expect and taught them how to counter each weapon. "If a man thrusts a spear at you he will be beyond your reach. He will aim at your face. Move to one side, like a boxer slipping a punch. Since he will have put all his weight behind the thrust, as his arm comes forward his body will turn moving his shield to the left. Simply step forward and stab him in his belly. Don't hesitate. Get him before he can recover his spear. If a man tries to whack you over the head with an axe, don't try to parry it with your shield: he'll smash it. Step forward so the axe blade will miss your head and stab him while his arm is extended. If he tries a sweeping blow from the side, duck under it, step forward and catch him as his body turns. Treat swordsmen the same way. Remember, the Saxons need space to swing their axes and swords. They will be spaced about two metres apart. There will be three of you in front of each of them. Protect your neighbour on your right. His attacker has no shield on your side."

They practised with wooden weapons, some being Saxons and the others Romans. There were many bruises and the odd broken nose but soon the men were confident they could deal with such attacks. They had quickly grasped that if they held their close order and kept in line the Saxons would have little chance to hurt them.

The cavalry too had to practise as well as breaking in new horses and training them to battle. Horses had to be trained to smash into bodies of men rather than try to jump them or to veer off sideways. They had to be trained not to rear so as to prevent enemy infantry stabbing the exposed belly. They had to respond instinctively to pressure from the rider's legs, to turn, go forward or back or to stop.

The men had to learn how to charge in line, none getting ahead and none lagging behind. They became proficient in hitting home with their spears, practising galloping at stuffed dummies and striking them without losing hold of their weapon and recovering it as they rode past. They became expert in the use of the long cavalry sword, more often used as a slashing weapon than for stabbing. Many of them had bows too and had to practise shooting from the saddle. All had to be competent in the use of javelins, practising riding at targets and throwing a succession of javelins to hit them as they rode past. The new recruits grew daily in confidence. All were equipped with chain mail armour, cavalry helmets and narrow oval shields. Artorius had brought all his spares with him, and there had been enough and more for three extra turmae.

Saddles had been a problem. One had been given to the carpenters who had taken it apart and then fashioned more to the same pattern. No-one had yet heard of stirrups, so saddles were still of the old Celtic pattern, two curved wooden frames across the horse's back linked by thin curved slats that would bend downwards under the weight of a rider. Each frame had two wooden horns that curved inwards so that when the rider sat in the saddle and depressed the wooden slats they closed over his thighs giving him a very secure seat. It was not unknown for a cavalryman to be killed in battle yet not fall from his horse. The whole assemblage was covered with soft padded leather to prevent chaffing and a sheepskin was placed beneath it to protect the horse.

All this extra equipment had to be made on site. The camp was not just a residential town: it was an industrial enterprise too. Forges worked day and night. Potters turned out thousands of crude bowls and cups and skillets for cooking. Carpenters were busy making saddles, wagons, new buildings as well as repairing hafts of tools and weapons. Blacksmiths toiled at their forges to turn out weapons and tools. There was even a tannery to produce leather. Bones from the many animals that fed the troops were kept to be boiled down to manufacture the glue used to make the three-ply shields which would be lighter and stronger than those of the Saxons. Fully half the strength was on work duty while the rest were training. All this activity made the camp a noisy and smelly place.

Each day wagon trains arrived full of supplies. Ambrosius had sent tax collectors out to all the towns and to the large villa estates demanding payment in kind. He did not want coin. He needed food and fodder and raw materials. Some landowners had tried to fob off the collectors, claiming poor harvests or the sale of all their surpluses but the collectors were all now trained troops and soon searched out the stuffed barns. They developed a degree of contempt for the fattened proprietors of great estates who were unwilling to play their part in the war that threatened them all. Some had even tried to sell produce at inflated prices, seeing the war as a means to make themselves even richer.

Artorius shared this contempt. He had committed his men to save and restore the Roman Diocese of Britannia. What he had discovered of its leading citizens made him wonder if it was worth the saving. If the war succeeded, he could see the great citizens queuing up to gain lands reconquered from the Saxons. They would have put little of their wealth into the war but would expect to gain from it. Many would produce forged deeds to properties in Cantium (Kent) so as to gain estates near to continental trade. He was sickened by them.

He felt for the common folk who had little means and eked out an existence as tenants of the landowners. With money now scarce, they paid their rents in kind and bartered their surpluses for such essentials as pottery and tools. These were the people he would fight to protect. He was a Christian and saw his duty as protecting his Church and its flock from the heathens. He had heard that they always burned down chapels and slaughtered clergy. That was reason enough to fight, he thought. The rich could be dealt with after the war.

The winter wore slowly on. December and January were cold and wet. Often there was snow and weapons practice was difficult when feet slipped and were numb with cold. Still the work went on. The long distance patrols had had to cease for lack of available fodder for the horses, but there was little need. The Saxons had gone home or set up new homesteads and were busy surviving the winter. They would not advance further nor raid westwards again until the spring.

Ambrosius, Gerontius and Artorius began to plan their spring offensive. The main Saxon settlements were still far away to the east. Cantium was heavily occupied by Hengest's people. A small offshoot of these had gone to the north country but they were very few and were easily contained by the Dux and the army of the Wall. There were heavy settlements to the north of Camulodunum (Colchester) and these had expanded westwards over the Ermine Street south and north of Lindum (Lincoln) and around Ratae (Leicester). This was largely empty land. There were few villas there and few towns. Where there were Roman settlements they were industrial rather than agricultural, potteries and smithies and glass works. This had been an area of Imperial estates worked by slaves for the benefit of the State so there were few private villas and towns. The land was flat and largely forested and the soil heavy. There were many broad, slow flowing rivers that would impede the advance of an army. There were many marshy areas, particularly around the Wash, which the Romans had avoided as unhealthy except where they could be drained.

"We have to ensure that Londinium and Camulodunum remain safe under our control," said Ambrosius. "They are the key. While we hold them, the Saxons in Cantium cannot unite with those further north. If we can push the Saxons away from them, our task will be easier."

"We will need to put troops into both," said Gerontius. "If we stiffen their defences, we could launch punitive patrols against any Saxon expansion. At first we should be content to contain them where they are. If we prick them hard enough and often enough, eventually they will come out in force to fight us and then we can attack to destroy them."

"It strikes me that Hengest should be our main target," opined Artorius. "He is a noted war leader, famous for his fighting ability and for his guile. He is virtually King of Cantium. If we defeat him, his people will fragment without leadership. The Saxons further north arc family groups with no central authority. We could push them well away from Londinium without too much risk of their uniting against us."

"So we start from Londinium. It will be hard to get there without Hengest knowing we are coming," said Gerontius.

"I'll range ahead with my cavalry," said Artorius. "We can move fast and appear and disappear at will. Hengest will know we are moving but not where our army is, nor its destination."

"Then we must decide how to get there," said Ambrosius. "We could go via Venta Belgarum (Winchester) and Calleva (Silchester), the easiest route. We could strike north east to Corinium (Cirencester) and go via Verulamium (St. Albans). That way is longer, but we would be covered from view by the hills."

"We want Hengest to know we are moving," said Artorius. "He would expect us to go via Calleva and he will be watching that route. If I go that way, he will think you are following. When you don't appear he will be confused and off balance while you march around him farther to the north and reach Londinium before he can intercept you."

Gerontius agreed, saying that the main army would be north of the Tamesis (Thames) which had few places where it could be crossed easily. Small detachments of troops could be sent to guard the fords and discourage any Saxons from crossing the river. They could easily reach Londinium without any major ambush.

Ambrosius thought the strategy good. He said to Artorius, "You will be the most at risk. You will be south of the river and nearest the Saxon forces if they come out in strength. I don't want to lose too many of my precious cavalry. You must be very careful. Avoid pitched battles. You will have to cross the river before we get to Londinium - the Saxons will certainly try to block your access to the bridge there."

"I can cross the river almost anywhere. Horses can swim, even with men on their backs. It will be easier to use a ford but not essential. The main thing is to prevent Hengest getting accurate information as to where the main army is. There are two Saxon settlements in the gap in the hills where the river goes through towards Londinium. They were planted there by Vortigern and are long established. They must be prevented from sending any intelligence to Hengest. It is not a major problem. They are a different people and isolated. If a small cavalry garrison is placed to over-awe them and keep them at home, that should suffice."

"So be it," said Ambrosius. "We march via Verulamium while Artorius moves parallel to the south. We march quickly. Londinium has supplies, so we only take what we need for the march. No wagons and oxen - they will slow us down. Each man must carry what we need. Extra supplies can follow after we reach Londinium."

"Some practice marches will be useful," said Gerontius. "The men will have to get used to marching with very heavy packs. We can't afford them becoming exhausted on the real march. We'll make it competitive, each century against its neighbour, a twenty mile marching race. It will be good for morale as well as toughening them up."

"Good idea," said Ambrosius. "We have one more month before spring in which to prepare. I want to move early, before Hengest expects. That way we keep the initiative. We won't give him time to prepare. He must already know we are gathering an army but will not expect us to move so soon."

The strategy was good. Its only weakness was that the cavalry could move much faster than the infantry and might get too far ahead. Artorius knew this and determined to limit his advance to twenty miles a day. He would set out first and ride to Venta Belgarum where he would halt until the day appointed for the infantry to set out. Then he would advance on a broad front in short rushes to confuse the enemy if they had any scouts so far west. He would pause again at Calleva while the army caught up to the north. His aim was to be one day's march ahead as they approached Londinium. As they got near they would need to be more cautious and slow down. He would cross the river some twenty miles west of Londinium and join Gerontius for the last day's march.

The last month of winter was spent practice marching. Weapons practice was stepped up. An air of expectancy pervaded the camp. The men were excited and itching to put into practice what they had learned. Century vied with century to prove they could march further and faster and were better at fighting in close order. Morale was high.

Chapter 3: The March.

The day before Artorius was to set off, Ambrosius called a full parade of the troops. They formed up outside the camp, some two thousand men, in neat ranks behind their century standards. The cavalry formed up mounted behind the vexillum of each turma. Ambrosius rode a horse to the centre of the parade which had formed in a hollow square. He was in full armour and wore the traditional red cloak of a general. He halted to address his army.

"I am Governor of Britannia, elected by the Council of the Cities of Britannia. I do not pretend to be a military man. Like most of you, I have never fought in any war. However, my position requires me to lead the defence of this Diocese against the Saxons who have invaded and colonised it. To do this effectively I have called on Gerontius and Artorius and their experienced men to train this new army.

"When the Emperor raises new legions, he names them after himself. You will be named after me, since we have no contact with the Emperor in Ravenna. You will be called the Ambrosiaci and will fight in my name for the Provinces of Britannia.

"Since I am no real general, I appoint Artorius, my Magister Equitum, to be Dux Bellorum, Commander-in-Chief for the duration of the war. Gerontius will be his deputy. Under their command, you can be sure that you will not be asked to do the impossible, nor be committed to battles you have no chance of winning. I am too old to lead a long campaign and have too many other responsibilities. I will come with you to Londinium and then leave the planning and campaigning to Artorius and Gerontius. You know them. You know they are competent. You know what they will expect of you. They will bring you victory.

"Tomorrow, Artorius will lead his Cavalry eastwards. Four turmae will remain here to screen the infantry who will march two days later. We go to Londinium but in such a way that the Saxons will not know where we are, how strong we are nor where we intend to strike at them. We go fast, twenty miles a day with full packs and no baggage train. It will be a long, hard trek - but I am confident you can achieve it. You are now the best troops in Britannia. The Dux at Eboracum would be jealous of you.

"Make no mistake: this will be a long, hard war. The enemy are far more numerous than we and are settled in the east. We go to pen them in where they are until we can gather more strength to push them back into the sea. We fight for Britannia and for Christianity.

"You are all that stand between your kin and friends here in the west and the heathen horde to the east. You must not fail. When you fight, fight for your families and friends, to save them from slaughter or slavery. Remember, you are all that stand between civilisation and chaos."

Ambrosius had broken with normal Roman practice. Roman armies had always been based on the legion infantry and the Magister Militum had always been superior to the Magister Equitum, the cavalry being seen as merely the support for the infantry. Ambrosius had realised that in this new war, against the Saxons who had no horsemen, the cavalry would become the main means of defeating them and the Magister Equitum had to be the overall commander.

Artorius was impressed. Ambrosius had given his army a name. That was important for any army unit. It was what united them as one family. He had given them an objective. They knew what they were to do. He had told them what he thought of them, as the best in Britannia. He had acknowledged his own inexperience and had appointed experienced men to command.

Artorius was very conscious of how far he, himself, had risen. Six short months ago he had been a simple Tribune with a small command. Now he was a Prefect and Dux Bellorum for the whole of Britannia. It was a huge responsibility. He prayed he was up to the task. Ambrosius' promise of victory had laid a heavy responsibility on Artorius and Gerontius. His first act as Dux was to promote Bedwyr to the rank of Tribune to command the four turmae who would go with Gerontius and Ambrosius. The infantry had to have a cavalry screen. Bedwyr had proved competent and wise. It was a logical choice.

Next day Artorius led eight turmae of cavalry out of the camp and took the road to Venta Belgarum. They went there first rather than direct to Calleva so as to get extra supplies. Calleva had suffered much from the Saxon raids and would have little to spare for the army. If they went fast they could reach Venta in two days. There they would get the extra supplies before moving on to Calleva. One turma rode ahead as scouts while the rest followed the road to Venta.

Two days later, the infantry set out along the road to Corinium, leaving a token force behind to train more men and maintain weapon production. They marched six abreast with Bedwyr's cavalry scouting ahead and on either flank. Ambrosius and Gerontius rode in the centre of the column. A plume of dust rose above the trudging men and their armour jingled as they went. As was fitting for a new corps, all bore shields painted with Ambrosius' badge, the boar, and each century standard was topped with a boar rather than the traditional hand.

Their route went north-east to Corinium before bending to the west for Verulamium. Like all major Roman roads there were inns spaced about every ten miles along the route where news or rumour could be got. Bedwyr's horsemen made a point of visiting these for any rumours of Saxon activity nearby. One turma was despatched to take the old prehistoric ridgeway along the crest of the hills to their south to ensure no Saxon eyes overlooked their line of march.

Further to the south, Artorius had made good progress. The roads were still good even though they lacked maintenance. Scrub had grown up alongside them so the advance guard had had to be vigilant for possible ambushes but they had reached Venta Belgarum without incident.

There they had got a lukewarm reception from the Senate Prefect, Caradoc. He was a rich landowner of British descent. His father had been City Prefect before him and, despite being very young, he regarded Venta and all the lands of the Belgae almost as his own kingdom. He knew Ambrosius was Governor and perforce had to recognise Artorius as Dux Bellorum when shown his letter of appointment under Ambrosius' seal. He did not see that he should give supplies to any army marching east. He made it clear that he did not agree with the war. The Saxons were a long way away and were no threat. Venta was strong and its people quite capable of defending themselves. He needed no help from Ambrosius and thought that the move to Londinium would be a provocation to the Saxons.

Artorius was exasperated. "We are not talking about Venta," he said. "We are defending the whole of Britannia. Venta may be strong but is Calleva? We are all in this together. The strong must be prepared to help the weak. If you will not give supplies, I will use my authority and take them, if need be at the point of the sword. Afterwards you may beg pardon of Ambrosius if you are to keep your position and rank. He is not someone you can afford to anger. He has already threatened to replace the Senate of Glevum with a military Governor. He could do the same here."

Caradoc backed down. He was angry, and showed it, but allowed Artorius to take food and fodder for his men and horses. They camped outside the city. Artorius wanted little to do with Caradoc and his Senate. He saw them as too parochial, too concerned with their own little bit of Britannia and uncaring of the rest. It was best his men did not discover Venta's lack of support for the war and suffer a drop in morale.

He sensed that Caradoc was puffed up with his own importance and disliked any interference or opposition to his own ideas. He was the sort of man who would bear grudges and remember any slights. By his blunt speaking, Artorius had made an enemy.

Next day they marched to Calleva with three turmae riding ahead on a broad front as an advance guard. The road was good but much of the farmland and many of the villas were abandoned. The Saxon raids had not reached this far west but fear that they might had led most of the landowners to move away. They rode on past fields full of sodden, rotting grain.

At last they came to Calleva. Here things were quite different. Much of the city was in decline. Many of its people had fled to Armorica and almost all of the villas to the east had been abandoned. The surrounding lands were still open around the villas but were neglected, with weeds and scrub growing over what had been fields. Erstwhile tenants still scratched a living from the farmland around them but surpluses no longer came to the city. The townsfolk had taken to farming land within the walls and pasturing herds by day immediately outside. Corn drying kilns had been built within the walls. It was as though the city was under close siege, even though no enemies were surrounding it.

The Senate was reduced. Two thirds of the senators had gone to Armorica taking their portable wealth and many of their tenants with them. Artorius was welcomed warmly. He toured the city to inspect the defences. They were in a poor state. Like most cities, Calleva was ringed by a stone wall some four metres in height. In many places the parapet had collapsed. The great ditches outside had been partially filled with rubbish and silt. The gates were rotten and ill-fitting. Projecting from the walls were semi-circular bastions equipped with ballistae - but these were old and in poor repair. Artorius thought they were more of a danger to the defenders than to any enemy outside.

He took his findings to the Senate. "You need to repair the parapet. If you lack masons, use timber. Clean out and deepen the ditches. Make new gates out of thick timbers. Repair the ballistae if you can or else throw them away and rely on archers on the bastions. The Saxons are not good at assaulting walls, so you should be safe enough. Gather supplies and store them - enough to feed your people basic rations for six months. The Saxons cannot maintain a siege that long. If you lack cut stones, demolish some of the empty houses and use that material. The owners won't be coming back. Clearing abandoned houses will give you more land for cultivation."

The Senate thanked him for his advice and offered food and fodder for his men and horses. Artorius declined. He had taken enough, he said, from Venta, and Calleva needed all it could store. "If my campaign succeeds, you will be safe. The Saxons will not come here. If I fail, they will. Don't expect any aid from Venta. The Senate there is only interested in protecting its own. Put your defences in order, store supplies and pray that Ambrosius wins this war."

He left next day to continue moving eastwards. The three turmae now went ahead on a broader front so that any Saxon scouts would be confused as to where Artorius' main force was. If they encountered any Saxons in arms they were to scatter them and then retire out of range of any pursuit. Because he had advanced so rapidly to Calleva, Artorius was able to slow to ten miles a day so that the army to the north could catch up.

That army was making good progress. The road to Corinium had been good and they had been accepted there. The people of Corinium knew that their city was part of the richest agricultural area in Britannia and was thus an excellent target for Saxon raiders. They were pleased to see Ambrosius' army and happy that it was moving east to block any Saxon advance. Even so, some of the Senate were less than happy to give any supplies to the army. From there the army had struck out along the road to Verulamium. A strong detachment was sent southwards towards the great gap in the hills where there were two small, long-established Saxon settlements. Gerontius himself led the way. The gap in the hills was of huge strategic significance and the Saxons living there had to be neutralised. The cavalry on the ridgeway advanced there too to block any escape through the gap.

The Saxons were soon aware of armed men in their vicinity. They came out to fight. They took position on a low hill and waited. Two hundred warriors stood in line facing the advance of three hundred trained Roman soldiers. They watched as they marched forward in column and then deployed into three ranks. They noted the second line of three ranks some twenty metres behind. They saw the cavalry deploy on either wing. The Romans halted. The Saxons waited, weighing up their chances. Then came disturbing news. More cavalry were coming from the ridgeway behind them. Their villages were at risk. Their women and children were in danger.

They marched back to defend their homes. They knew it was hopeless. If the Romans wanted, they could march straight in. Two messengers were sent south to take news to Hengest but both were pursued and ridden down by horsemen.

The Saxons waited as the Romans came on. They halted outside the bigger village and an officer rode forward. He halted just outside. The Saxon chief went out to meet him.

Gerontius sat on his horse as the man came out. "I have no wish to kill your men nor to burn your village," he said. "I could do it easily and leave your women and children to fend for themselves. You are too few to threaten me and this is only a small part of my army. I offer you terms. You can stay here and farm your lands if you promise to offer no aid or intelligence to Hengest or any other Saxon war band that comes this way. If you so swear, by whatever gods you worship, I shall leave you in peace. If you refuse, I shall raze this village to the ground. Go back to your men and tell them what I offer. Bring me their reply in one hour."

The chief went back to his villagers. As they talked they watched cavalry riding round and round their village. They had never seen horsemen before and were over-awed. It did not need the hour. After fifteen minutes the chief came out with his leading men. They stood before Gerontius. The chief stepped forward.

"We accept your terms. They are generous. We swear by Woden to offer no aid to your enemies."

"So swear you all?"

There was a murmur of assent.

"So be it," said Gerontius. "To ensure your compliance with these terms and to remind you of your oath to Woden, I shall station horsemen on the hills nearby. They will watch your coming and going. If you march out armed as for war, they will swoop down and burn your villages. You will not be able to stop them nor to catch them afterwards."

He rode back to his troops and marched to the second village where the same ritual was repeated. A garrison of one half turma of cavalry was stationed on a small hill overlooking the settlements with orders to defend their base with a ditch and rampart and to patrol the area around the villages.

Two Saxon settlements had been neutralised without a blow being struck and the march could continue in safety. Gerontius marched in double time to rejoin the army on the road to Verulamium. Ambrosius was pleased at what had been achieved and congratulated Gerontius. No men had been lost, and the half turma left behind could patrol the gap in the hills and give ample warning if Hengest tried to come that way.

Further to the south, Artorius was moving steadily eastwards. He was now in land that had been ravaged by the Saxon advances and raids. He passed burned and abandoned villas and had to pause to bury the skeletons of their people. It was a grim business. Small groups of survivors were found hiding in the woods, fearful of all armed men. They were traumatised by their experiences. The Saxons had killed all they caught and burned many buildings after pillaging their contents. These people now lived in huts made of sticks and thatched with bracken. They had nowhere to go and fed off what they could get by hunting or gathering in the woods. All were emaciated and starving.

Artorius gave them food and told them to go west to Calleva. Calleva needed more people to man the walls, he said. They would be welcome there and much safer. He was appalled at what he had seen. Many of the skeletons showed that the Saxons had hacked their victims to pieces. Some they had hanged in the doorways to the villas where the skeletons still swung. Of these some were missing hands or feet showing that they had been tortured, probably in an attempt to extract from them the whereabouts of any treasures. His men were sobered by what they had seen and were quieter than before. Their faces had a set expression of determination to avenge what had been done to defenceless people. Now they knew for real why they were fighting and Saxon warriors could expect no mercy from them.

Much the same was reported from the advance screen. They too had stopped to bury the pitiful remains scattered about wrecked settlements. It was the tiny skeletons of babies and toddlers that most affected the men. Some were reduced to tears at the sight and in camp the night silence was broken by the steady scrape of whetstones on sword blades.

Artorius sensed the cold rage that now gripped his men. He called in all the decurions for a council of war. They crammed themselves into Artorius' tent to hear what he had to say.

"You have all seen the horrors that happened here. You are all angry. Husband that anger. Keep it ice cold in your hearts. It will stand you in good stead when it comes to fighting: but, hear me, keep it cold. If you explode into red rage you will lose your discipline and do rash things that might lead your men to disaster. They feel the same as you. You must be their cooler head. Keep them on a tight rein. Keep them disciplined. We will avenge these horrors but clinically and coldly. We will teach these

Saxons to fear us as their implacable foes. They will learn that we are the vengeful angels of Britannia and bring death to any Saxon who bears arms against us. Now go back to your men and tell them what I have said. We advance on Londinium at speed. We will cross the Tamesis some miles upstream of the city where there is a good ford. If we spot any Saxon warriors in our way, we will sweep over them and kill them all."

Next day the march resumed, now at a trot. Trotting without stirrups was uncomfortable and tiring but speed was needed. They no longer stopped to bury the dead but rode on in grim determination. Twice small bands of Saxon warriors were seen. Artorius rode his men around them and then charged through and over them. None survived. They left the dead for the wolves and rode on.

Hengest by now had learned that an army was moving towards him. He was gathering his own and sending men to guard the approaches to his territory. He could not know how fast cavalry could advance, never having seen horsemen before. He was expecting an infantry host capable of no more than ten or fifteen miles a day. He had no idea that Gerontius could maintain at least twenty daily. He had to get intelligence as to where the Romans were. The two small Saxon bands were some of his scouts. Their failure to send reports told Hengest only that hostile forces were to his west, south of the Tamesis. Where could they be heading? If they stayed south of the river, he could meet them with full force. If they crossed to the northern bank it would be harder to come at them. He sent some stronger forces to watch the fords. Meanwhile his host was growing and he was nearly ready to march out of Cantium.

Gerontius had had much the same idea. The army had reached Verulamium without incident and had replenished its supplies. It now had only a two day march to reach Londinium. Artorius was due to join them soon. To do so he would have to cross the Tamesis. Gerontius suggested that it would be good to guard the fords. It would prevent any Saxon reconnaissance from south of the river and would give safe passage to Artorius. Ambrosius agreed and detachments had been sent to watch the northern bank of the river. One turma of cavalry was sent to patrol between the picquets at the fords.

When Hengest's scouting force arrived near what is now Maidenhead, they were amazed to find Roman troops on the opposite bank. They had assumed the Romans would be much further to the west. Numbers on both sides were about equal, so the Saxons advanced to attack. The Romans quickly formed in three ranks with their oval shields almost overlapping to the front. After standing on the opposite bank, screaming and shouting and banging swords and spear hafts against their shields, the Saxons advanced into the ford. They came at a run but soon had to leap to avoid the slowing drag of the water around their feet. In midstream they were in water over their knees and had to wade. Their charge lost all impetus.

As they reached shallower water and began to move faster again they came within range of Gerontius' men. Pila were hurled against the Saxons. Some fell but most caught the missiles on their shields only to find them embedded in the wood and bent. The shields were flung aside and the Saxons came on with spears, axes and swords swinging high. A second volley of pila did much more damage. So many Saxons fell that those behind were impeded by the dead and wounded. The attack halted. Those at the rear began to waver and those at the front, sensing this, began to withdraw backwards.

It was then that disaster struck them. As they edged their way towards the south bank a full turma of cavalry crashed into them from behind. Men were hurled aside by horses only to be swiftly despatched by thrusts of cavalry spears. Some tried to flee along the river and drowned when they left the edge of the ford. One or two reached the bank and ran but they only got a few metres before they were felled by slashing cavalry swords.

Part of Artorius' advance guard had arrived and their hatred of what the Saxons had done made them the most efficient of killing machines. Coolly and calmly they rode down the Saxons, stabbing with spears or slashing with swords. It was soon over. Not one Saxon warrior survived.

Gerontius' infantry looked on in awe. They had played only a bit part in this drama. The cavalry had been supreme. They marvelled at the precision of the attack, the cold ruthlessness of the cavalrymen and their implacable mercilessness towards their beaten foes. After all was over and the red stain of blood had flowed away down river they welcomed the troopers. They camped together that night while waiting for the rest of Artorius' men. The remainder of the advance guard had arrived at dusk and Artorius in the early morning. He had had news of the 'battle' and had ridden through the night to ensure that all was well.

There were still Saxon corpses strewn over the ford when he came. He viewed them dispassionately and ordered that any useful armour be stripped from the bodies and weapons recovered from the ford. They should not be left for other Saxons to find and use, he said. Roman pila were extracted from Saxon shields and straightened. He congratulated the young decurion, Gawain, who had led the charge. "You did well," he said. "You waited for the right moment and hit home when they could least oppose you. You kept your men in check and made them effective when it mattered. That is the mark of a real commander. I will tell Ambrosius what you did."

Gawain was a charismatic officer. He seldom had to discipline any of his men. They did what he wished because they wanted to obey him. He had a ready wit and a light hearted air that kept morale high. He looked for the good in his men and readily praised them. He was popular with the other decurions too. Artorius liked him for his flair and his readiness to take on any task no matter how difficult it might be.

Artorius spoke to the centurion who had held the far bank with his infantry. "You did what was needed. You held your men steady in line and waited for the enemy to come in range of your pila. Gawain tells me that you behaved exactly as you have been trained and it worked. Well done. You have faced your first battle and won without loss. I now know I can rely on my infantry."

They marched north east to meet with Ambrosius on the road from Verulamium to Londinium and found him in camp that night, one day's march from the city. By now Artorius was reeling with exhaustion. He had ridden through all the previous night desperate to catch up with his advance guard who were engaged with the enemy. Now he had ridden through all the next day to reach Ambrosius. His men and their horses were foundering. Ambrosius greeted him warmly and sat him down in the headquarters tent to eat and drink.

"You're spent," he said. "You need rest, you and your men. I saw how they fed and watered their horses and groomed them even though they themselves were dropping from fatigue. You all need a good night's sleep and a good meal. We will pause a day here. There are no Saxons within two day's march of us, so we can afford the delay. Tomorrow you can tell me what you found on your march and next day we go on to Londinium."

"Hengest knows we are moving," said Artorius. "We killed two of his scouting parties and the fight at the ford shows that he seeks to hold the banks of the Tamesis. When we get to Londinium, we should move fast to catch him as he comes out of Cantium."

"Save that for tomorrow," said Ambrosius. "Tomorrow you will have a clearer head and will be able to think things through better. Tonight you must eat, drink and sleep. We are safe here, out of Hengest's reach. He does not know where we are. He thinks we are south of the river. He will look for us there and find nothing. In the meantime we will get ourselves safely into Londinium. You have done your job superbly."

Ambrosius was right. The only news Hengest had received was of troops south of the river. He had sent out scouting parties to range far to the west, but they had found little or nothing to report. There was no sign of the passage of a large army, no sign of marching camps. They found the remains of the two scouting bands and the remains of the battle at the ford. They found burned Saxon settlements. Enemy troops had been there but they had vanished.

All this had taken days, and Hengest was totally unaware of the great army that was poised near Londinium. Even had he known, there was little he could do about it. His host was not fully gathered. He had not expected the Romans to move so soon nor so quickly. He was also quite old. He had come to Britannia as a youth and had led his folk in a long war. He lived on his reputation as a great war leader and warrior but he knew now that his fighting days were really over. He could inspire his men but he could no longer lead a charge.

A day's rest was good for all the army. The horses, that had become lean on the long march, gorged themselves on grain. The men set to to repair equipment, mend worn boots, sharpen swords and rest around camp fires.

Artorius reported what he had seen to Ambrosius and Gerontius. They were horrified at his account of the slaughter and torture inflicted on defenceless civilians by the Saxons. "They are like ravening wolves," he said. "They spare no-one. They kill for the sake of it. Women, children, the old, the sick - none are spared. They hack their victims to pieces as though they are butchering meat. My men are of the same mind as me. We cannot let them continue to live in this island. We must kill them or throw them back into the sea."

"We will need many more men for that," said Gerontius. "For now, all we can hope to do is pen them in. If we hurt them enough and force them back to lick their wounds they might remain quiet while we gather greater strength."

"The one thing that I noticed," said Artorius, "was that they have no experience of cavalry. They cannot face a full cavalry charge. They are confused and frightened by horsemen. That is our great advantage. We should recruit more horsemen to harry them, to break up their battle lines, to threaten their settlements. Hit and retire to hit again - that is how we will wear them down to the point that they will want to leave Britannia."

"That is for the future," said Ambrosius. "Tomorrow we go to Londinium and then advance on Cantium. We must force Hengest to fight and then beat him. It will be the end of his reputation as a great war leader. He will be finished as 'King' of Cantium. His people will fall to bickering among themselves and will have no-one to unite them for war against us."

Next day they marched and soon covered the distance to Londinium. They arrived outside the city towards dusk and camped. Londinium stood on the north bank of the Tamesis. Roughly rectangular in shape, it was walled on all sides, the river adding to the defence of the south side. A long wooden bridge crossed the river which here was nearly a mile wide. A small suburb stood at the southern end of the bridge but this had been abandoned. Inside the walls were all the usual town buildings. A great basilica formed one side of the forum and the Senate House and the church, built on the site of a former temple, formed another. There were many town houses and tenements crammed together around the forum. There were also open areas which were now under cultivation as in Calleva.

Ambrosius, with Artorius and Gerontius and an escort of two turmae of cavalry rode into the city. The City Prefect came to meet them. He was effusive in his greetings and ordered that a large empty house be given to Ambrosius as his headquarters. The cavalry were billeted in the city and a Senate meeting was called for the next morning. To Artorius, Londinium seemed much like Calleva. Much of the population had fled to Armorica. Empty houses were already showing signs of neglect. Open spaces within the city which were under cultivation showed it was safer to grow crops within the walls. It was a small city despite its being once the largest in Britannia. It covered no more than a square mile beside the wide river which was crossed by the long wooden bridge. Wharves occupied the north bank with warehouses behind them but there were no ships loading and unloading - the Saxon rebellion had killed all maritime trade.

The defences, however were in good order. The walls were well maintained and all the gates were manned. A strong wooden palisade had been added along the riverside in front of the warehouses to strengthen the defences towards the south. A forest of sharpened wooden stakes had been set in the mud of the river bed at low tide to impede any attempt to ford the river. The remaining citizens were not afraid and had looked to defend themselves. Artorius was confident that they would hold out.

The Prefect told them that the city was struggling. It existed because of the bridge over the Tamesis and because it was the safest place to come into Britannia by sea. Traders had flocked to it and it had grown rich. All that had changed after the Saxon rebellion. Traders would not risk the voyage around Cantium and the bridge was an open invitation to Hengest. That was why so many people had left. Luckily the granaries were full and crops could be grown close to the city as well as within the walls.

Ambrosius pointed out how important the place was. It was the cork that could keep the Saxons bottled in Cantium. It sat in the centre of a huge bowl. To the south the North Downs were a natural barrier atop which garrisons could watch for any movement out of Cantium. To the north another escarpment faced the Saxon settlements that had spilled across the Ermine Street. "I will leave troops here to hold and patrol all that area," he said. "If we place garrisons strategically and link them with cavalry patrols, I doubt you will see any Saxons."

The City Prefect was impressed. "We'll put it to the Senate tomorrow," he said. He bade them good night and left them to relax after the long march. They were all tired but elated. They had achieved their objective. They had marched from Sorbiodunum to Londinium quickly and secretly. Hengest was unprepared and unaware. He had no knowledge as to where they were nor as to their numbers. He knew they were on the move but had been unable to find them. He had believed them south of the Tamesis and was still searching for them there.

They could sleep well that night, secure in the knowledge that they had wrong-footed their enemies and were poised to strike them before they could prepare any defensive strategy. It was a good feeling.

Chapter 4: The Medway.

The Senate meeting was good. Unlike so many other City Senates, that of Londinium was welcoming. The army was granted permission to camp within the walls. The troops were seen as guardians rather than as extra mouths to eat stored supplies. Supplies were granted as a matter of course. Ambrosius was deferred to as Governor and Artorius and Gerontius were recognised as Prefects, equal in rank to any Senator. Their account of their march and their minor victories over what Saxons they had encountered was listened to attentively.

The proposed wider defence of Londinium was discussed. The Senate saw the sense of it but protested that it would drain too many men from Ambrosius' army. After much talk, the senators proposed that their own citizens should form the guard garrisons on the crests of the hills and that Artorius should only have to lend them some cavalry until such time as they could develop their own force to patrol from garrison to garrison. The establishment of the garrisons would have to wait until after the current campaign. Ambrosius would need every man he had for that.

When Ambrosius told them that the army was going to strike directly towards Durovernum Cantiacum (Canterbury) by following the great road, the Senate promised to send wagonloads of supplies to follow. His field army operating between Londinium and Cantium was the best defence they had. It was only right that they should maintain it.

Artorius noted how the co-operation of city Senates depended on their proximity to the Saxons. Glevum and Venta had been surly and unwilling, as had some of the senators of Corinium to some extent. Calleva, Verulamium and Londinium were eager to help. The decision of the Emperor Honorius that the British cities should organise their own defence had in reality broken the unity of Britannia. Vortigern had been a great statesman and had succeeded for some years. He had contained and pushed back the Irish settlers in the west and had secured the east. He was from Glevum and so had its support but, when he continued to require taxes of the other cities, they had refused and rebelled. Parochialism had become stronger than any sense of Diocesan unity.

Ambrosius told the Senate that he would remain in Londinium while the army went forward to fight. "I am no real soldier," he said. "My presence with the army is not necessary. Artorius and Gerontius have enough to do without worrying about protecting me. I shall be safe enough, here, with you. They must be free to fight the war and make whatever strategic or tactical decisions they need without having to defer to me. Artorius will command as Dux Bellorum and Gerontius will act as his deputy in the field. They are both fully competent and professional. It is they, rather than I, who have created this army and they know best how to use it."

Artorius told the Senate that speed was of the essence. The army would move next day. They had to strike at Cantium by surprise, before Hengest could organise a proper defence. Their aim was to force him to rush to confront them in open battle and to defeat him so thoroughly that his credibility as a war leader would be destroyed. "Gerontius and I have much to do today," he said. "We have to plan our march in detail and decide where we will fight. With your permission, we will leave you to continue your meeting. We have to plan and then confer with our officers and issue orders for tomorrow's advance."

They left and returned to the headquarters. The day was spent in planning. Cantium had only one major natural frontier on the line of the road to Durovernum, the river Medway. If Hengest got news of their advance, that was where he would try to halt them. The road crossed the river by a bridge and bridges were easy to defend. A small force could hold an entire army at bay at a bridge. However, there were several places further upstream where the river was shallow and could be forded on a wide front. That was where they would have to cross. If the crossing was defended, it would be difficult and costly. They had to get there before the Saxons could fully concentrate.

"We must use guile," said Gerontius. "We make them think we are going to the bridge and force them to defend it. Our main force uses the fords and thus we outflank the defence."

"But then they will merely retire and Hengest is free to pick his own battleground." objected Artorius. "He'll only defend the bridge with a small force. His main army will be held back. We have to force him to confront us with his full strength."

"How?" asked Gerontius.

"By double bluffing him. We send a large force to the ford. We make it obvious we intend to cross there. We keep a large cavalry force well hidden to the rear. We draw Hengest's army to defend the ford and we attempt to force a crossing. Once battle is joined, the cavalry cross further upstream and more force the bridge. We hit him on both flanks at the height of the battle. His men will not know how to respond and will break."

"It will be difficult," said Gerontius. "Timing will be important. My infantry can advance over the ford but they must not get too far. They must allow themselves to be pushed back and draw the Saxons into the ford after them. We have to prolong the fight to give the cavalry time to make their own crossings and ride round for the final assault. We will be fighting in the middle of the river and if anything should go wrong for the cavalry, our own men might break. Remember, they have never fought a pitched battle before, except for my Cornovii."

Artorius was conscious of the risk. "Keep some of the best of your men in the reserve. If the men in the ford begin to waver, put fresh men into the fight. That will steady the rest and gain time. The cavalry will cross the river. There is little the Saxons can do to stop them. If the water is shallow enough they can gallop across. If the fords are too well defended, they can swim across where the river is deep and there are no defenders. One way or another, the cavalry will get there in time."

"I pray God you are right," said Gerontius. "My men will have to know the plan and will have to have absolute faith in the cavalry."

"Your men have absolute faith in you," said Artorius. "I hope they have faith in me. They will have to know that I will arrive and pick the right time for my attack. If I strike too early we might fail. They must endure until I judge the moment is right and we can utterly destroy the Saxon host. We do not want any significant part of it to escape."

They then planned their march. It would be too much to hope that Hengest would not get word of their movements once they were on the edge of his territory but they could still confuse him. They would march in small detachments about a mile apart and would camp separately. Cavalry would go as scouts and as flanking forces. If any Saxon scouts came near, the most they would see would be one or two detachments and that is what they would report to Hengest. Their reports would be contradictory as to numbers. All he would know was that Roman forces were moving towards Cantium. Having no clear idea of their numbers, he would be forced to move his whole host to oppose them and that was exactly what Artorius wanted him to do.

They marched soon after dawn. The cavalry clattered across the long wooden bridge over the Tamesis and advanced nearly a mile to screen the crossing of the infantry. When all were over the river, the order of march was begun. The infantry marched in ten detachments, each about a mile behind the detachment to their front. Cavalry probed far ahead and rode on either flank and more cavalry brought up the rear. Artorius was confident that this unorthodox formation would be safe. Each detachment was strong enough to withstand ambush by small Saxon forces and the cavalry would easily discover any larger concentrations of the enemy in plenty of time for the army to halt its leading units and allow the rest to catch up. The road passed through open country dotted with farms and villas, now mostly abandoned. Patches of woodland punctuated the landscape and these had to be carefully probed by the advance guard lest they held Saxon scouts.

The first day was uneventful but on the second the cavalry screen began to encounter enemy scouting parties. Hengest had heard they were coming. Most of these parties were slaughtered by the cavalry. They rode them down as they tried to flee. A few fugitives managed to escape to make their way back into Cantium. Artorius let them go. Their reports would worry Hengest. Their inability to estimate the Roman numbers would worry him most of all. He would soon have to move.

The third day would bring them to the Medway. Artorius halted the leading detachments until the rearmost had caught up. It no longer mattered if Hengest got accurate reports as to their numbers. By now he had to be marching his host to defend the Medway. The army halted behind the crest of the hill above the river that wound its way northwards towards the Tamesis. Artorius and Gerontius rode to the top to spy out the land. The river was a wide silvery band below them meandering its way towards the estuary. The road was a broad, straight slash through the woods going down to the narrow bridge.

A turma of cavalry rode down the great road towards the bridge over the river. This was built of stone and the Saxons had no means of breaking it. Instead they had blocked the passage with a wooden palisade and had some three hundred warriors behind and on the far bank of the river. Gawain rode back to Artorius with the news. "The palisade is not high. Our horses could leap it easily. We could charge over it and scatter the defenders."

"We will," said Artorius, "but not yet. We will face them with a small force while the rest of the army turns along the bank to advance two miles upstream to the ford. The cavalry will hold back out of sight. We want Hengest to face us at the crossing, so we must make our intentions obvious. He must be nearby. We camp on this bank and set men to probe the depth of the water - that will force him to rush his army to face us. Once he is committed, the cavalry can begin to move further upstream to find other fords."

Artorius was right. Hengest was encamped some two miles behind the bridge. He had marched for two days to get there and his men were fired up for battle. Before they had set out they had offered sacrifices to Woden and then marched in their various war bands led by their chiefs. It was a huge mass of men and very disorganised. Each chief had his own idea as to how to fight the Romans. Each wanted a position in the battle line where the most glory could be gained. They had donned all their finery, gold armlets, gold collars, jewelled helmets, armour and sword belts.

Their men were less finely equipped but each had the heavy round, solid wooden shield with the iron boss at the centre that was capable of crushing an enemy's skull when thrust with force into his face. Many had the long-handled battleaxes with the broad blades that could slice heads from shoulders. Others carried the long, heavy spears that gave them the advantage of a long reach. Each war band had its own standard and some of them were remarkable. Most were long poles with devices mounted on the top. Some had simple cross bars from which streamed wolves' tails while others sported the entire skin of a totemic animal. Others were topped by animal skulls or stuffed birds, ravens being popular. Hengest's standard was one of the tallest and had a horse's head at the top and two horse tails streaming from a crossbar below it.

Few of the men had any armour other than simple helmets. Some had little in the way of clothes, going to battle stripped to the waist. Each was certain of gaining glory and prestige in the fight. It was a motley army but very dangerous for all it lacked organisation. Each warrior was skilled in the use of his chosen weapon and sheer numbers made it formidable. Hengest had, indeed, brought his whole host to the Medway.

Like most barbarians, the Saxons saw military strength in terms of numbers. A chief's power was measured by how many men he could bring to battle. Most of these were not full-time warriors but farmers who equipped themselves for war when called upon by their chief. Battles were won by the force that had the larger number of men.

Hengest had soon heard of the cavalry who had investigated the defences of the bridge. Soon after he learned of the main Roman force marching upstream. He followed on the other side. The Romans marched more quickly than the Saxons, so when Hengest reached the ford it was to find the enemy setting up camp on the other bank. Men were in the river using poles to measure its depth and marking where there were deeper patches.

The river was wide here and very shallow. Hengest was sure that this was where the Romans would cross. With his vastly superior numbers, he was sure he could stop them. They would not attempt to cross now because it was too late in the day. The battle would be tomorrow.

Artorius watched the Saxons settle down for the night. There were thousands of them. They had few tents. They made rude bivouacs of sticks thatched with leaves for the important men and the rest simply settled on the ground wrapped in furs and cloaks. Artorius posted sentries to guard against any attempt at a night raid across the river. He had already sent some cavalry to find other fords upstream and to discover if the entire opposite bank was being watched. It was not. There was a narrow ford some three miles upstream, the scouts told him. Horsemen might cross it three abreast. It would suffice. So far his plan had worked. Tomorrow would be the real test.

The morning came and the Romans were roused by trumpets. Horns called the Saxons from their rest soon after. Gerontius took his time. He took fully three hours in forming his men up to face the Saxons, each century in turn marching into position. He treated it like a parade and the Saxons watched, fascinated. He meant them to watch. While they watched him they would not be watching Artorius as he led his cavalry quietly away a mile to the rear to move upstream.

The Saxons had never faced uniformed Roman troops. They were impressed by the lines of men in off-white tunics and trews with glittering scale armour and large oval shields painted red and bearing the white boar badge.

Towards noon Gerontius made the first move. His men were drawn up in three ranks, eight centuries in front and eight more twenty paces behind. He sent the eight front centuries into the river which was here about two hundred metres wide. They marched steadily forward to mid stream and halted. The Saxons did nothing. For Gerontius' men this was a nerve wracking time. They were conscious of their lack of numbers, the thinness of their line and their lack of experience. Their centurions and optios were kept busy keeping the ranks straight and encouraging the men. Gerontius ordered his men further across the river until they were close enough to throw their pila. The Saxons were now jumping about and yelling insults, banging swords and spears against their shields. At a word from Gerontius, the front Roman rank threw their pila. It had an instant effect. Many Saxons fell while others found their shields useless from being impaled.

The result was exactly as Gerontius had hoped. The Saxons rushed into the ford to close with his men. A second volley of pila threw their charge into confusion and the third broke it. The Saxons withdrew to the bank to reform. The space between Gerontius' men and the far bank was littered with dead and dying. Red stains flowed downstream towards the bridge. Roman morale was raised. The Saxon charge had been broken without loss to the Ambrosiaci. Gerontius ordered his men onward again. They walked forward in perfect line, their shields making an almost unbroken wall to their front, their sword points glittering in the narrow gaps between the shields.

The Saxons were not used to this sort of fighting. Their battles were warrior against warrior, a headlong charge followed by hand-to-hand combat in a wild melee. In their war against Vortigern's volunteers that was how the fighting had been. Now they were facing trained, professional troops. They were unnerved by the tight formation of silent, armoured men walking towards them. They had not expected missiles to come at them. Their front ranks wavered. Only the press of men behind them kept them in place. The men behind were eager to get into the fight and pushed forward spilling the front ranks into the water. Before they could gather themselves for a charge, the Romans broke into a run at them.

Gerontius knew that it was dangerous to meet a charge standing still. He sent his men forward at a slow trot. When the forces met there was much clashing of shields and many Saxons fell. They could not break into the Roman line. When they hacked at an opponent's head with their axes, he simply stepped forward inside the reach of the blade and jabbed with his sword. Spearmen found they had no space to wield their weapons effectively and when they did manage an over-arm thrust, found their opponent had dodged the point and then stabbed home with his sword. Some Romans fell but the gap in the line was always filled from the second rank.

More and more Saxons poured down from the bank to join in the fight. Gerontius, riding with Cato just behind his fighting line, judged it was time to draw them on further. He ordered his men to give ground, moving slowly backwards as though the Saxon numbers were pushing them back. In reality it gave Gerontius' men an advantage. They were moving back onto clear footing while the Saxons had to clamber forward over the bodies of the dead and wounded.

Hengest, who was watching the fight from behind, was convinced he was winning it. The Romans were being forced back. He ordered the rest of his army into the ford to increase the pressure. The Saxons were now about ten deep, pushing forwards. Only Hengest and his small bodyguard were left on dry ground. The pressure was almost too much. Gerontius sensed the line beginning to waver and called in his reserves. They marched forward and the line steadied.

The Saxons had scented victory and redoubled their efforts. Things were beginning to get a little desperate in the ford. Just when Gerontius had begun to plan how to extricate his men in good order, he heard a trumpet sounding on the enemy's side of the river. He saw Hengest's standard suddenly withdraw and then came the thunder of hooves. "It's Artorius!" he cried and his men took up the cry, "Artorius! Artorius!" Five turmae of cavalry swept along the bank to crash into the rear of the Saxons. Panic ensued. As the cavalry ploughed their way into the press, men began to run. The pressure was suddenly relieved and Gerontius' infantry surged forward to cross the ford and clamber onto the far bank.

Another trumpet call came from downstream. Gawain and two turmae of cavalry had forced the bridge and came galloping to cut off and cut down the fleeing Saxons. Some few escaped but most fell to the swords and spears of the horsemen. Some Saxons formed tight knots of men in an attempt to make a fighting withdrawal. Gerontius' infantry pushed them back and the cavalry overwhelmed them. Soon all was quiet save for the groans of the wounded and the rasping breathing of the troops. Artorius rode to meet Gerontius.

"Well done," he said. "I watched your battle from the edge of the woods for ten minutes before I judged it time to charge. I had to let Hengest think he was on the verge of winning before I struck. The surprise had to be total. Your men were superb. They held their line and kept their discipline. You should be proud of them."

"I was about to call them back when I heard your trumpet. I think that was the sweetest sound I have ever heard! I was beginning to think our plan had gone awry, but you promised you would get here, and you did."

The army set up camp beside the battlefield. Roman dead were buried and the wounded handed to the care of the surgeons. The corpses of the Saxons were stripped of armour and weapons. A heap of gold jewellery was gathered outside Artorius' tent. It was a considerable pile. The weapons were not of much use, not being suited to close order fighting. However, some of the swords had richly gilded, jewelled and enamelled hilts which were detached and added to the pile of booty. The blades of swords and axes could be smelted down and be re-forged into Roman types. Armour was gathered from those dead Saxons who had worn it.

They counted the Saxon dead. It was remarkable. Hengest had brought a host of seven thousand against them and over five thousand had been killed. The Saxon host was effectively destroyed. He would never be able to raise as many men again and the few he could would be raw recruits. The threat from Hengest was gone.

This work was important. For most of Gerontius' men, this had been their first battle and it had been traumatic for them. Making them collect booty and count corpses gave them something to do rather than dwell upon the horrors they had just experienced. Even so, many of the youngest were seen to vomit at the sight of disembowelled Saxons and severed limbs. The stench of blood and faeces was new to them and unexpected.

Cavalry still ranged the environs of the battlefield seeking out fugitives. Any they found were killed. The troopers still remembered what they had seen on the march from Calleva and were merciless.

Artorius and Gerontius decided that they would only advance a little further into Cantium. They would harry the nearest Saxon settlements, burning huts and barns and sending their people back towards Durovernum. That should be enough to teach the Saxons to be more cautious about expanding to the west. When they marched back to Londinium, they would leave a garrison of cavalry on the hill overlooking the road and the ford. A rampart and ditch were made to protect the garrison. This was the only way a large army could quickly pass out of Cantium. To the south lay the great weald forest, dense woodland, through which an army would have slowly to hack its way.

They spent three days on these tasks and then marched back to Londinium. News of their victory had been sent ahead and when they reached the bridge over the Tamesis they were met by Ambrosius and the whole Senate of Londinium. They were given a joyous welcome.

Chapter 5: Securing Londinium.

The next months were spent in Londinium. Artorius was convinced that what was needed was a greater sense of security for its citizens once the army moved away. There was little threat to the southeast now that Hengest had been so comprehensively beaten but there remained many more Saxons to the north, straddling the Ermine Street and around Lindum and Ratae. There were also Saxon settlements along the coast on the north side of the Tamesis estuary. They were the nearest and had the easiest access towards Londinium but had taken no part in the rebellion that Hengest had raised.

However, they were Saxons. They were heathens. They lived apart and followed alien customs and laws. True, they were a different people to those of Cantium and seemed more peaceable. There were still many Romans living peacefully among them and these Saxons were too close to the great city of Camulodunum, which was well defended, to pose much of a threat.

Further north the picture was unclear. Saxon settlements had spread far and wide across the flat lands south of the Wash. This had been thinly populated before the Saxons came. The heavy soils and dense areas of woodland had been unrewarding. There were fewer villas and any Roman settlements were villages rather than towns. Much of the land had been taken as Imperial estates and was used industrially but with the advent of the Saxons the potteries and ironworks had closed and the villages had been abandoned. Now there were many clearings in the forests, each with a Saxon settlement. There was no central authority among them. They had come for land and had taken over the wilderness. Each settlement descended from one family group and, although they were all of the same people, they were scattered.

However, their population was constantly growing and, when a village outgrew its land, its surplus population went in search of new and better land to the west. It was a creeping colonisation. If ever they were to unite under one leader, they would be a very serious threat. They far outnumbered the people of Cantium and more kept coming from across the sea.

"We need to secure the Ermine Street," said Artorius. "It is the one link between Londinium and Eboracum. We also need to keep open the road to Camulodunum. While we hold Londinium and Camulodunum, the Saxons to the north and those of Cantium cannot aid each other. We need secure frontiers."

Ambrosius saw the sense in this. However, he had promised the citizens of Londinium that he would post garrisons on the escarpments to the north and south. If he kept that promise, his army would be reduced in numbers, too few to risk advancing along the line of the Ermine Street. "I cannot demand more taxes from the cities to support more troops. Vortigern tried that and failed. That is what caused the rebellion of the cities. We have to live with what we have got."

"Was not your father, Ambrosius the Elder, one of the rebels?" asked Artorius.

"Yes, but in the name of Justice and Law," replied Ambrosius. "He was exiled by Vortigern for daring to speak out when Vortigern allowed Hengest to increase his numbers. He had spoken his mind in a Council Meeting where men are free to say what they think. Vortigern counted him a trouble-maker and exiled him on trumped-up charges. He accused him of tax avoidance even though he was one of the few who actually paid his full assessment. His estates were confiscated and Vortigern made them his own. When the rebellion started, its leaders called my father back from

Armorica to lead them, knowing that he had been wronged by Vortigern who now seemed to be a tyrant. It was of no use. Vortigern and Hengest were too strong."

Artorius saw the problem faced by any central authority in Britannia. The Governor was elected by the cities and governed with their permission. He was not an Imperial appointee with the backing of an Emperor. He could only do what grudging Senates allowed him to do. If they cut off his supplies or refused taxes, he was powerless - Governor only in name. For the moment Ambrosius was strong. He had a victorious army. While he was successful, the cities would pay up. If he suffered reverses and needed much more in the way of men and supplies, they would not.

Artorius thought long and hard about the dilemma faced by Ambrosius. His promise to Londinium had to be kept but the army could not afford the necessary men. The people of Londinium had offered to man the garrisons themselves but they had insufficient people to do this adequately. The only possibility was to recruit more men and plant settlements along the crests of the hills which would be self-supporting. He thought of the Saxons of the Tamesis estuary. They had proved peaceful. They had not joined the revolt. Would the promise of fresh land be sufficient to entice some families to settle as federates around the edges of the Londinium basin?

True, they were Saxons and so, in British eyes, untrustworthy. However, their new lands would be wide open to punitive raids from Londinium if they broke their trust. They would be too vulnerable to rebel. He suggested this to Ambrosius who grasped at the idea. His only caveat was that the Senate of Londinium might not agree. Artorius said, "Offer them three turmae of cavalry based in Londinium to keep the federates under control. That might sweeten the potion."

The Senate was reluctant but saw the sense of what Artorius proposed. The presence of a strong force of professional cavalry was comforting. They fully trusted Artorius when he said that three turmae of horsemen would be quite sufficient to ensure the loyalty of any federates. It was just the thought of Saxons an easy day's march from the city that worried them. Eventually they agreed.

When emissaries were sent to the estuary settlements they came back with good news. The Saxons there had no love of Hengest. They were no lovers of the people further to the north either. Hengest was a Jute, from the northern tip of what would later be Denmark. The people further to the north in Britannia came from Angel, in central Denmark. They had fought the people to their south on the edge of the low country about the banks of the Elbe. The estuary Saxons had come from there, many as refugees. They were more than willing to guard Londinium from their former enemies.

Artorius rode the tops of the hills to find good places for new settlements. The chalk hills were capped with clays and flints but the soils were light enough to cultivate. On the dip slope of the escarpments wells could be sunk and there would be no problem over water. There were several villa estates which had supplied Londinium but were now abandoned. He selected places where new villages could be sited so that their people could observe way out beyond the escarpment. The houses would be about a mile or so from the crest of the ridges but their lands would extend to the tops. Not only could people live here, they could also have a ready market for their surpluses in Londinium.

It took months to organise the new settlers but the Senate of Londinium proved up to the task and managed it without needing Ambrosius or Artorius. This freed them to turn their attention to the north. It would be impossible to evict all the Saxons from the wide lands they had settled. The mere attempt could have united them and that had to be avoided. What mattered was the security of the Ermine Street and the road to Camulodunum. The army would march north in the spring.

Artorius spent some time writing to his mother. He told her of the march to Londinium and the horrors he had witnessed on the way. He recounted the defeat of Hengest, praising the infantry of Gerontius which had made the victory possible. He made only a passing reference to his promotion as Dux Bellorum with the rank of Prefect. Titles and rank meant little to him other than to enable him to achieve what he felt was his duty. He asked for her prayers and those of the nuns among whom she now lived.

Ambrosius stayed in Londinium. Before the army moved he called a full parade. Those men who had played a major role in the defeat of Hengest or who had showed conspicuous bravery in battle had to be rewarded. Gerontius and Artorius had given him citations as to the performance of many individuals and he meant to recognise them.

He had chided Artorius for not dressing in the uniform of a Prefect. Artorius had replied that he had come to war as a Tribune and had had neither the time nor the means to dress in finery. He liked his cavalry uniform. He trusted his gear. A fancy cloak and a polished cuirass would not make him a better soldier. He did not need them.

Ambrosius accepted this. He had come to like and trust this young officer who had proved so competent. He sensed that Artorius was not fighting for glory, nor to gain wealth and honours. He was fighting out of duty and for Britannia. Even so, he knew that status among the senators of the cities was measured in acres and bullion. If Artorius was to be heard in the Council of Britannia he had to appear the equal of any other senator.

He offered to grant Artorius some of the abandoned estates around Calleva but Artorius had dismissed the idea. "The army is my estate," he said. "It's better than land and villas. I can take it with me wherever I go."

Ambrosius had had to accept that Artorius would not seek material reward. He liked him even more. He would have to find some other way of showing publicly what Britannia owed Artorius.

Chapter 6: The sword in the stone.

The day of the parade came. The troops had spent much time polishing armour, cleaning and mending tunics and repairing campaign damage to their gear. The cavalry polished their chain mail by shaking it in sacks of dry sand. The parade was held outside the north gate of the city and a dais had been set up from which Ambrosius could preside. The troops formed up to form three sides of a square, two sides filled with infantry and the third by the cavalry. They looked splendid in their polished armour standing in ordered ranks behind their standards and vexilla. Artorius, Gerontius and the City Prefect sat on the dais with Ambrosius. It was the City Prefect who began the proceedings. He stood at the front of the dais to address the troops.

"You have won a great victory. You have saved Londinium from the heathen. You have fought a host more than three times your numbers and have destroyed it. Your deeds will go down in history as being equal to those of your predecessors, the Legions of Augustus, Vespasian and Titus. You are true heirs of the glory of Rome.

"I speak for the whole Senate of Londinium to express our praise and thanks for what you have done. Some of you will be recognised individually for heroic acts or outstanding leadership in the campaign. That is right and proper. All are deserving. The Senate has petitioned Ambrosius to grant honours to this army. You have an honourable title, 'The Ambrosiaci', and I can think of none better. You bear your standards and vexilla with pride. On them you have the emblem of Ambrosius, the boar - the peaceful beast that forages the forests but who is so deadly when threatened. It is an apt badge.

"Londinium has voted to decorate your standards. From this day on you will add the laurel wreath of victory inscribed 'Londinium' to your standards and vexilla. Ambrosius approves and so wishes. This is our mark of respect and gratitude. You have fully earned it."

He sat, to the cheers of the men. Ambrosius stood and raised his hand for silence. He then spoke. He told them how he regretted not being with them at the battle of the Medway Ford. He had learned from Artorius and Gerontius how they had fought, how they had held their line against overwhelming odds and then pushed forward to destroy the enemy. None had lost heart and tried to flee. All had been steadfast and had done their duty. He then came to individuals deserving of special mention. The young optio, Marcellus, had seen his centurion fall and his century waver. He had run to the front and had rallied his men, charging the Saxons with such fury that they gave ground before him. Marcellus was promoted to centurion rank and given a gold torque, captured from the Saxons, to wear on his armour.

The list went on. Each individual soldier who had caught the eye of Gerontius or Artorius received a decoration. When it came to some of the officers, their reward was promotion. The decurion, Gawain, who had forced the Medway bridge became a Tribune as did some others.

Finally Ambrosius came to Gerontius and Artorius. "I wanted to reward these men above all others," he said. "They led the campaign. They planned it. They gave you the training and confidence to do what you did. I wanted to grant them estates. I wanted to enrich them to make them equal to any senator in the land. All Gerontius would accept was as much gold as he could put in his saddle-bag without slowing his horse - and that was little enough. Artorius would not accept even that. How do you reward a soldier who spurns gold?

"I had an idea. I will show it you."

Beside him, on the dais, was a large object covered by a cloth. He pulled the cloth away. A large block of dressed, white stone was revealed. On its face was incised the word 'BRITANNIA' picked out in bold red paint. Set upright into the top of the stone was a cavalry sword with a jewelled hilt that glittered in the sun.

"Artorius came to me as Tribune commanding the Sarmatian cavalry. He came at a time when Britannia was bleeding to death, if not dead already. I know something of Sarmatian custom. When a Sarmatian warrior dies he is buried and his sword is set upright at his head. The custom is little followed now. A sword might be taken by an enemy, so a wooden replica serves in its place. This stone and the sword in it represent the grave of Britannia. Now I am going to demand that Artorius takes the sword from this stone and uses it to prove that, while it is in his hand, Britannia shall not die."

Artorius was embarrassed. He could not refuse. He knew the value of symbols to army men. This was a great symbol: it would become the mystical icon of the war against the heathen. He had to take it.

He stepped forward and grasped the hilt. He pulled upwards and the sword slid out of the stone. He held it aloft. Its blade was long and bright and the sunlight flashed off it. The men cheered. Ambrosius had pulled off a master stroke. He had given an immensely valuable thing to Artorius but, more importantly, he had given the army's General a symbolic totem. As far as the troops were concerned, Artorius was now Britannia. Britannia was no longer a vague idea for which they fought. Britannia was Artorius and the Sword of Britannia.

Afterwards, Artorius asked Ambrosius about the sword. "Don't fob me off with magical tales," he said. "The men are saying that it was the gift of a nymph from the Tamesis. They like the idea, so I have not denied it. Where did it really come from?"

"I had it made." said Ambrosius. "There is a skilled smith here, in Londinium. We took some of the sword blades you took from the Saxons and smelted them down. From the iron, the smith fashioned your sword. It is made from four bars forged together. They were heated and twisted and beaten, cooled and heated again and beaten again until the iron had become steel. It was very skilled work. Then I had the hilt fitted. The hilt is of wood wrapped in leather and bound with gold wire. It will not slip in your hand even if your hands are sweating. The cross bar and pommel are of cast bronze, gilded. The gemstones set in the guard were the gift of the Senate. The great ruby in the pommel is my gift. You would not accept estates or riches, so I decided to give you a better sword. After all, as you keep telling me, you are a soldier."

Artorius laughed. "In the manner of your giving it me, you have given me greater responsibilities. The troops will expect me to use it. They say it is invincible. I'll have to take care I kill all my opponents or they will lose trust in the sword and in me. But, thanks anyway. It is a superb weapon. Its balance is perfect. It fits my hand and is like an extension to my arm."

The sword was superb. Its blade, some ninety centimetres in length, was straight sided for most of its length and then tapered to a sharp point. As light played on its surface the blade appeared textured like flowing water. The hand-guard, which was narrow like all roman swords, was a bronze casting with intricate patterns on the surface picked out with enamel and set with semiprecious stones. The grip, too, was textured to fit the hand and was covered in soft leather bound with gold wire. The gilded pommel, which served as a counterweight to the blade and balanced it, held a huge ruby of a deep red colour. The ruby alone was of immense value.

Even the scabbard of the sword was rich. It was covered with red, tooled leather and decorated with embossed gold and jewelled plaques.

The chape was gilded bronze. With it came a new military belt of leather with gold plates set with jewels. The clasp was of Saxon work, captured in the battle. It was solid gold and decorated with intertwining, grotesque animals fashioned in enamel and with garnets set as their eyes.

To complete the ensemble there was a new helmet. It was made of two semi-hemispheres of iron joined and reinforced over the crown by an iron crest piece. Cheek and ear guards extended on either side and a nose guard was set as an extension of the crest ridge to the front. At the back a shallow neck guard was fitted. In form it was a fairly standard cavalry helmet.

What made it different was what the jewellers of Londinium had done to it. The entire helmet had been gilded and designs had been chased, etched and embossed over its surface and then silvered. Each cheek piece was engraved with a rearing horse and scroll patterns covered the rest. Jewels were set around the headband. At the top of the crest ridge was a socket into which a plume of white horsehair had been fitted. It was a beautiful object.

"Now you will look like a Dux Bellorum," said Ambrosius. "I can't have my Commander-in-Chief going around in the uniform of a Tribune. Gerontius is getting a new helmet too. The army expects its commanders to look the part."

He was right, of course. Commanders have to be visible to their men, instantly recognisable at a distance. Their presence and conduct on the battlefield was what maintained morale. This gilded helmet, flashing in the sunlight, would become a better rallying point than any standard.

Artorius stammered his thanks. Estates meant nothing to him, but this new gear was serviceable as well as rich. It marked him out as what he was, a soldier with high command. He knew the troops would be proud to see him in it and so accepted it graciously. He also had to accept a new suit of scale armour with each scale gilded. When he rode in front of his troops he would appear to be clad in gold and in sunlight he would glitter.

Chapter 7: Securing the roads.

Next day the army, all but three turmae of cavalry, marched north. The men, still elated by victory, were confident and eager. They crested the hills north of Londinium and looked out over the great plain that lay before them. Far to the north, beyond the flat, hazy horizon, was the Wash and the fenlands that lay about its edges. To the northeast lay the ancient territory of the Iceni, now densely populated by Saxons. To the east was Camulodunum, the oldest of all the cities of Britannia and the ancient capital of the Trinovantes. Due north was the territory of the Coritani, whose capital was Ratae.

Ratae was still in Roman hands, as was Camulodunum, but the great forested plain was now home to many thousands of Saxons. Their settlements spread south of the Wash and as far west as what would later be Northampton and even as far as what would be Warwick. They lapped around Lindum to its west and north. Through the centre of these settlements passed the Ermine Street to Lindum and then on to Eboracum.

It seemed to Artorius that the road was the key to controlling this area. Armies could move most easily along the roads. If the roads were denied to the Saxons, their armies would have to move cross-country, through much forest and marsh and that would slow them down. What was required was a series of defended outposts from which cavalry could patrol the roads. If any Saxons who dared to use the roads were captured or killed, the Saxons would learn to fear the roads and they would be left to the Romans.

They advanced. At every road junction they paused and scouted about for places where small garrisons could be safe and overlook the road ahead. Where they found such places, defensive earthworks were dug. Then they moved on.

News of their presence went before them. The Saxons were wary. They had heard of the defeat of Hengest. Now his vanquishers were here, marching into their new lands. They had no leader of the status of a Hengest to oppose them. They kept to their settlements and awaited events. For some, events were sudden and fatal. Any settlements within five miles of the line of the road were raided, their huts burned and their crops taken or ruined. Artorius was ruthless. He would clear a wide swathe beside the road. Where underbrush and trees had grown within thirty metres of the carriageway, they were cleared. No ambush sites were to be permitted along the route.

At the same time, the road itself was repaired. It had long been neglected and weeds had grown over it. Here and there bridges had fallen and blocked culverts had permitted flooding that had washed away the surface. Bridges and culverts were repaired and the ditches beside the road were cleaned. It was time-consuming work and progress north was slow.

They advanced no more than five miles a day but it was enough. News of their coming panicked the Saxons near the road. More and more abandoned settlements were found where the Saxons had moved to be further away. Cavalry patrols sent ahead to find any enemy reported nothing. It seemed the Saxons would not risk a fight.

It took most of the summer to get to just south of what would later be Cambridge, the area around which was heavily settled by Saxons. Here a low ridge was crossed by the road. Artorius inspected the terrain. The ridge faced towards what would later be the city. Behind, some low hills protected it. It was the perfect place for a permanent garrison and the perfect place for a settlement. He would suggest that federates from the Tamesis estuary be planted there.

It was time to march back to Londinium. As they went they left small garrisons of cavalry at each of the prepared sites. They would patrol and watch the roads. Altogether there were seven such garrisons and they guarded all the approaches to Londinium and Camulodunum. If the Saxons concentrated and moved, Camulodunum and Londinium would get ample warning. Next year the work could continue northward towards Lindum.

The biggest problem Artorius faced was the drain of manpower. Cavalry were the best troops to garrison and patrol the roads but he had too few. Each garrison, however small, weakened the main army. There was an urgent need to recruit and train more horsemen. More horsemen would need supplies and horses. That was the difficulty. Artorius was confident that news of the defeat of Hengest would encourage men to join the army, if only for excitement, glory and booty. The matter of supplies and horses was something that the Council of Britannia would have to agree - and that was made up of rich, tight-fisted senators like those of Glevum.

They would be perfectly willing to accept the need and approve the idea but once it threatened their own pockets, they would demur. Ambrosius was going to have to get very tough with them.

When Artorius got back to Londinium he found Ambrosius was sick. Londinium was notorious for fevers. It was low-lying beside the great river and its marshes. It was damp and very subject to fog. The people who lived there were used to the climate and had some immunity but incomers like Ambrosius from the healthier uplands of the west country were subject to becoming ill. Artorius reported to Ambrosius' sick-bed and recounted what he had done and what he still needed to do.

Ambrosius saw at once that Artorius was right. The army had to be enlarged. The major need was cavalry and that required horses as well as men. He did not know whence they could come. Artorius had seen the abandoned villas and fallow farmland on his march to Londinium. "Lands abandoned by their owners should be requisitioned by the State," he said. "The surviving tenants should farm them to supply the army. That could bring in the corn we need. The Cotswolds are where the army has always bought its horses. In time of war, they could be requisitioned too. The Council might object, but they cannot legally refuse."

"They will object," said Ambrosius. "They will argue that since they elected me, they can depose me too. They deposed Vortigern after the massacre of the first Council."

"Vortigern was in the pocket of Hengest," replied Artorius. "He had no power any more, neither military nor moral. You have me, and an army. They dare not attempt to depose you while I stand at your side. For the moment the Saxons are cowed and penned in. We have time on our side to sort out the Council of Britannia. We should leave most of the army here to defend what we have won. We go with a small but significant force back west to convene the Council. We ask for men and supplies. We give them the chance to do their duty. If they refuse, we get tough."

Ambrosius agreed. He was sickly, but they could carry him in a litter. It would be good to get out of the accursed damp climate of Londinium. They would call the Council to meet at Glevum. "We might as well beard the lions in their den," he said. "How many troops should we take with us?"

"Three turmae of cavalry and two centuries of infantry." It was clear that Artorius had thought things through in advance. "I will leave Gerontius in overall command here. Bedwyr will command the cavalry, including the garrisons on the north road. Gawain will come with us and Marcellus who will command the infantry detachment."

"You have it all worked out," said Ambrosius.

"That is why I am your Dux Bellorum," laughed Artorius. "It is my job to think ahead and plan."

Two days later, after having explained all to Gerontius and Bedwyr, they set out. They first took Ambrosius to his villa near Sorbiodunum. He was still unwell and Artorius was fearful he might not be able to attend the Council meeting. "If need be, you go in my place," said Ambrosius. "I will back whatever you decide needs doing." He had developed an implicit trust in the young officer.

The Council members from Londinium and Verulamium had come with them and had assured Ambrosius of their support. Artorius was sure that Calleva would support Ambrosius as well. Messengers had gone to every city summoning the Councillors to Glevum. The meeting was scheduled for three week's time. Artorius prayed that Ambrosius' health would improve enough before then.

It did not. If anything it worsened. Artorius reluctantly accepted that he would have to speak for Ambrosius. He did not relish the idea. The Councillors were all educated men. They all had training in oratory. They had had plenty of leisure time in which to play politics and were skilled at playing one city off against another. Would they listen to a military man with no experience of speech-making, no flowery turns of phrase? Would they even let him speak, since he represented no city Senate? True, Artorius now had the rank of Prefect which made him the social equal of any senator but he had no lineage behind him to impress men who prided themselves on inherited wealth and status. They would view him as an inexperienced upstart, lacking education and urbanity. They would be outwardly polite but stubbornly determined to thwart whatever he proposed just to keep him in his place.

Chapter 8: The Council of Britannia.

Artorius went to Glevum so as to arrive on the evening before the meeting. He sent Gawain ahead with a letter for the City Prefect requesting accommodation for himself and his men. Gawain had had to wait outside the gates for an answer. When he got it he was angered. Artorius was permitted to enter Glevum but not his troops. When he showed the reply to Artorius, Artorius had laughed. "The same as before!" he exclaimed, "but this time they are not dealing with a mere Tribune."

On the morning of the meeting they marched to the gate. The sentries opened it to allow Artorius passage and then were amazed when Gawain and a turma of cavalry swept through and secured the way for all Artorius' men to march in. There was nothing they could do except watch as the column marched to the forum.

Artorius rode in the midst of the column in full armour. His helmet flashed bright in the sun and his polished and gilded scale armour sparkled. A great red cloak draped the flanks of his horse. When he dismounted, he left his men formed up in the forum facing the doors of the Senate House. He beckoned Gawain and Marcellus to come with him and strode up the steps and into the chamber.

The Councillors were already gathered and were seated along the sides of the chamber. The President's seat on the praesidium was occupied by the City Prefect of Glevum, a middle-aged man, corpulent and fleshy, who was a little nonplussed by the sudden appearance of Artorius with two officers who stood on either side of the doors. He was even more discomfited at the sight of a detachment of troops in the forum.

"I thought I had given orders that your men stay outside the city," he said.

"They are," said Artorius. "They are far to the east, in Londinium and along the great north road and in garrison overlooking the Medway fords. These men are my bodyguards and wherever I go, they go. It is the norm that a Dux Bellorum has a bodyguard. I assumed you could not be meaning them."

The Prefect looked abashed. He had not meant to display any opposition to Artorius so soon.

"Of course. I understand. You are welcome. I hear that Ambrosius is unwell and that you are here to speak his wishes. So be it. In his absence, the Council has elected me to preside at this meeting."

"I defer to the Council, as far as is legal. I am here as Ambrosius' representative and in my own right as Dux Bellorum of Britannia. That gives me the right to speak in any Senate in this Diocese and in this Council too. I will listen with interest to your deliberations and then tell you what your Governor requests." He was conscious of the intended snub. As Ambrosius' representative he should have been given the right to preside. He sat on a side bench and began to listen as Senator after Senator rose to speak at the tribunal.

Every speech started with a congratulatory reference to the army and its great victory over Hengest. Artorius was praised as the saviour of Britannia. His troops were lauded for their courage and endurance. Ambrosius was praised for raising and training such an army. Then the speeches turned to deal with the problems faced by the cities. Trade had declined. It was no longer possible to get fine wines. The women were complaining that fine silks and cottons were not to be had. The potteries were closing. Too many craftsmen had fled the Diocese. One Senator demanded why it was no longer possible to find an artisan who could repair a mosaic floor.

Once he had heard enough, Artorius rose. He walked to the tribunal but did not stop there: instead he went up the steps onto the praesidium. He kept his helmet on his head so that he seemed to tower above the City Prefect and addressed the Council.

"You all are worried why things are not as they were. You mourn your inability to obtain the luxuries to which you are accustomed. You deplore the lack of trade. The reason for your discomfort lies here, in this Council.

"When Honorius gave you the authority to rule and defend this Diocese, you set up the Council of Britannia. You delegated the responsibility of defence to Vortigern whom you appointed Governor and you were happy when his policies seemed to succeed. You approved when Hengest asked to increase his numbers. You shouted down the one man who spoke out against more federates in the east. To you, the greatest threat lay with the Irish to the west, in Demetia (Pembrokeshire), Dumnonia (Devon and Cornwall) and the Lleyn peninsula.

"When Vortigern required more supplies to maintain his federates, supplies that you had been very willing to vote when danger threatened, you refused him and Hengest rebelled. After seven years of war and when Hengest was on the point of utter defeat you agreed a truce and went happily to meet him at his hall in Cantium. There the first Council of Britannia perished and a resurgent Hengest launched his hordes towards the west.

"This Council, the successor to the first that so signally failed, must redeem its reputation. The lack of trade stems from the isolation of Londinium and the dangers for traders in sailing round the coasts of Cantium. While Saxons are there, there will be little or no trade. There are new Saxons on the south coast near Noviomagus (Chichester). They are contained. I have men watching them. They are a threat to trade coming into the south.

"Great swathes of our lands have been invaded and colonised by the heathen. Cities are threatened. Londinium, Camulodunum, Ratae, Calleva, Lindum - all are threatened. And where are their senators, their great men? Run away to Armorica taking their riches and tenants with them. Those riches could have raised an army three times the size of mine and those tenants could have served as troops.

"At the outset of this war Ambrosius had to plead for aid from the Dux at Eboracum. He allowed Ambrosius just three hundred cavalry. They marched here from Deva and were refused entry to this city and food for their continued march. Their Tribune was sickened that, in a time of war, men prepared to fight and die were refused all hospitality by the richest city in Britannia.

"Ambrosius knows he cannot prosecute this war without more men.

He needs more cavalry. He needs recruits and horses and grain. He is Governor of Britannia and has the right to impose whatever taxes he needs in time of war. He does not so wish. He wishes that this Council shows its support for the men who are fighting and dying in the east by volunteering what is needed.

"Will you so vote? Will you grant him three thousand extra troops and horses and the supplies to maintain them for at least five more years?"

He stood while the City Prefect put the proposal to the vote. The Councillors of the eastern cities all voted in favour. Glevum and Venta Belgarum voted against as did all the rest once they had seen which way Glevum went. The vote was narrowly lost.

Artorius spoke again. "You have voted to protect your riches from tax. You have put your self-interest before that of the Britannia you pretend to serve as its Government. In time of war a duly appointed Dux Bellorum is supreme in all that pertains to the fighting. He represents the Emperor. He has the right to levy supplies for his forces. He has the right to station them wherever they are needed." He drew his sword and held it pointing at the senators. "He has power of life and death over all who impede his campaigning. That is the Law. Any Senate who refuses him supplies or bars his passage is deemed to be in rebellion. Rebels suffer death and the confiscation of their estates." He sheathed his sword and continued in a gentler tone.

"I have no wish to use my army to force Senates to give me what is their duty. Abandoned estates, those that were left when their owners fled to Armorica, will be farmed for the army. That might suffice for a while. Each Senator will give a horse to the army - and a good one at that.

"If you do not, you will see what I have seen. The Saxons will come. You will see burned villas and wrecked farms. You will see the skeletons of the dead scattered on the ground after they were hacked to pieces. You will weep over the bones of babies and toddlers. You will mourn the skeletons of your bailiffs hanging in the doorways to your burned houses minus a hand or a foot from being tortured to divulge where you had buried your bullion to conceal it from the tax gatherers.

"You will live within the walls of your cities, growing what food you can inside the walls like they do in Calleva or Londinium. You will be surrounded by Saxons and not dare to leave the safety of your walls. There will be no trade. You will find you cannot eat gold. When your reserves dwindle you will learn what hunger is. When the rats leave the city for fear of becoming your dinner you will know your end is near.

"You will pray God for miracles. You will pray that the Dux at Eboracum will come. You will appeal in vain to the Emperor in Ravenna. You will ask forgiveness for lives of luxury and greed but it will be too late.

"I am going to give you one more chance. I will put Ambrosius' request to you again and allow you another vote. I will note down which cities wish to be considered in rebellion. As Dux Bellorum, I will deal with them later."

The City Prefect stood to put the proposal once more to the vote. He was shaken by what Artorius had said. He believed him. Who was this Dux Bellorum? He was too confident, too self-assured, to be bluffing.

One by one the Councillors stood to vote. Each looked at the grim soldier standing on the praesidium and glanced out at the troops outside. The vote was unanimously in favour.

Artorius thanked the Council. He would send collectors to gather in the extra supplies. He promised to be fair in his assessments. It was not his nor Ambrosius' intention to impoverish anyone. Obviously the rich would have to pay more than the poor. He would be appealing for recruits for the new cavalry. He trusted no-one would be refused permission to volunteer. He trusted that never again would soldiers in their army be refused entrance to any city. He would remain in Glevum for two more days. He trusted the City Prefect would grant them suitable accommodation.

With that he left. He waited, mounted, until the City Prefect came out to lead him and his men to a large palatial house. This was to be the officers' quarters. The troops would be billeted among the townsfolk. The City Prefect came in with them full of apologies for the misunderstandings and the contrary vote. Artorius grinned at him and doffed his helmet. "I was not surprised. I had experienced Glevum hospitality before. I was that Tribune who was refused supplies for my men."

The Prefect was abashed. "I am sorry. The men at the gate were only following Senate policy. The Senate was concerned about the safety of Glevum at a time of crisis. You might have been Saxons trying to gain access by guile."

"That is the problem," said Artorius. "In time of crisis each city thinks only of itself. It is natural but it breaks the unity of the Diocese. That is why there has to be a Governor with supreme authority. Without that the Saxons will pick you off, city by city. Ambrosius has proved a good Governor. Alone of all his class he has thrown his wealth into the fight. It was he who raised and supplied his forces - he got little or nothing from those he was trying to protect. He was refused drafts of men from among their tenants. He was refused supplies. He has no illusions about the loyalty of the different Senates. He knows that most senators have as their first concern the preservation of their wealth rather than the safety of their Provinces and their people."

The City Prefect knew that Artorius was right. He himself, like his father before him, had spent his adult lifetime evading taxes and piling up wealth. He had done what all the rich did. It had seemed the natural thing to do and old habits die hard. Status among the senatorial class was indeed measured in acres and bullion. Each competed with the next to have larger, more palatial houses, to eat off silver platters, to have the most sumptuous mosaic floors, to import the finest wines - their importance was measured by what they had rather than by what they did.

When the Emperors, fearful of senatorial conspiracies, had stopped appointing senators to military commands, the various senates had indulged in politics without risks. The link between wealth and military obligation had been broken and with it any sense of political realism.

The senators were cultured, urbane, educated men. They knew their history and their law. They could quote the great poets. They vied to have the largest libraries. What they lacked was realism. They assumed that the Empire would last forever. The current crises were just a temporary blip. The Emperor would reassert authority, send an army to Britannia and expel the barbarians.

None saw that the Empire was in its death throes. None saw the anarchy that already reigned in Gaul. None realised that the Emperor in Ravenna had no effective power. The world was changing but they could not change with it.

There was one other factor that made the situation in Britannia unique. In Gaul the barbarians had come in to be part of the Empire. They wanted to share in its wealth and civilisation. The Saxons merely wanted better land and a better climate than that they had had in their homelands. They were not buying into the Empire. They were taking what they could and were not prepared to adapt their culture nor to learn from a more sophisticated one. In Gaul the wars were about political control: in Britannia it was a cultural conflict.

The Saxons did not take over the empty villas they found. They had no need of towns or cities. They marvelled at buildings they could not copy, thinking them the works of gods and then set up homesteads of wooden huts in clearings in the forests. They drank home-made ale and mead rather than wine. They had no need of trade. They grew just enough food for themselves, not seeking surpluses to sell. They used no coinage and their luxuries were what their craftsmen could make or what they could loot from the Romans.

The war in Britannia would be more bitter and more pivotal than the wars in Gaul. What was at stake was the survival of anything of Roman civilisation. Would the Diocese remain Britannia or become Saxonia?

Chapter 9: The new Army.

Artorius returned to Ambrosius with the news that the Council of Britannia had voted the extra men and horses. He explained that troops would be needed to extract the promised supplies because the vote had been grudging. He suggested that a strong place be prepared to store the supplies. The camp at Sorbiodunum would be just about large enough for the new recruits and their horses but a secure supply depot near to the places where horses were bred and much grain grown would be useful.

Ambrosius suggested that one of the old hill forts could be re-fortified quite easily and would have the capacity to store supplies in transit to the army. Gawain was despatched to find such a place. He chose the smallish hill fort at South Cadbury. It was small enough to be re-fortified quickly and was close to the roads along which supplies could come. It was close to the villa lands of the plain which had been Imperial lands farmed to supply grain for the army and for export to Rome. The work was put in hand by the infantry under Marcellus. A new gate was constructed and the ramparts were strengthened with rough stone revetments and a strong palisade. Wooden store-houses and stables were set up inside.

Meanwhile, Gawain's cavalry toured far around seeking recruits. The news of the battle of the Medway Ford had spread far and wide and the reputation of the cavalry that had won the battle so spectacularly made them glamorous. Many men came to volunteer. Some of these were sons of senators with hopes of command in the new army. Artorius disabused them from the first. "Promotion will be by ability, not by social rank," he said. "You all start as troopers. The most proficient will become decurions. Of those, the best might be made Tribunes. You have to prove yourselves in training and in battle."

Artorius knew that troopers had little respect for officers who had not risen through the ranks. They needed to know that their decurions and tribunes had all served time as troopers and had earned their promotions. Only men of such a record could command the trust of their men in battle and in the many other tasks that cavalry could expect.

Some men volunteered as infantry. Artorius accepted them and promoted Marcellus to be the Tribune in charge of training them. Once again the great camp became a hive of activity. Infantry training went quicker than cavalry training. Soon the four new centuries were able to take over the task of ensuring that supplies were collected efficiently, freeing the cavalry to concentrate on schooling the new recruits.

The new cavalry had scale armour since there was no more chain mail and the horses were protected with leather rather than mail. Chamfrons of leather protected their heads with pierced and domed eye guards made of bronze. The protection would not be quite as good as mail but would be adequate. The horses of heavy cavalry needed such protection. They were used for shock tactics, galloping straight into the enemy, knocking men aside and trampling them. Some frontal armour was essential.

After some months, when Artorius was satisfied that all was going well and that he could safely entrust all to Gawain and Marcellus, he set off back to Londinium with an escort of one turma of horsemen. It was time to be back at the front and to plan the next summer's campaign. Ambrosius was still frail and would stay to convalesce at his villa. His presence there would keep the western cities docile and somewhat more willing to pay their dues. Artorius took a great train of grain wagons with him and was readily welcomed as he neared Londinium.

He left instructions that, as troops proved competent, they should be sent to Londinium. After a few weeks a steady stream of fresh cavalry was added to the army. Some of these new recruits were sent to replace the garrisons along the great north road, the garrison by the Tamesis gap at Ambrosden, those by the Medway and those on the South Downs above the South Saxons. Artorius decided that a token army presence in the west would be appreciated by the western cities and despatched a turma of cavalry to set up a fort guarding access from the Lleyn peninsular which was still an Irish Kingdom. They would provide a cavalry presence to aid the Votadini of Gwynedd who were all infantry and lacked scouting mobility. The base still bears their name, Dinas Emrys, the fort of the Ambrosiaci.

More troops were stationed at Ambrosius' villa to which defences were added. This site, Amesbury, also still bears their name. Ambrosius would have to have troops with him to remind the Senates of the basis of his real authority. Three more garrisons guarded the confluence of the Avon and Severn rivers. Saxons might pass via the Vale of Evesham but they were really there to ensure the Senates of Glevum and Corinium would not back-track on their agreement as to the extra supplies.

At last Artorius had what he needed. He had just sufficient infantry to hold any Saxon frontal assault but he now had a preponderance of cavalry who could be used as long-range scouts, mobile detachments and as the deciding, overwhelming element on the battlefield. He was confident that he could now turn events further in his favour.

That summer the new army was despatched to harry the Saxon settlements to the west of the great north road. Federates were settled on the ridge facing Cambridge. The way was opened as far as Lindum. Camulodunum was secured with a strong garrison.

The new troops were good. They proved well disciplined. Their officers were drawn from Gawain's old command and Artorius decided that the enlarged army needed a better command structure. Bedwyr, Cato, Gawain and Marcellus were promoted to the rank of Prefect. Gerontius remained as Artorius' deputy in over-all command of the infantry but Cato was given his own cohort charged with the defence of Camulodunum. Gawain commanded the garrisons and all the scouting parties that went out to raid Saxon settlements and to gather intelligence as to what the Saxons were doing. Bedwyr commanded an enlarged garrison at Londinium as the mobile reserve and as a guard over any access out of Cantium. Marcellus was responsible for the defence of the west, the depot at Sorbiodunum and the forces sent to contain the Irish.

Artorius himself had his body guard, commanded by Vortipor. Vortipor had distinguished himself at the battle of the Medway Ford and was an able cavalry commander. He had almost succeeded in capturing Hengest.

This was a more flexible army and thus more efficient. The Saxons were everywhere contained and cowed. The Irish in the west were contained too. All was going well.

Things went well for a couple of years but then came bad news. Ambrosius was dead. His sickness had lingered and had developed into pneumonia and this had proved fatal. With his death all was back in the melting pot. A new Governor would have to be chosen and that Governor could change the command of the army. If he chose, he could dismiss Artorius and Gerontius, appointing others as Dux Bellorum and his deputy. All depended on the vote of the Council of Britannia.

Artorius had no illusions. The City Prefect of Glevum would seek the post for himself and had the means to buy votes. Caradoc of Venta was also ambitious and would certainly oppose any who would keep Artorius as Dux Bellorum. Each city would jockey for power, hoping its Senate president would gain the Governorship. The cities of the west would seek to reduce the army to save costs. The cities of the east would vote for the status quo, knowing the Ambrosiaci as their only security.

There was going to be much political manoeuvring, much bribery, much slanderous accusation and Artorius himself would be the butt of most of it. He had presumed to tell the Councillors some unpalatable home truths about themselves and their class. Some may have recognised the truth of what he had said. The majority would resent it. He knew he was not popular with the senatorial class. They had had to accept him while Ambrosius was Governor but most of them would now happily remove him.

Artorius mourned Ambrosius. He had proved an able and conscientious Governor. He had striven to defend the Diocese while his fellow senators had merely sought to defend their own wealth. He had been honest and wise and patriotic in contrast to the duplicity, stupidity and greed of so many of his class. He had achieved much with little thanks. He had also proved a good friend. Artorius was conscious how much he owed to Ambrosius.

Artorius was forced, much against his will, to lobby the Senates of the eastern cities. The Council, in electing a new Governor, had to have a two thirds majority for their choice. If the cities of the east voted as one block such a majority would be impossible. The west would be forced to compromise or to fail to appoint any Governor at all.

What the Councillors might not remember was that, until a new Governor was appointed, all appointments of the previous Governor continued with full legal authority. If no Governor was elected, Artorius would remain as Dux Bellorum.

It was a distraction he could do without. He had a war to fight. He should not have to guard his back and lobby for support. He was a soldier and had a soldier's dislike of politics. The Senates of Londinium and Calleva were supportive. They knew him as their saviour and would not support any candidate who meant to remove him. Calleva was particularly opposed to Caradoc of Venta who had refused any aid to them when the Saxon raids had swept about them.

Between them the Senates of Calleva and Londinium began to lobby in favour of Artorius. Emissaries were sent to Camulodunum, Ratae, Verulamium, Noviomagus and Lindum. If all these cities supported a candidate favourable to Artorius, nearly half the votes in the Council would be safe. The west would not get a two thirds majority.

Glevum and Venta were busy lobbying too. However they were not united. Their policies were the same, a reduction in the size and cost of the army, the removal of Artorius, a truce with the Saxons - but each lobbied and attempted to bribe in favour of their own man.

The result was that the Council was deadlocked. The City Prefect of Glevum could not get the needed majority without the support of Venta Belgarum. Glevum would not support Caradoc. The eastern cities could not get enough support for any of their candidates. No Governor was appointed. Artorius was not surprised. The cities would never agree unless they were faced with an immediate danger and thanks to him and the Ambrosiaci they were not. He would continue the war as Dux Bellorum and demand his legal right to supplies. There was nothing the Council of Britannia could do to gainsay him.

Several minor battles were fought over the next two years against Saxon war bands who had come together under one or other ambitious chieftain. All were won by the Ambrosiaci. Their reputation grew. The lesser folk lauded them and willingly gave a tenth of their surplus grain to feed what they saw as their army. The landed gentry were less enthusiastic, grudging what the army claimed. Those who had sons who had joined up were willing enough. Those who had lost manpower from their estates were resentful.

Artorius and Gerontius had forged a powerful and efficient force. It was the only fully Roman field army left in the Western Empire. In Gaul, Aegidius hung on to the last vestiges of Roman power with a small field army that relied increasingly on whatever barbarian allies he could bribe to support him. They were notoriously unreliable, changing sides at will, even in the midst of a battle. The result was that Gaul had sunk into a state of anarchy. In the south and in Hispania (Spain) was the large Kingdom of the Visigoths - ostensibly federates of Rome but in reality totally independent. In the north, Franks had settled across the old Rhine frontier and had spread as far as Paris. Britons had colonised Armorica. Saxons had a presence in the Seine delta and in what would become Normandy. Alemanni and Suevi had carved out territories for themselves. All fought each other, with Aegidius and, later, his son, Syagrius, holding the ring with their small army.

Only in Britannia was the picture clear. The Romans held the majority of the land as a coherent, well defended territory. Saxons held much of the east but were contained. Tiny Irish kingdoms clung to the extreme west but were weak and disunited. The northern frontier along Hadrian's Wall held.

This was the achievement of Ambrosius Aurelianus, Artorius and Gerontius. It had little to do with the cities of Britannia. It was the cities, dominated by over-wealthy landowners, that had nearly brought the Diocese to its knees. It was those same landowners who, in time of crisis, had either fled or had sought to deny what Ambrosius needed.

Artorius had to continue what Ambrosius had begun. As Dux Bellorum he had the authority and with his new army he had the means. He sought to put pressure on the Saxons to force them to unite against him and fight the great battle that would destroy them. This meant a war of attrition. It would take time, but time was on his side. Each campaign gave his new army more experience and confidence. Each campaign made the Saxons more fearful.

Chapter 10: Icel.

Hengest died soon after Ambrosius. He had been the architect of the Saxon invasion of Britannia. He had built his power and had tried to conquer the Diocese. Where force had failed he had used guile and had nearly succeeded. He had lacked sufficient men to win the whole of Britannia. He had made his bid for power too soon and then faced Artorius at the Medway and had gone down in defeat. He was not greatly mourned by his people. They were still licking their wounds and fearful that their new-won lands might be invaded by the resurgent Romans. They were not united. Hengest had drawn his people from all the Saxon lands. The Saxons of

Cantium were mixed, Jutes, Friesians, Angles and Rhinelanders. Their figurehead had been Hengest and now that he was gone there was nothing to unite them.

Artorius was glad at the news. There would be no new King in Cantium. The people would be like those of the middle lands, small communities without a central authority , easy to over-awe or to push back.

Then came grimmer intelligence. For years the Saxons to the north had been receiving fresh drafts of settlers from across the sea. Now their King had come to join them. It seemed that since the majority of his subjects had gone to Britannia, King Icel might as well go there too with all that was left of his people. Angel in Denmark was left empty and abandoned.

King Icel claimed descent from a long line of kings. He started his genealogy with Woden, the god of war. He was the one figure who could unite most of the Saxon settlers in Britannia. He would never get the allegiance of the Saxons of the Tamesis estuary. He had fought them in the past. He would not have the allegiance of the Saxons in Cantium. He could, however, claim to rule the vast majority of the Saxons in Britannia.

This was a threat that Artorius could not ignore. He would have to force Icel to battle before he could consolidate his rule. Since Icel had set up his royal hall at Venta Icenorum (now named Caistor by Norwich), he was too far north to be easily tackled from Camulodunum or Londinium. Lindum and Ratae would have to become the army's forward bases. The war of attrition would have to be stepped up. Saxon settlements to the west of the Ermine Street would have to be harried and their people forced east as refugees. Ratae could be an excellent base from which raiding parties could sally south and west against the Saxon villages.

The army marched north. They went openly and steadily. Artorius wanted Icel to know they were coming. He wanted Saxons to observe the dense columns of cavalry and the ordered ranks of infantry. He wanted the Saxons to be afraid.

They were welcomed in Lindum. Like Londinium, Lindum had been surrounded by Saxon settlement and had withdrawn its people behind the safety of its walls. Artorius' first priority was to clear the Saxons from near the city. Cavalry rode out daily on raids, riding into abandoned villages and burning them. Any stored grain was hauled back to Lindum. The Saxons, who had invariably fled into the forests, would find only embers and no food when they returned. The patrols on the Ermine Street soon began to report of refugees fleeing east.

Artorius kept up the pressure. At last came news of Saxon war bands gathering to the east. Artorius moved south to the banks of the Black Water where he set up a large camp about two miles from the river. He would let the Saxons come to him. His cavalry kept him informed. They could ride up to view the Saxon forces quite openly, aware that they could ride away without any chance of being caught. Artorius soon knew the Saxon numbers and, from the number of standards and totems, how many chieftains were coming against him.

Three times he beat back such war bands with heavy losses. He told his men to make a point of killing the chiefs. "You will know them by their weapons and dress," he said. "They will be the ones with swords and some element of armour. They will be dripping with jewellery. Kill them and their men will tend to flee." He reasoned that if these Saxons had a King they would have an aristocracy too, who would be the leaders of war bands. The more he killed of these, the more likely it would be that Icel himself would come with a great host to fight him.

So far Artorius had suffered few losses among his troops and still had many men eager to enlist. The close order of the infantry had held each Saxon charge and the cavalry had always been able to sweep through the enemy once they had fought to a standstill. The Saxons still had no answer to a determined cavalry charge. Once they broke and began to flee they were easy quarry for the horsemen. Most of their casualties came in retreat.

The Saxons were learning that isolated war bands could do little harm to Artorius and his army. They knew they had not faced his full strength. He had left troops in garrison at Lindum and Ratae. More were at Londinium and Camulodunum. He had some four thousand men at the Black Water. The only way to beat him would be to bring overwhelming numbers against him.

King Icel decided to do just that. He gathered every fighting man he had.

All his chiefs came with contingents. The sons of those who had already been killed were keen to avenge their fathers. A war host of some ten thousand men was gathered and marched towards Artorius.

Icel planned to outflank the Roman line. He would split his force into three. The largest contingent would lead a frontal assault on Artorius' infantry and engage the whole length of his line. Then the other two would try to turn the flanks and roll up the line from either side. The flank attacks would be by dense blocks of men. Icel reasoned that the Roman cavalry were most effective when their opponents were in open order. If his men kept close together they might withstand a cavalry charge.

It was a simple plan and could have been very effective but Artorius had ideas of his own. He knew the numbers coming against him. He knew they would be able to extend their line much further than his. He changed his dispositions.

He would divide his infantry, reinforced by the garrisons of Ratae and Lindum, into two divisions with a wide space between them. This had the effect of extending the line. Behind the central gap a strong force of cavalry would be formed ready to charge through it at the centre of Icel's line. Smaller cavalry forces would be positioned on the flanks and a strong cavalry reserve would be placed so as to strike at any part of Icel's force that seemed to gain ground. He would allow Icel to attack but would aim to push him back to the banks of the river and there pen him in.

To make this easier, he advanced to only half a mile from the river. Icel would have to cross if he wanted to fight and then he would have no easy line of retreat.

He explained his plan to Gerontius. "Much will depend on your infantry," he said. "They will be attacked in front and possibly from the sides too. The centuries on the ends of the line must be able to rotate to face a flank attack. If they do, it will be easier for the cavalry to charge the flanks of Icel's army and rout them towards the river."

"I'll brief their centurions," said Gerontius. "They can do it. They have practised such movements on manoeuvres. It will not be easy in the press of battle but they have the discipline and the training. We'll put our best centuries on the flanks. It might be best if two centuries rotate on each end. It will draw the attacking Saxons round and they will get in the way of their own flank attacks."

They only had to wait in camp for a couple of days. Then they saw Icel's host. A vast mass of men began to deploy on the other side of the river. They were a dark shadow over the ground with hundreds of standards and totems proclaiming how many chieftains had come with Icel. Artorius noted how they formed in three separate divisions. He pointed out to Gerontius that the two smaller masses of men would be the flank attacks. "He'll commit his centre first and then call in the rest to come at you from the sides. We must allow them to come. Only when they are involved can the cavalry deal with them."

Artorius drew up his lines. As usual, half the infantry were held as a reserve some twenty paces behind the front ranks. Icel saw the gap in the centre but it was too late to change his plans. He sent his army across the water and formed again opposite the Romans. The Saxons made a lot of noise, shouting war-cries, sounding horns, drumming weapons on shields: if it was meant to terrify the Roman troops it failed. They stood in their ranks in silence.

Then Icel launched his centre. They came at a run, each man vying to be the first to reach the Roman line. They were met by a hail of pila that felled many of them and disordered those who followed. A second and then a third volley of pila nearly halted the charge but it came on, a yelling mass of men. When they were some ten metres from the line, the Romans charged. They went at a trot, keeping in line, shield to shield and crashed against the Saxons. It was a battle of hacking and slashing and stabbing. The Saxons could not break the line.

Icel's centre had begun to run into the wide gap between the two Roman front line divisions and had begun to swing towards the ends of the Roman lines when they were hit by five turmae of cavalry that charged into them from well behind. The Saxons were in no sort of order in the gap and were swept aside. The cavalry passed straight through Icel's army to halt and reform on the bank of the river.

Icel was confused. He had enemy horsemen to his rear, blocking his line of retreat. He had to win the battle now. He ordered his flank attacks to move. Gerontius saw the two masses of men begin to run forwards and had a trumpet sound. Instantly the two centuries at either end of the line gave ground, wheeling back to face outwards. Their Saxon opponents swung around with them so that when the flanking charges came in, they first hit their own men from behind. For a moment confusion reigned. Then Artorius struck. Cavalry took the Saxons on either flank, smashing into their lines and breaking the impetus of their charge. They broke backwards and the wings of Artorius's army advanced pushing them further back and inwards. The infantry reserve marched to help envelop the Saxon army.

Icel's huge numbers were now his undoing. Most of his men were crammed together unable to swing their weapons. Most were out of reach of any Roman. All they could do was stand and wait till the men in front of them fell so that they could join the fight.

Icel himself was caught up in the crush. He could see little of what was happening. He knew things were going badly wrong but could do nothing. Roman horsemen were riding round and round the battle, cutting down any Saxon who had the sense to flee and launching constant pin-prick charges against the Saxon rear. Icel's army was shrinking towards its centre. Gerontius' men were now almost marching forward, each pace being over the body of a Saxon warrior. The ends of his line had wrapped themselves around the Saxons, most of whom could not lift a weapon.

A trumpet sounded. The Romans halted and backed off several paces still in their close ranks. Eight turmae of cavalry stood behind the Saxon mass with spears levelled. A strange silence fell.

Artorius rode to the edge of the Saxon host. "Lay down your weapons," he cried. "You are surrounded. You are defeated. If you continue to fight you will all die. I would speak with your King. I will offer him terms. If he accepts, you will be able to march home to your wives and children." His words were translated by one of the Saxon federates he had brought from Londinium.

There was a movement within the mass of Saxons as Icel pushed his way to the front. Artorius ordered his men to give more ground so that a wide space was made into which the King stepped. Artorius towered above him on his horse.

Artorius looked down at him. Icel was of middle age. His hair and beard were greying. He was really too old to be fighting in any battle. Artorius sprang down from his horse, sheathed his sword and offered his hand to Icel.

"Your plan was good," he said. "Against any army but mine it would have worked. You should not be downhearted. Your men obeyed you and fought well."

Icel took the proffered hand. "Your men were too good for us. Man to man, my warriors might win but your men fought too close together for mine to gain advantage. Yours is the victory. I am now your prisoner, as are all my surviving men. You may do with us what you will."

"Peace is my will," said Artorius. "You are a King. It is my will that you remain so, as my friend rather than as my foe. You can still command your men. You can still rule your people. However, it must be on my terms. We must agree firm frontiers. There must be no further expansion into the lands of Britannia. You will admit that in Britannia you will owe loyalty to its Government. If we can conclude a firm treaty between us, you can rule your people in peace."

Icel was surprised and gratified. "You are generous in victory. That is noble. You speak like a King, yet you are not so. I will parley with you. We will have much to discuss. Let my men camp here tonight and tomorrow we can talk and come to terms."

Artorius was pleased. Icel did not grovel in defeat. He had dignity. Yes, he could deal with this man. He could make a treaty that would hold. "If your men lay down their weapons and promise not to try to escape, they can camp here for as long as it takes us to reach a lasting agreement. They will have my permission to bury their dead and their wounded will be tended by my surgeons."

Icel turned to his men and ordered them to lay down their weapons. He told them the temporary terms that had been agreed. They were to bury the dead and camp.

It took two days to draw up a formal treaty. Icel was treated with deference. He was allowed to retain his sword. He discussed long and hard as to where the frontier of his lands should be but had to accept that Artorius wanted clear frontiers. Finally Artorius proposed that the Black Water should be a clear enough frontier to the north and that the Ermine Street should be a clear enough marker to the west. The Saxons would be allowed settlements up to within two miles of these lines. Their plough lands could reach to the frontier but their houses had to be two miles back. Saxon settlements would be allowed to within ten miles of Camulodunum to the south.

Icel agreed. He would call back all the settlers he could who had crossed the Ermine Street and find them lands within the bounds set by Artorius. Artorius said, "If your people multiply and your lands become too crowded, send those who wish to start new settlements in virgin land over the sea. They could go to Gaul or to Germania. The old lands of the Franks are now very nearly empty. They could settle there."

The settlement was drawn up in writing. Icel, who could neither read nor write, set his mark to it alongside Artorius' name. Then he made an offer that Artorius was not expecting. "It is a custom among my people that any formal agreement should be confirmed by connecting the two parties together in some way whereby to break their word would be a public dishonour. I have a daughter. I will give her to you as wife. You and I will thus be kin. I will be as a father to you, and you will be as my son."

Artorius was nonplussed. He was single, so he could not refuse on grounds that he already had a wife. He said that he would have to think about this generous offer. He would have to meet the girl and satisfy himself that she was willing. He would not have her forced against her will. Did he want a wife? Would the girl want him? Yet if this treaty depended on such a marriage, could he really refuse?

Icel said that his daughter would of course be willing. She would do her duty by her father. She was honourable and obedient. There was no way that she would refuse to marry Artorius. She knew she would be married to a man of her father's choice and trusted that he would choose carefully. He had found Artorius noble and merciful. He thought him eminently suitable for her.

Artorius was flattered. Icel's offer was generous and genuine. To refuse would be difficult and risked offending the King. "I will accept, on one condition," he said. "Your daughter must choose to marry me of her own will. She must not give herself to me out of duty to you nor out of loyalty to her people. She may dislike me when she sees me. She may find me abhorrent to her. I would not want to commit her to life with someone she cannot love."

Equally, he thought, he could not commit himself to someone he had never met. She might be horrendously ugly. She would be a heathen and not understand his Christianity. She would not speak his language and he did not speak hers. The negotiations with Icel had had to be via interpreters. It would take time for her to learn his language. She would have to adapt to Roman culture. She would have to learn Roman customs and manners. It would be very difficult for her.

Artorius said, "Among my people it is the custom that a man and a woman be betrothed for some two years before they marry and each has the right to withdraw before marriage if they find the other unacceptable. I am willing to betroth myself to your daughter but she will have the right to refuse me at any time within the betrothal and to return to you in full honour. That is as far as I can go."

Icel agreed. He did not understand the Romans fully but if that was their custom, so be it. He would return home and send his daughter to Artorius. The wedding would take place within two years.

Artorius had won a great battle. Nearly half of Icel's army lay dead. Roman casualties were small: some two hundred had fallen. More importantly, he had won a great peace. The Saxons were to abandon a vast tract of Roman territory and live within fixed bounds. The most numerous and best politically organised of all the different Saxon peoples, and therefore the greatest Saxon threat, had been neutralised.

He could now be free to turn his attention to the other threats against Britannia. The Irish in the west still had to be dealt with. He could leave garrisons at Londinium, Camulodunum, Lindum and Ratae to watch the new fixed boundaries and move the bulk of his army to Deva. First he would go to Camulodunum and await the arrival of Icel's daughter. He did not even know her name! He was curious and not a little nervous as to what he had committed himself. He hoped he might like her. He prayed that she might like him. It would be very strange conducting any sort of courtship through interpreters.

He would have to find her somewhere to live while he went campaigning. He owned no house. His home had always been the barracks or a campaign tent. He had no great wealth. His pay was simply the rations issued to the army and a share of any captured booty. He ate and drank what his men ate and drank. Now he had to maintain a princess. For all the Saxons seemed primitive in Roman eyes, their great men lived in some style. She would be used to the best.

Gerontius laughed at his concerns. "You are Dux Bellorum of Britannia. You are entitled to the proper pay of such a rank. You are entitled to half the booty captured in battle. The men would not grudge it you. They love you for living like one of them, but think you are a little mad not to take what is your due."

"The Councillors will not like it if I become rich like them," said Artorius. "They will claim that I am continuing the war merely to enrich myself. They will be more inclined to refuse supplies if any larger portion is to go to me. They will not like my betrothal. They will not willingly accept a Saxon Princess as their social equal. There will be much slander against me. Rumours will circulate that I am siding with the enemy. They will see me as another Vortigern - he married Hengest's daughter."

"Let them think what they will." replied Gerontius. "They are a spent force. They proved that when they failed to choose a new Governor. They cannot agree among themselves even on the most trivial of affairs. They cannot do anything against you. The east supports you and, more importantly, the army supports you. You could make yourself Governor if you so chose."

"I don't want that. I am a soldier. A Governor has to be a politician and deal with the likes of Caradoc of Venta. I have no experience of plotting and secret deals. I want nothing to do with all that." Artorius was adamant. He was no politician. He disliked faction and intrigue.

They marched to Camulodunum to await the arrival of a Saxon Princess. The surviving Saxons, their wounded having been patched up by Roman surgeons and having had their weapons returned as a mark of respect, marched home.

Chapter 11: Winnifhoere.

It was a full week after they had reached Camulodunum that news came of Saxons coming towards the city. Fifty warriors marched as escort to a covered ox-wagon. Beside the wagon was King Icel himself. They had been challenged on the road by a cavalry patrol which had now added itself to the escort so that it was an impressive sight.

Icel had dressed for the occasion. He wore a long, fur-trimmed tunic of a rich red over yellow trews that were gathered close about his legs by cross gartering. A rich sword belt at his waist had a huge, solid gold clasp. His arms were decorated with heavy gold bands and a short blue cloak edged with ermine was fastened with a large brooch. His long hair and beard had been curled into ringlets and he wore a jewelled, gold circlet on his head. To Roman eyes he was a typical barbarian but he was a splendid one in his finery.

Artorius rode out, in full armour, to meet the cavalcade. With him went Gerontius and the City Prefect and one turma of cavalry as an escort. They processed into the city. Icel was hugely impressed. He had never seen a large Roman city. Venta Icenorum was very small, poor, run down and virtually abandoned. He marvelled at the buildings of brick and stone - materials the Saxons had not mastered. He was amazed by the massive city walls and the many semicircular bastions that projected from them and the tall towers that flanked the gates. He was overawed at the size of the central church. The forum with its Senate House and basilica, even though, in Roman terms, dilapidated and in need of some repair, seemed to him to be the work of gods and not of men.

How could he have had the stupidity to think he could defeat a people who could make such works? He felt humbled in the face of the outward signs of civilisation.

They went first to the Senate House where the senators had been gathered. It was important that Icel be given a Kingly welcome. This was a State visit and all the due courtesies had to be paid. Icel was given a seat to one side of the praesidium alongside Artorius. Speeches were made, praising Artorius for his victory and Icel for concluding a treaty which promised perpetual peace.

All this took time, since all had to be translated, sentence by sentence for Icel. He too made a speech. "I have come here to keep my promise. A King must ever be true to his word. I made a pact with Artorius who beat me in fair fight. I have ordered my people back within the bounds we agreed. I have forbidden any to cross those bounds in the future. I have made my sons swear to abide by the treaty so that it will hold after I am gone. I have brought my daughter with me to give into the care of Artorius. They are betrothed and will marry if they both so wish within the next two years." He rose, went to the doors and fetched in a young girl. "This is Winnifhoere, my daughter."

It was said with pride. Winnifhoere was slender and beautiful. She was dressed in a simple robe of the finest wool dyed a pale blue. Over her shoulders she wore a long cloak of a rich red colour fastened on each shoulder with large gold brooches. A belt of gold chain hung at her waist with a richly enamelled clasp. Her yellow hair was worn long in two plaits that reached to her waist and a jewelled circlet topped her high, intelligent brow.

Artorius was struck by her beauty and by her demeanour. Her grey eyes had glanced all around the Senate chamber as she entered, not with amazement, but with interest. She had then fixed them on Artorius with a somewhat quizzical look, as if weighing up his possibilities as a future husband. It was as though she knew and sympathised with his predicament. He was being saddled with an alien wife whom he might not like.

He did like. He warmed to her from the first. She looked fragile and vulnerable and he wanted to protect her. She walked to the praesidium on her father's arm and he placed her hand in that of Artorius.

"This is the daughter of my later years," he said. "All my other children were sons. She is special and precious to me. I give her into the care of

Artorius who has proved noble and gracious. Among my people those are the attributes of a King. I think it right that Artorius should wed a Princess."

Spontaneous applause broke out among the senators. Something special was being enacted before them. They had seen the softened look on the face of Artorius: they had approved the quiet dignity of Winnifhoere. It did not matter that she was Saxon and he Roman. Somehow it seemed utterly appropriate that these two should be together.

They adjourned to the basilica for a State Dinner. Artorius had been asked what should be served to a barbarian King. He had said that the Saxons ate much of roasted meats, breads and stews. Roast beef would be acceptable and some good wines.

All the senators and their wives were there, plus sons and daughters. All fifty of Icel's bodyguard, of whom three were his sons, also had to attend. Gerontius and the Tribunes represented the army. At the top table were seated the City Prefect with his wife and daughter, Artorius, King Icel and, of course, Winnifhoere. She was the focus of attention.

Artorius had dreaded this. The matrons of Camulodunum would watch her like hawks for any lack of Roman manners. They would delight in recounting any social solecisms she might commit, proving her 'barbarity'. As they had walked hand in hand to the basilica he had gently squeezed her hand in encouragement and sympathy. She had squeezed his back, looking sideways and up and giving him a shy smile.

Winnifhoere had never eaten a Roman meal with a full setting. She did not know what forks were for. Saxons simply carved their meat from the joint with a dagger and put it to their mouths with their fingers. Icel's sons and the rest of the escort did just that, ignoring the fancy two-pronged forks. Winnifhoere copied what Artorius did. It was clear she was not used to a fork but she was proving no 'barbarian' in public. Icel too copied his hosts.

She soon noticed how Artorius regularly dipped his fingers into a finger bowl of water and dried them on a cloth before taking wine from his glass having wiped his lips first. She did likewise. If all was unfamiliar to her, she did not show it. She was pleased that Artorius noticed what she was doing.

He grinned at her and winked. She sensed he cared and she felt strangely at home. If this was the worst she would face in becoming a 'Roman', she could cope.

She looked down the length of the long trestle tables at which were sat the guests. She marvelled at the elaborate hair styles of the women, their painted faces, their fancy robes of silk and fine cotton. She did not then know that the dresses were all old and kept as 'best' because silk and cotton were no longer to be had. She wondered at how the women painted their faces. They must have slaves to do it for them. Again, she had no experience of a mirror.

Many of the men wore white tunics with a purple band. She wondered why they did not wear colours, not knowing that these tunics were a badge of rank. The other Roman men were clearly warriors. They wore mail armour with fancy belts from which hung their swords. They wore leather boots. They were much the same as any other warrior except that all dressed almost the same.

She listened to the babble of conversation. The Romans spoke the British tongue. She could not understand it, but it sounded musical and expressive. It was something she was determined to learn. She could hear the Saxons chatting among themselves and watched, amused, as they attempted to communicate with the Romans by sign language.

Icel was painfully chatting to the City Prefect through the interpreter. The conversation was slow and stilted but they seemed to be getting on good terms. Because Winnifhoere had no-one to talk to, she had time to be an observer and she was fascinated. When she spotted a woman staring at her, she responded with a smile - and often received one back.

Artorius noticed this and thought, "Bravo! She's winning them to her side." He felt a surge almost of pride. She was intelligent, this Saxon Princess. She was not afraid. It was almost as though she was already his wife.

After the banquet, all retired to the quarters prepared for them. The Senate had agreed that Artorius should have a private house in Camulodunum rather than live in the army headquarters. That was not the appropriate place for a betrothed couple. A large empty town house whose erstwhile owner had fled to Armorica had been commandeered and put in order and a wing prepared for Winnifhoere. It was a very large house in the form of three wings with a courtyard garden. The front had the usual double doors that opened into the atrium and offices to either side. The two wings that flanked the garden had the kitchen and store rooms, the dining room and, at the far end of one wing, the bath house. These were rare in town houses - only the super-rich could afford private amenities. On the top floor were bedrooms. Servants had been engaged, a cook, a housekeeper, a maidservant, steward and gardener. Artorius had insisted that a Saxon woman who could speak the British language be employed as a companion for Winnifhoere. She must have someone with whom she could talk in her own tongue. Artorius' quarters were in a separate wing.

It had been a good day. Artorius was captivated by Winnifhoere. She had dignity and grace. She was obviously intelligent. She had adapted to strange surroundings and unfamiliar manners. Most of all, she had made an impression on the hard-bitten senatorial wives whose tongues were like razors and whose lives revolved on malicious gossip. He liked her. He felt she might come to like him. She had responded to all his gestures of sympathy and encouragement. She seemed to understand exactly what he was trying to communicate by gesture, smile or facial expression. She had responded with her own and he had found he understood too. It was a good beginning.

There would, of course, be problems. He was Christian. He did not know, nor understand, the beliefs of the Saxons. The Church, in the person of the Bishop of Camulodunum, would not approve this union. Roman Law had forbidden pagan worship within the Empire for over half a century. While the law had signally failed in the countryside, it had been enforced in the cities. Whatever Winnifhoere believed, she would not be allowed any public manifestation of her faith. He felt for her.

There would be little time for him to court her, either. Their time together would be limited. He had grave responsibilities that would drag him away for long periods. He could not take her on campaign - she would be in danger if he lost a battle and concern for her safety would be a great distraction. He had to go west very soon. He could not be seen to be neglecting the wars because he had a Saxon girlfriend! Icel had given him a great gift but with it came ties and extra responsibilities. Would she understand?

Winnifhoere went to bed that night with her own concerns. She liked Artorius. He seemed affectionate and sympathetic. She had been impressed when she had peeped out of the covered wagon when he came to meet her father and his escort. He had seemed to be a part of his horse and was clad in brilliant, glittering armour. He was obviously worshipped by his soldiers. She had been excited by this new environment and all these new experiences. She was pleased to have a Saxon companion with whom to talk. That had been very considerate of Artorius. It would take time to get used to this new life, whether or not she married him.

It was all strange. Even the bed was strange with its linen and cushions. She had been surprised to be given a night robe. It seemed the Romans dressed to sleep. She had so much to learn. She decided that her first priority would be to learn the language. She wanted to be able to talk to Artorius, to discover what he was really like. All she knew was what her father had told her. He was noble and generous. He was merciful. He was a great war leader with a powerful army. But did he laugh? Would he be really caring of her? Would he marry her merely to cement his treaty with her father or would he choose her despite the political advantage?

She already knew he was to go away to the west without her. She determined to master some of the British language before he returned. That at least would demonstrate her commitment to this strange new world.

Chapter 12: The gathering storm.

Next day, King Icel left with his sons and his bodyguard. He said his farewells to Winnifhoere and told her that Artorius had given him permission to visit her regularly. That had been generous. He had also said that Winnifhoere was free to visit her erstwhile home whenever she wished. She was pleased. Artorius saw her as having family and friends and would not seek to cut her totally from her old life.

Artorius and Icel parted as friends. Icel respected Artorius and Artorius had developed a deeper understanding of Icel as leader of a nation. He gave him due honour. Vortipor was sent to escort Icel home. There must be no misunderstandings with the cavalry patrols on the roads. Artorius was sure the treaty with Icel would hold. He could reduce the garrisons at Ratae and Lindum and move west against the Irish. The remaining troops were to assist King Icel in calling back the settlers to the west of the Ermine Street. There had been raids from Ireland against the northwest coasts and towards the Solway Firth. New Irish settlements had to be averted. He would march to Deva and despatch troops from there to face whichever threat seemed most serious.

Yet again he sent letters ahead to his mother at Deva. He wondered what she might think of him getting betrothed to a Saxon, albeit a princess. She had been proud of his appointment as Dux Bellorum and had congratulated him after the battle of the Medway Ford. She had told him that he was living up to the standards his father had set and that she had expected nothing less. Now she was going to have to accept his possible marriage to a barbarian. He hoped she might understand.

News of the great victory on the Black Water had gone before him. He was feted by the common people. Cities like Glevum, whose Senate complained that Artorius should have submitted the treaty with Icel to the Council of Britannia for approval, had already begun to question whether the army needed to be maintained any longer at its present strength. Artorius ignored their carping. Whilst camped at Deva he received the news he had long expected. Venta Belgarum was refusing its supplies. Caradoc was in rebellion. He had failed to gain the Governorship. The Council of Britannia had failed to remove Artorius from his command. As far as he was concerned, Venta Belgarum would be independent.

Artorius sent Gerontius with a strong infantry force to demand his rights and to force Caradoc to obey Roman Law. Meanwhile he would advance north, into the lands of the Dux Britanniarum to aid him in securing the western end of the Great Wall. Irish raiders were to be expelled from the lands about the Solway.

Once there he had to fight just one battle north of the Wall to restore all to order. Immediately afterwards he received very grim intelligence. Gerontius was dead. He had reached Venta Belgarum and had learned that

Saxons had occupied the Isle of Vectis (Wight). When he heard they were landing at Portsmouth, near the old fort at Portus Adurni (Portchester), he had marched with Caradoc to oppose them. At the height of the battle, Caradoc's men had turned and sided with the Saxons. Gerontius had extricated most of his men but was killed whilst withdrawing them. It seemed the Saxons of Vectis were Caradoc's federates.

Artorius was enraged at the treachery. He mourned his friend. Cato was promoted in his father's place with an assurance that he would be avenged. The army marched rapidly south. More bad news followed. The Saxon chief, Oesc, who had been confined near Bamburgh by the Dux Britanniarum, had escaped by sea and gone to Cantium. There he was gathering a host. The Saxons of Vectis had come from Cantium. Would Caradoc ally himself with Oesc? Artorius marched post-haste to Sorbiodunum. He called in the garrisons from Lindum and Ratae. He ordered the cavalry at Londinium to step up patrols on the borders of Cantium.

A breathless messenger arrived from the garrison watching the South Saxons by Noviomagus. King Aelle was on the march with a host. He had passed into the great Weald Forest where cavalry would be hampered.

This had all the smell of a conspiracy. It probably had Caradoc as its instigator. It had obviously been planned for some time. Caradoc would trust that Artorius would rush east to confront Oesc. There, or on the way there, he would be ambushed by Aelle and the men of Venta. If he stayed at Sorbiodunum, the three armies could unite with overwhelming force against him. Worse, Caradoc knew whence Artorius drew his horses. He could pass through the Tamesis gap and strike at the Cotswold villas. Then he could advance west towards Glevum.

Artorius sensed that Caradoc had a grudge against Glevum. Its Senate had refused to vote for Caradoc as Governor. That would be his real objective.

Artorius called a Council of War. He placed before his officers all he knew and what it might signify. All depended, he said, on what Caradoc did. He could not advance east while Caradoc threatened his flank or his rear. He needed to know where was Aelle, would Oesc too pass via the great Weald Forest and which direction would Caradoc take from Venta. It was clear they were going to avoid the roads. Cavalry could outdistance them along them and bring Artorius intelligence. Caradoc knew that.

Gawain spoke up. "If they aim for the Cotswolds by way of the Tamesis gap, they will need the permission of the two Saxon settlements there. They are of Icel's people. Let Icel know that they are in danger and let him reinforce them. Then the enemy would have only two ways to follow. They could go along the old ridgeway where our cavalry could have a field day because the land is open and treeless, or they would have to use the Kennet valley and come out on the northern edge of the Sorbiodunum Plain. We could wait until we know which way they will come and pick a battleground to our advantage."

Artorius saw the sense in this. Cavalry were to scour the area to the east to discover where the enemy forces were. Caradoc was to be watched, and if he moved, Artorius was to be told which way he went. Would he strike north towards Sorbiodunum, or would he move eastwards to meet Aelle and Oesc? Artorius thought the latter most likely. Caradoc was a bully and, like most bullies, a coward. He would never risk facing Artorius alone. No, he would link up with his allies.

News came from Londinium. Oesc was passing south of the North Downs following the Holmesdale, the valley of the River Mole. This was open land to the north of the Weald forest where there had been villa estates. The gap in the downs where the river flowed northwards to the Tamesis had been guarded by a strong cavalry screen but Oesc had gone on westwards.

A message was sent post-haste to King Icel. His reply was warm. He had sent two thousand of his warriors to aid his people by the Tamesis. That should be sufficient to bar the way to Oesc. He told Artorius that Oesc was now calling himself a King. Icel was not impressed. His was a long lineage descended from Woden - Oesc was an upstart with no pedigree.

Because the Saxons were passing mainly through forests they were very slow. Artorius' horsemen soon had glimpses of them. An army camping gives itself away by the smoke of campfires. An army thrashing its way through woodland leaves a trail of flattened underbrush. It soon became clear that both Aelle and Oesc intended to meet at one of the fords over the Tamesis near the gap in the hills.

All now depended on what would Caradoc do. At last he marched. He set himself at the head of his Saxon federates and headed northeast. As Artorius had guessed, he too was going to meet up with Aelle and Oesc.

Artorius posted cavalry to hold the ridgeway, in case the enemy went that way. He doubted they would because they feared cavalry and the ridgeway favoured horsemen. "If Icel proves honourable and bars the Tamesis Gap, they'll come through the Kennet valley. That's where we will have to fight."

He rode there with Cato, Gawain and Bedwyr. The valley was broad and mainly flat with the river winding through towards the Tamesis. There was no clear place within the valley where they could gain much advantage from the ground. As they returned Artorius noticed how the valley suddenly narrowed. A forested spur thrust southwards across it just where the road from Venta Belgarum to Cunetio (Mildenhall) crossed the valley from the south. The road was built on a low causeway across the valley.

Artorius halted to examine the place. The causeway formed a low rampart across the valley. Here the valley was narrow enough for his army to completely block the way west. The spur from the north could hide any reserves from view. To the east the land was fairly open. Two abandoned villas were there and their farmland, though covered in weeds, was still clear of trees. The open land extended for some four miles eastwards. Two miles to the east a low hill was crowned by one of the old Celtic hill forts.

Artorius thought of putting a garrison in it, but his scouts reported that although it had a formidable double ditch and could easily be held, there was no well. A garrison had to have water. Artorius abandoned the idea. He would fight at the road. If his army was defeated, the Saxons would have a clear passage across the north of the Sorbiodunum Plain towards Glevum and Aquae Sulis (Bath). It was a risky strategy but this site offered the best chance of success.

They returned to Sorbiodunum for detailed planning. They might have as much as a week to prepare.

Chapter 13: Badon.

The armies of Aelle, Oesc and Caradoc met. They camped by the Tamesis. Before they moved on, they had things to decide. First and foremost they had to appoint a Commander-in-Chief. This was not easy. Oesc had brought the largest contingent and assumed thereby that he would command. Caradoc had forged this alliance and knew where to strike. He assumed he would lead. Aelle was a King with a better lineage than Oesc and would not permit his men to be led by a self-proclaimed King with no pedigree.

There was much discussion. Several times Aelle threatened to march his men home. Eventually they agreed that Aelle would command with Oesc as his deputy. Caradoc had to be content with the command of the right wing.

Next they had to decide their route. Caradoc was for going through the Tamesis Gap and Aelle sent men to negotiate with the two Saxon settlements there. They were to persuade them to join the expedition. They came back with the news that King Icel had sent warriors to block their path. If they attempted to force their way through, King Icel would take that as a declaration of war. He would invade Cantium. Oesc had immediately vetoed any attempt to pass through the gap.

Aelle proposed that they pass by way of the ridgeway. Caradoc agreed it was a possible route. Oesc opposed it. It was too open he said. Artorius almost certainly had troops up there already and his cavalry could hit them again and again without their being able to reply. His people knew what Roman horsemen could do. They would have to pass to the south of the hills. Thus it was agreed that they would pass through the Kennet valley.

This actually favoured them. The eastern end of the valley was forested. They could pass almost unseen and safe from horsemen if they avoided using the road towards Aquae Sulis. They marched and vanished into the woods.

Artorius soon had intelligence of their move. King Icel's men had informed him of the approach to use the Tamesis Gap. Artorius had had the great camp watched and thus soon knew when it broke up. His men on the ridgeway had seen no Saxon host. It was to be the Kennet valley.

Artorius issued orders and his army moved. Each division knew where to go and what to do. They camped behind the great forested spur that jutted into the valley. Cavalry occupied the hill fort to observe the first signs of the Saxon advance. Until it came they could get water from the river that ran past it just to the south.

Artorius ordered the chaplains to say daily Masses for the troops. This would be a crucial battle and it was right that the men be fortified by religion as well as patriotism. He himself took to wearing a cloak with the image of the crucified Christ embroidered on it. This was to be a fight for the very soul of Britannia and Artorius would make it a crusade.

They waited. The valley was silent and peaceful. It was empty. It took two days for the Saxon host to march through the forest to reach the open farmland. As soon as it appeared, the garrison at the fort rode back to Artorius and he deployed his men.

Cato's infantry were to hold the causeway. It would be a thin line of three ranks and would have no reserve. They would have to absorb the Saxon charge and hold it. Behind the spur, Artorius held the majority of his cavalry. More were placed behind a small hill to the south. A token force of horsemen were to deploy openly behind the infantry.

Artorius wanted the Saxons to come on in a frontal assault. Once their charge was held, the infantry were to give ground as though the Saxon pressure was too great for them. Once they had moved back enough into wider ground, the cavalry would sweep out from behind the hills and take the Saxons in flank. It would be very hard for the infantry. Any backward movement could easily break the line and could lead to a rout. The lack of a second, reserve line made this more likely. Discipline would be everything. Artorius himself would be with the cavalry behind the line with Bedwyr. Cato would be immediately behind his infantry. It was important that the Saxons see the small cavalry force. They would think their few horsemen all they had with them and that would embolden them.

When the Saxons debouched onto the open land and looked ahead, they soon saw Artorius' line along the causeway. They advanced rapidly and deployed. Caradoc's men were on the right, Oesc's formed the centre and Aelle's were on the left. They advanced at a loping run to halt some three hundred paces from Cato's thin line. Cato was outnumbered by some ten to one.

The Saxons took some time to reform their own lines. Because Cato's infantry filled the entire width of the valley, they could not use their numbers to overlap and then turn his line. They would have to smash through it. They began to advance in a solid mass. Then they charged.

As usual the charge was rather like a race. Each warrior wanted to be the first to reach the Roman line. Their front became jagged as the fastest men got ahead. Cato's men were in the normal three ranks. The first rank waited, their pila gripped in their right hands. Cato rode back and forth behind them. "Wait my order," he called. "Keep steady. Wait."

When the Saxons came near enough, he cried "Loose!" and, with the sounding of a trumpet, a flight of pila flew into the front ranks of the Saxons. Men sprawled as they were hit. Others tripped on the shafts of pila that had impaled their shields. The charge faltered and then came on pushed forward by the men behind. A second and third volley of pila brought many more Saxons down. The approach to the causeway was littered with dead and dying and the Saxon charge had to run over them.

The lines met with a crash of shields. Cato's men, in close order, could stab at whichever Saxon exposed his body as he wielded his heavy weapon. The pile of dead and wounded grew. The cavalry closed up close behind the fighting line and assisted the infantry with archery and javelins.

"Give ground," cried Cato and, with another trumpet signal, the whole line took three paces backward. The Saxons surged forward. "Again!" cried Cato. The line withdrew some more. Gradually, a few paces at a time, the Romans backed away. The Saxons were in high spirits. They had lost hundreds but they were pushing the Romans back. They were winning the battle!

Cato kept up the backward movement. It was not easy. The line was now no longer as straight. He rode back and forth encouraging his men. "Hold till the line straightens! Move back a bit more! Straighten your line!"

He was taking casualties too. More and more of the second rank were having to plug gaps in the first and his men were getting very tired. However he had done enough. Artorius, riding behind the lines, could now see sufficient space at each end. He drew his sword and raised it high. This was the signal. From either side cavalry poured onto the battlefield and smashed into the flanks of the Saxons.

Chaos reigned among them. As men were bowled over only to be stabbed by Roman spears, the leaders took to their heels. On the right wing, Caradoc and his bodyguard fled back while his men tried vainly to stop the Roman charge. On the left wing, Aelle left the field too. Oesc watched them go, saw the rout that was beginning, and followed them. Thousands of Saxons at the rear of the battle broke and ran. Cato's men, sensing the faltering of the Saxon line, began to advance, a wall of shields and sword points.

Artorius galloped forward to join Gawain who had led the cavalry attack on the left wing. "We must stop them reaching the woods!" he cried. "Send your men after and past them to block their escape!"

Ten turmae of horsemen, recalled and re-formed by trumpet calls, set off at a full gallop down the valley. They passed right through the Saxon rout without stopping and on past the hill fort almost to the end of the open farmland. There they halted and faced about. The fleeing Saxons were now running towards them.

Back at the battle site the slaughter went on. Cato's infantry advanced, an implacable wall of mail and shields. Horsemen rode on either flank, herding the Saxons back. Any who slowed to try to fight were ridden down. The rout became general. The entire Saxon host became a torrent of terrified, fleeing men, running blindly in a vain attempt to outdistance and outrun the horsemen. They were hunted across the farmland.

Caradoc led the rout. He was the first to see the long line of red-plumed horsemen barring the way to the woods. He veered to his left, splashed through the shallow river and clawed his way up and into the hill fort. Aelle and Oesc followed. At least the horsemen could not follow them there.

Soon the fort was almost filled with Saxons. They were the survivors: the rest were spread in heaps across the open land or lay in piles where they had fallen in front of Cato's line.

Artorius' cavalry rode round and round the fort, penning the Saxons in behind its double ditches. The Saxons manned the ramparts and threw up barricades in the entrances. At last they felt safe.

The fort was at the western end of a low ridge, at its highest point. It was small. Roughly circular in shape, it crowned a low escarpment. The hill fell steeply from it on three sides, north, west and south. To the east the ridge sloped gently away towards the distant woods. On this side there was just one ditch and the three and a half metre high rampart. On the other sides the ditch had been doubled. The entrances were to the north and to the south and were approached by steep winding tracks between the ramparts. It would be a difficult place to attack, and impossible for mounted men.

Artorius brought up his army and halted below the fort. He called Gawain, Bedwyr and Cato to his side. He asked by what name the fort was known. "It is called Mons Badonicus", said Bedwyr. They looked up at the ramparts above them. "We have them penned in," said Artorius. "They will be expecting us to attack on foot and so lose many men. We won't give them that chance. We sit out here and wait. They have no water. We block them from the river on the south side and wait. After three days they will be mad with thirst. They'll break out and then we will have them."

The army camped. Constant patrols circled the besieged Saxons. Infantry set up camps opposite both entrances. The Saxons lining the ramparts were noisy, yelling insults and waving weapons. Gradually they quieted. Reality began to dawn on them. They were trapped in their stronghold with little food and no water.

As night fell, they looked down on the Roman army. They were ringed by camp fires. Wagon loads of supplies had been brought up for Artorius' men. They listened to them singing, laughing and feasting. The smell of roasting meat wafted up to the fort. Some of the Saxons tried to sneak away under cover of darkness. They blundered into Artorius' patrols and were swiftly despatched.

Their leaders were at odds. Oesc blamed Caradoc for the rout. He had been the first to run, he said. He was a coward. Aelle blamed Oesc. Oesc should have kept men in reserve as they had planned but he had let all charge in one go. Oesc knew him to be right but he had been unable to hold any back. They had all wanted the glory of victory and the chance to prove themselves.

They bickered through the night. They had no plan. When dawn came the Romans were up and ready. The cavalry still circled the fort. The river was guarded. The Saxons had been amazed at the cavalry attack. Artorius had hidden more than half of his army and had more cavalry than infantry. The Saxons waited for Artorius to offer them terms. He did not. They saw him riding with his officers. The sun flashed off his gilded helmet and armour. Who was this man who had so easily defeated them, they wondered. Was he a god? Maybe it was the magic of his famous sword. Only some sort of wizardry could have beaten their great army.

The day wore on and Artorius did nothing. He rode openly around the fort, stopping to chat with outposts and sentries. He seemed to ignore the Saxons on the ramparts who shook fists at him and spat in his direction. He seemed so very confident.

Aelle had a plan. Small parcels of men should slip away at night and make for the woods, there to hide. If three or four groups of fifty men made it, they could disrupt the Romans when the rest made a break for it. It was the only plan they had, so that night they tried it. Fifty men clamboured over the rampart on the east side, across the ditch and out across the open slope of the ridge. They practically crawled across the open ground. They made it to the woods.

The second group that left an hour later, just after moonrise, was spotted by a cavalry patrol. Trumpets sounded, cavalry came galloping and the fifty men had to run for their lives. Only ten reached the safety of the woodland. They found none of the first fifty hiding there. They had gone on homeward. Among them was Aelle himself. This was the part of his plan he had not shared with Caradoc and Oesc. He despised Oesc as an upstart and Caradoc as a cowardly bully. They had drawn him into their scheme with the promise of certain victory. In defeat he felt only anger and contempt for them and had no wish to stand and die alongside them.

Oesc was furious to discover next day that Aelle was gone. His men were hungry and thirsty. They had watched the Romans taking water from the river and leading their horses there to drink. They had watched Romans bathing. It was maddening. Now their Commander-in-Chief had deserted them. They roared their anger.

Artorius heard the commotion. "They'll break today," he told Gawain and Bedwyr, "or perhaps tomorrow at the latest. We must be ready for them. Caradoc will break to the south, the shortest route to Venta. The rest will break east. Have your men ready to catch them in the open ground before they can reach the woods. I'll guard the south with Cato. We have a score to settle with Caradoc."

All day they watched and waited. The Saxons stayed in the fort. A third night passed. Numerous Saxons were caught trying to sneak away. Their cries as they were speared by horsemen deterred the rest.

By mid-morning next day the Saxons were desperate. Oesc was for the entire force breaking to the east but Caradoc would not. "I go south," he said. Oesc was angry. This division of their forces would weaken them but Caradoc could not be persuaded. Too late, Oesc realised that Caradoc was only interested in saving himself. He was indeed a coward.

At noon they poured out of the fort. Oesc's men flooded out onto the open land to the east and formed a compact mass. They ran for the woods. Half way there they were hit by cavalry from both sides. A desperate fight began and as they neared the trees more cavalry rode out to meet them. The gently sloping ridge made a perfect cavalry killing ground. They stood no chance. Oesc fell with most of his men. The few survivors who reached the trees ran on.

Caradoc had come out of the south gate and led his men headlong through the Roman camp. He did not think to wonder why there was no-one there to stop him. They ran south across the river towards the old abandoned villa halfway up the slope on the south side of the valley and there discovered Artorius and Cato waiting for them. They were met with a full downhill cavalry charge that halted their progress and shattered their ranks. They broke in all directions, running mindlessly to avoid the horsemen. Cato's infantry advanced to herd the Saxons further into the path of the cavalry. In the midst of this chaos Artorius saw Caradoc.

Artorius urged his horse through the press to reach the City Prefect of Venta Belgarum. He sprang off his horse with his sword drawn. "Stand and fight!" he yelled. Caradoc spun round to see Artorius striding at him, sword raised. There was nowhere to run. Caradoc swung his sword at Artorius, who parried the blow easily with his shield. Desperately Caradoc backed off, sweeping his sword from side to side to keep Artorius away. Fear made him strong but he was facing a man who was full of ice-cold fury. Artorius was totally focused. He parried every thrust and slash almost automatically. He advanced inexorably upon the man who had betrayed Gerontius and Britannia. Caradoc made a last attempt to swing his sword towards Artorius' face. Artorius side-stepped the blow and thrust. The point of his sword took Caradoc in the throat and he went down, jetting blood.

Artorius stood, breathing heavily, over the twitching body. He felt no elation. He felt drained. He had avenged his friend, Gerontius. He had dealt justice to a traitor yet he felt numb. He let his cold anger subside. Vortipor, the commander of the bodyguard, rode up. "That was some sword play," he said. "We knew you as a brilliant commander but now we see you as a skilled swordsman too!"

Cato's infantry toured the battleground despatching dying Saxons while the cavalry hunted down fugitives. None were spared. When all was done they marched back to the camp. Gawain and Bedwyr were already there having finished off Oesc and his men before. As Artorius, still spattered with Caradoc's blood, rode into the camp, one of Cato's men shouted, "Artorius, Imperator!" Immediately the cry was taken up by others. It swelled into a roar. The entire army took up the cry, drumming their shields with spears and swords.

Artorius was embarrassed. He had not expected this. He did not want it. He had won a great battle and now his men wanted to make him Emperor. He rode to the headquarters tent followed by a mass of exultant soldiers. There Gawain and Bedwyr met him. "Did you put them up to this?" he asked.

"No," said Gawain, "but there will be no gainsaying them. They have made you their Emperor and you have no choice but to accept."

"He's right," said Bedwyr. "They want it and will have it. Not a bad choice, though. I can't think of anyone else who could do the job."

Artorius knew they were right. There was a very long tradition that the army could make an Emperor. Often an ambitious general would engineer the acclamation but this was spontaneous. He could not refuse. The army knew what he had done. He had fought and won three major battles, the Medway Ford, The Black Water and now this at Mons Badonicus. He had smashed the Saxon threat. He had saved Britannia from a major barbarian conspiracy and had destroyed a traitorous rebel.

"We camp here for a few days," he said. "We bury our dead and collect our booty. Then we march for Camulodunum. From there we will send news to all the cities of Britannia and tell them of my promotion."

They camped. The Roman dead were buried. The cavalry had lost some twenty horses. They too were buried, between the hill fort and the forest ridge on its western side, in two mass graves and low mounds of earth were raised over them. Cavalrymen are sentimental about their mounts. They grieved over them as though they had lost kin. They would not leave their corpses for the wolves. The Saxon dead were counted. Nine hundred and sixty Saxons had perished attempting to escape the fort.

To mark the battle-site, a wide breach was made in the eastern rampart of the fort, the soil being thrown down into the ditch, and a wattle and daub chapel was erected within the gap. The slope of the ground was such that the nave had to be stepped, the west end being higher than the chancel. Artorius decided that it should be dedicated to St. Martin, the one-time soldier who had become Bishop of Tours and was one of the founders of western monasticism. One of the chaplains was delegated to remain and say masses for the souls of the dead of the battle.

As always, the Saxon dead were stripped of armour and weapons and a mound of jewellery was gathered to Artorius' tent. There was much booty.

Chapter 14: An Emperor.

The march to Camulodunum was like a triumphal progress. They went first to Venta Belgarum where Artorius ordered the Senate to elect a new City Prefect loyal to the Empire. What were left of Caradoc's Saxon federates were penned on the Isle of Vectis and forbidden access to the mainland. A strong garrison was based in the city commanded by an able Tribune, Agricola, father of Vortipor. The troops were there to remind the senators that they now had an Emperor who was backed by a victorious army.

Next they marched to Calleva where they received a rapturous welcome. The city had been in a state of alert when the Saxons had advanced but its repaired walls and gates had deterred any Saxon attack and the city had suffered no harm. The Senate entertained Artorius and his officers with a banquet and a lot of high-flown speeches.

Then they went to Londinium. The garrison there had been active chasing the survivors of Oesc's host back into Cantium. They had enjoyed the task. The Senate met and offered addresses of praise to Artorius and his officers and yet another banquet was held in their honour.

Finally they marched to Camulodunum. Word of their coming had gone before them and the entire Senate and most of the people lined the road from Londinium as they arrived. The City Prefect stood just outside the west gate with Winnifhoere and her father, King Icel.

"Welcome home," said the Prefect. "We are honoured to name our city your home. You have saved the whole of Britannia from gravest danger. You have broken the power of Cantium. You have quashed the ambition of Aelle. You have destroyed the traitor, Caradoc. We welcome you not just as our liberator but as Emperor of Britannia. The army has acclaimed you and so do we. This is now your Imperial City and we are proud it should be so."

Artorius was beginning to tire of accolades. He had received bucket loads of flattery all the way. Doubtless he was going to get more, even here.

"I merely did my job," he said. "The Saxons attacked us and it was my duty to fight and beat them. I am no super-human. I am still the man I was when I rode to join Ambrosius. I am a simple soldier who has done what had to be done."

The City Prefect begged to disagree. He might have been a mere tribune at the start of the wars but he had risen by merit. He was the real architect of the army that had proclaimed him and it was he who had devised the strategies and tactics that had brought victory. That was more than the role of a mere tribune. Britannia owed him its very survival. That was more than enough to qualify him for the Imperium.

The army camped and Artorius went into the city. Tomorrow there would be a Senate meeting. For the rest of today Artorius and the army should rest. He went to his house. He had been away much longer than he had planned. A quick expedition to the north had become a three month, desperate campaign in the south. He feared Winnifhoere would have been lonely. She only had the one companion who spoke her tongue. He had smiled a greeting to her at the gate and she had smiled back. She had stood silent while the Prefect had made his speech of welcome. She had remained quiet while her father praised Artorius and was praised in return for his aid in blocking the Tamesis Gap. She had gone ahead to check that all was ready for Artorius in the house.

There she waited for him at the door. When he arrived, she said, "Welcome home!" Artorius was amazed. She had spoken in British! She continued, "I have had your quarters cleaned and aired. The furnace for the bath house is stoked. You will want to get out of your armour, bathe and change."

Artorius was stunned. Her British was not perfect but she had learned a lot in a short time. She must have made a huge effort. A surge of emotion gripped him. He caught her to him, embraced and kissed her. He knew she had done it for him. She cared. This had been no act of duty - it was affection and he saw it for what it was.

"You are my Princess!" he said. "You are all and more than I could have hoped. If you will have me, I will marry you. I will make you my Empress."

She grinned at him. "I will marry you. I loved you from the first, when you squeezed my hand to reassure me before that banquet in the basilica. I knew then that you were the right man for me."

There was something else he noticed. Around her neck she wore a gold chain and from it hung a cross. "What is this?" he asked.

"I have become a Christian," she answered. "At first I wanted it just to please you. I went to the Bishop for instruction. I listened to what he taught and then wanted it because I found it true, more reasoned than my old religion full of false gods and magic. I still have much to learn but I was baptised three weeks ago."

Artorius was even more amazed. There would now be no religious impediment to their union. Indeed the Bishop would now thoroughly approve. "And your father, what does he think of this?"

"He says that if that is what I now believe, he can have no objection. He loves me and he admires you. He wants my happiness. My faith is part of that."

Icel went up in Artorius' estimation. Not many heathen fathers would be prepared to countenance a daughter abandoning the ancestral gods. He would have to strengthen his friendship with the Anglian King.

They went in and Artorius went to his quarters to change. He went to the bath house, stripped and cleansed himself of the grime of three months campaigning. He finished by swimming thrice round the cold plunge bath and then climbed out. In the doorway stood Winnifhoere holding a warm towel for him. She looked at his nakedness frankly and without compunction. He took the towel and wrapped it around his loins.

"You should not see me thus until we are married," he protested. She laughed. "My people bathe in the rivers," she said. "I have seen all manner of men naked. Women too. It is nothing. It is not the same as the bed-chamber." Her grey eyes laughed at his embarrassment. Perforce, he smiled back.

She pulled the towel off him and dried him. She had brought a fresh tunic and trews for him to wear and helped him put them on. It seemed so natural, this intimacy. For a moment he forgot he was the Emperor. He was just a man enjoying the company of a woman who loved him. It was only when she gave him a new cloak, dyed purple and embroidered with a patterned gold edging, that his new rank became real to him.

Next day he dressed the part. White trews, a white, long-sleeved tunic with a gold military belt, the purple cloak to be fastened at the shoulder with a large bejewelled gold brooch, and white kid boots. He did not know whence these garments had come but suspected the Senate of Camulodunum had had something to do with them. He hung his sword and his dagger at his belt, fastened the purple cloak with the jewelled brooch and was about to leave for the Senate meeting when Winnifhoere stopped him and offered him a gold circlet fashioned as a wreath of bay leaves.

"The Emperor must wear this," she said. "It is the badge of his rank. It is even more apt when he is a victorious general." He put it on his head. It felt strange. He was used to his helmet but this felt different. He went out to find Vortipor and his bodyguard waiting. They saluted, crying "Ave Caesar!" and when he had mounted his horse in the midst of them, set off to the Senate House.

They passed through cheering crowds. When they arrived the senators all stood as he entered and he was ushered to the praesidium. As Emperor he would preside in any Senate in any city. He waited until the senators' applause had subsided, held up his hand for silence and announced the meeting in session.

There were many speeches. Each senator wanted to catch the eye and ears of the Emperor. All wanted to make flattering references to his achievements and impress with flowery oratory. At last they were done and Artorius could speak.

"I thank the Senate for its loyal congratulations. You have praised me, unduly. The real praise is due my army. Without its steadfast courage and discipline I could have gained no victories. Tomorrow I will parade the men and reward them. There is still much to do.

"The Irish in the west are now the most pressing threat to the safety of this Diocese. They must be expelled, contained or absorbed. Their independent kingdoms must be eliminated. It will take time but it must be done. The Dux at Eboracum needs a more secure frontier. The tribes immediately north of the Wall have proved unreliable even though their chiefs are all of Roman descent. They must be brought under closer supervision and strengthened to impede the Picts. Those are the tasks that now face the army.

"The civil administration must be restored and reformed. Corrupt magistrates must be replaced. Recalcitrant Senates must be purged of men who are self-serving and complacent. Bribery must become a capital offence, both for the official who accepts a bribe and for the man who offers it. Justice must be available for all and affordable by all.

"Only thus can Britannia be made to prosper again. I have no illusions. This will be a greater task than defeating the barbarians. It is a different sort of war. We must accept that life will never again be as easy or luxurious as it was before Hengest came. The economy has been shattered. Gaul is in the hands of the barbarians and little or no trade will come from there. The mint at Trier is in the hands of the Franks. Aegidius is no more and his son, Syagrius, his replacement, is weak. We will get no new coin and have no adequate source of bullion from which to mint our own.

"Our ravaged lands will take years to restore. We lack the people who could re-occupy and farm the wrecked estates. Too many are gone to Armorica. We lack craftsmen. We can no longer build in brick and stone. We must make new foundations for our State. We must not look back with regret and bemoan what we have lost: we must look forward into a new and uncertain world and make the most of it.

"We retain our Roman heritage and values. We retain Roman Law. We keep faith with our religion. Those are the fundamentals we must protect and guard. These are the foundations on which we will build a new and greater Britannia. Gaul has gone down to the Franks. Italia is in the hands of the Goths. Hispania is a Visigothic Kingdom. Mauretania has fallen to the Vandals. Only here, in Britannia, do the barbarians have no power.

"We are the last of the Romans in the West. Let us be a glimmer of light in the darkness that has fallen over the whole of the Western Empire. Let men in the future look to Britannia and say, 'There Rome survived!'"

He sat to thunderous applause. He had spelt out the ruination of the old way of life. He had pointed out the futility of trying to save what had already been wrecked. It could have been a depressing analysis of the situation but he had offered hope. Their values could carry them through and into a new world. They could retain their identity. They could maintain their principles and not become like the barbarians. They had a proud heritage that was worth preserving.

Artorius had surprised himself. He had delivered a rousing speech with an oratory equal to any trained rhetorician. The phrases had rolled off his tongue without effort. He meant what he had said. He put passion into it because he believed it. Perhaps that was all it needed to be an orator.

After the meeting he was congratulated by the City Prefect. "That was a fine speech. It was what we needed. You showed that you have a grasp of what needs to be done. You have a clear policy. You will be a great Emperor."

"I will only be that if I can carry the Senates with me. There will be many senators who will disagree. There will be many who laud what I say and work against me behind my back. I will upset many. I will remove their pet magistrates who let them off their crimes in return for bribes. Some I will bar from the Senates and they will take their affront and resentments to their friends. This will be a long, hard war fought out in cabals and plots. I hope I am up to the task."

Next day the parade was held outside the walls. Once more Artorius praised his men. They had been superb, he said. They had proved steadfast and loyal. They had marched and fought and marched to fight again. They had faced impossible odds with determination. He was immensely proud of them. He decreed another decoration for their standards and vexilla.

He gave a eulogy for Gerontius. He had been a loyal friend. He had shown no jealousy when Artorius had been promoted to Dux Bellorum. He had been generous in allowing his Cornovii to be absorbed within the Ambrosiaci. He had been courageous in battle, always close to the fighting line so as to encourage his infantry and to be ready to reinforce them as needed. He had given his life in saving his men from Caradoc's treachery. Now it was time to repay his generosity. The Cornovii were to be reborn as a separate corps. Cato would command them, as was fitting. They would return to their old job of confronting the Irish in Dumnonia and Cato would have the title of Comes Dumnoniensis, Count of Dumnonia. He would include the territory of Venta Belgarum in the area of his command.

Bedwyr, who had proved so capable and trustworthy in all that he had been asked to do, was promoted to Comes Britanniarum, commander of the field army. Gawain became Magister Equitum and Count Cato, Magister Militum. Vortipor, the young son of Agricola and commander of the Emperor's bodyguard would have the title of Protector. Agricola and Marcellus were to take an army to Deva and hold it ready to move either against the Irish in the Lleyn Peninsula or in Demetia. Agricola, promoted to Prefect, would command with his cavalry and Marcellus would be his deputy in command of the infantry.

Artorius himself was going nowhere immediately. He was going to wed. He felt entitled to some time for a honeymoon, he said, to rapturous and ribald cheers from his men.

Then he turned to the business of awards for individual bravery or merit. Most of these went to the infantry. They had had the hardest fighting at the Battle of Badon. They had endured the most and had displayed conspicuous courage. Each man had a citation from his officer read out and then marched forward to receive an award of a silvered plaque for his military belt or a gold torque to wear on his breast or an arm-band. There were plenty enough to give out: much booty had been gained at Badon.

The Parade had lasted most of the morning. At its end, Artorius had dismissed the men with a day and a half leave. They were free to enter the city and use the taverns and the shops and the public baths. They cheered him loudly, broke ranks and streamed into the city.

Artorius went to the Bishop. "Father," he said, "I am minded to marry tomorrow. I would prefer you to officiate, since it was you who brought Winnifhoere to the Faith. She told me she wanted to become a Christian just to please me but that you genuinely converted her. It is only right that you perform the ceremony for us."

The Bishop was surprised. He thought that the betrothal would last longer. Surely they needed more time to know each other. Artorius replied, "I am an Emperor and a soldier. From day to day I know not what will occur to drag me to one or other end of the Diocese. I went away for three weeks that became three months of perilous war. I will not risk that again. We are agreed. We wish to marry. We do not wish to wait longer. King Icel is still here, and it is right he should give his daughter in marriage."

"Then I shall bless it, with all my heart. Winnifhoere is a child of Grace. I know her conversion genuine. She came to the church every day you were absent to pray for your safe return. She will prove a loyal and loving companion. She is intelligent. She learned our language very quickly and now is learning to read and write in Latin. She will be invaluable to you."

When news of the forthcoming wedding got out, the city went wild with jubilation. The streets were decked in greenery. The Senate hastily convened to vote gifts to the couple. Soldiers volunteered to give up part of their leave to line the streets and escort Artorius to the church.

It was autumn, so the church was decked out with roses, the only flowers that bloomed so late in the year. The Senate offered to supply a wedding gown for Winnifhoere but she graciously declined. She knew what was appropriate for her to wear, she said. She had been planning her wedding for months.

The day dawned brightly. Artorius set out to the church first with Vortipor and an escort. Gawain would escort Winnifhoere. Once there, Artorius waited impatiently for his bride. King Icel waited at the door of the church. He knew nothing of Christian ritual but his daughter was to be married and he would not refuse to attend just because he was not a Christian.

Artorius heard the cheers of the crowds as Winnifhoere approached. He was nervous. He was more nervous about this than he ever felt before a battle. His heart was thumping in his chest when the trumpet sounded to signify Winnifhoere's arrival. He looked back towards the doors to see her being led into the church by King Icel. She was wearing the robes she had worn when he first saw her, the pale blue dress, the gold chain belt, the red cloak and the gold circlet on her head. He felt again what he had felt then.

The service was simple, as all marriage services are. They exchanged their vows, gave each other rings and then embraced to a ripple of applause. A solemn Mass followed in which they were the first to receive the Eucharist. The Bishop blessed them at the end and they left for the basilica amid the thunderous roars of the crowds.

A state banquet with much speech-making and much giving of presents by senators took up the afternoon. King Icel gave a large golden cup. "You should share this," he said. "A shared cup is a symbol that man and wife are one."

At last all was over. It was dusk and they were escorted back to the house by torchlight. They sat for a while smiling at each other, laughing at some of the more extraordinary presents and at the behaviour of some of the senators' wives who had drunk a little too much wine. Artorius dismissed the servants and said it was time to retire. He would bathe and come to her afterwards. He went to the bath-house, stripped off his finery and sweated off the grime of the day in the hot room. When he moved to the tepid room he found Winnifhoere. She was unplaiting her hair. As he watched she let fall her cloak and drew her dress over her head. She turned to face him, naked as he was and totally unabashed. "I thought a bath was a good idea, so I have come to join you," she said.

They bathed and then walked to Artorius' bedroom. They lay on the bed. They took wine from the great gold cup and sat beside each other. Artorius found he could not keep his hands from drifting over her body. She was so beautiful; her skin was so soft; her breasts were so responsive to his touch. He kissed them often, and she laughed. She looked at his body. It was well muscled and proportioned. He was a handsome man. She traced the white lines of the scars of old wounds on his thighs. Cavalrymen often received cuts to the upper legs in battle and such scars were almost a badge of their profession. They settled down on the bed and pulled the linen sheet over them. They lay entwined and later slept.

The next day, they bathed again, dressed and prepared for visitors. King Icel was to depart that day but would not leave without bidding his daughter good bye. The City Prefect was bound to come with him. Bedwyr, Gawain and Cato were also likely to come to pay their respects to their new Empress. She did not know them other than by sight and from what Artorius had told her. Also, of course, there would be a procession of senators and their wives, the former seeking influence and status, the latter weighing up the Empress.

Artorius was under no illusions as to their motives. He was the new power in the land and these men hungered for power themselves. If they could not get it on their own, they would seek to be near the source of power. They would want their wives to be 'friends' of the Empress and thus, through her, draw Artorius to favour them.

Artorius told this to Winnifhoere. "We must be polite and welcoming, but not allow ourselves to become too close to any of them. If we appear to favour one, the others will become jealous and I will have more enemies."

"How childish they are," said Winnifhoere. "All they need do is to do their jobs well. You are a just and fair man. You reward those who work well. Don't they know that?"

"They have been used to forming groups and parties to push their ideas in the Senates. They will want me to be part of their politicking too."

It was as Artorius had predicted. Senators came with advice, pet projects, warnings as to the unreliability of certain of their fellows, recommendations as to which senators were his real supporters and so on. Their wives engaged Winnifhoere in small-talk about fashion, cosmetics, furnishings - each evincing friendship, admiration as to her choice of bridal wear -"It was so different, yet so right!"- and generally trying to impress their sincerity on the Empress.

King Icel spent some time alone with his daughter before coming to say his farewells to Artorius. "My daughter tells me she loves you and you love her. That is for what I had always hoped. I know she will be happy with you which is all I have ever wanted for her. You are now the Emperor and she is an Empress. I did not expect that but I will get used to it. My daughter now ranks higher than her father!"

"I did not expect it either," laughed Artorius, "but neither of us will take precedence in your Hall. We are one family now. We can be comfortable together."

Bedwyr, Gawain and Cato came for dinner. It was a cosy informal meal. Winnifhoere questioned them about their campaigns. Gawain entertained her with amusing anecdotes about some of his troopers. She grew to like these hardened warriors.

After the meal, Artorius asked them to bring all the senior officers to the house next day before the army moved off to its various postings. He had an idea to put to them. When asked to tell them first, he demurred, saying he would keep his secret until next day. They left.

Artorius and Winnifhoere breathed a sigh of relief. It had been a long and exhausting day. Artorius told her of the sycophantic manoeuvring of the senators and how he had not risen to the bait of agreeing too much but had expressed platitudes such as, "An interesting idea! I will have to think about it." Winnifhoere laughed about the wives and their attempts to get close to her. She had been invited to fifteen different houses to inspect bed linen or furniture or decor. She had found none of the women much to her taste as friends. They chatted contentedly, took a nightcap of wine and retired to bed.

Chapter 15: The Fellow Countrymen.

Artorius was up early next day. He had preparations to make. The housekeeper was set to organising things with the aid of the gardener. There was much moving of furniture and stools. All was ready after a couple of hours of activity and Artorius waited in the atrium for his officers to arrive. They came as ones or twos and were told to go into an inner chamber and make themselves comfortable. Agricola came too, having been summoned earlier by Artorius. When they were all arrived, Cato being the last to come, Artorius and Cato went in too.

The room had been furnished with a circle of tables, and stools had been set around the outside. A cup had been set on the table by each stool. All but two of the stools were occupied, Cato and Artorius taking the last two vacant seats. Artorius noted how the officers had divided themselves into two distinct groups, cavalry and infantry. There had been a babble of voices before he entered, but this had ceased and they had all begun to stand as he came in. He bade them stay seated.

Artorius sat and began to speak. "I wanted you all here before you go your separate ways to different postings. We all belong to one big organisation, the army. We each have our particular loyalties within it. Some are cavalrymen with an affinity for others of their kind," he gestured to the group of cavalry officers, "and others are infantry with a different esprit de corps.

"Each is an officer commanding men and under command himself, save perhaps for me. If things go wrong, I cannot blame my commander: I don't have one. This is how armies are organised. Each man knows his place. Each man obeys his orders. Each man believes his unit the best in the army. The army is the sum of all its different parts.

"But an army should be more than that. It should have a sense of purpose. It should stand for something more than just fighting invaders."

He paused and drew his sword, laying it on the table before him, its point towards the centre of the circle.

"This sword has been called 'The Sword of Britannia' and 'Caliburn', hard striking steel. Many of you will remember how Ambrosius Aurelianus had me accept it. Some of you believe it to have magical powers. It has become something of a mascot to the army. To the men it is Britannia.

"To me it is something else. It is Justice and Righteousness. I wield it for those ends. I use it to protect the weak and the defenceless. I use it to bring down traitors and criminals.

"You all know I have little time for rich landowners who are prepared to risk the safety of this Diocese rather than pay the men who fight and die for it. I think you all share my contempt of such.

"Such men have no right to this army. They should have no power over it. They should not be allowed to order its actions. This sword, in my hand, will deny them. This sword stands for the Law. It will support just magistrates who judge according to evidence and not according to how much they have been paid. It will support the just actions of you, my officers, and will accuse the unjust.

"This Diocese has been ravaged and impoverished by the barbarians. Some still have to be dealt with. The Law is flouted by the rich and does no longer protect the poor. This sword and the army it represents must become the means of setting things to rights.

"If you will support me in this, if you agree that the army is more than just a fighting machine to do the bidding of the rich, lay your swords on the table before you."

There was a rustle of movement as they drew their swords and set them before them.

Artorius continued, "You will have noticed that this setting is circular. There is no 'head' to the table. Each of us is, at one and the same time, at the head and at the foot of the table. Here there is no rank, no protocol. We are all equal here. The title 'Count' or 'Prefect' or 'Tribune', 'Protector' or 'Dux' or 'Emperor' is meaningless.

"What unites us is this circular table and the swords we have laid on it. What unites us is the matter of Britannia. By joining your swords with mine you have committed yourselves to Justice and Righteousness and Law. You have made your swords part of mine.

"We are a brotherhood. We should have a name. I propose we call ourselves the Combrogi, the Fellow Countrymen, to remind us that it is for Britannia we stand, a Britannia that is Christian, Just and Righteous."

He stood, went to a side table, took up a flagon and went around the tables filling the goblets with wine.

"Now we will pledge ourselves to always support the poor, to aid the defenceless, to put down injustice and uphold the Law. Let us drink to that."

He raised his goblet and drank. The rest stood and did likewise.

Thus was formed a unique institution, the Combrogi, an association of top officers committed to a common ideal and sworn to use their forces only in following that ideal. Artorius had forged a new weapon for the new sort of war he knew he would have to fight, the war against corruption in government. The different Senates, so adept at political intrigue, would seek to flatter his commanders, get them 'on side' and then use them and their forces to oppose the Emperor or frustrate his policies. By naming them the Fellow Countrymen, he had appealed to something more fundamental than loyalty to an institution such as the army or to a man such as himself or even to a vague idea such as 'Rome'. They would be loyal to Britannia and to the Britannia he had described for them.

Afterwards they adjourned for refreshments. They chatted, told ribald jokes, ribbed each other and behaved as army officers always do together. Then they left to march their various commands to their different postings. They had agreed that they would meet at least annually to renew the Combrogi. At that meeting new members could be admitted and they would recount what they had done.

Cato marched via Calleva and Venta with his Cornovii to confront the Irish in Dumnonia. He left a garrison at Venta to watch over the Saxons who still occupied the Isle of Vectis and to keep an eye on the Senate that had supported Caradoc.

Agricola and Marcellus marched via Verulamium to Deva. From there they could strike west at the Irish in the Lleyn Peninsula or southwest at the Irish in Demetia.

Gawain was sent north with a large cavalry force. His mission was to liaise with the Dux Britanniarum at Eboracum and bring his semi-independent command into the new army. The Dux was virtually 'King' north of the river Trent. He had a motley collection of troops, remnants of the auxiliary forces that had always manned the forts along the Wall and a small legionary field army, the remnants of the Sixth Legion, at Eboracum, that was woefully short of cavalry. Gawain's force would be useful, Artorius reasoned, and might sweeten the pill that the days of independent power for the Dux were ending.

A strong garrison was kept at Camulodunum. It had to man the various fortlets that watched the approaches to Cantium and guarded the Ermine Street. These garrisons were now to patrol and police the roads - there was no military threat from King Icel's folk. Artorius wanted the army to become the friend of travellers, protecting them from thieves and brigands.

Artorius himself was to progress through all the cities. They needed to get to know their new Emperor. He would travel with his bodyguard and would take Winnifhoere with him. In the east he was well known. Most of his campaigning had been there and he had earned the gratitude of the cities. In the west he had only been seen as demanding of supplies. He had threatened the Senate of Glevum. There he had little popularity. In the north he was virtually unknown, just a reputation built on rumour.

The cities had had to accept the new situation whether they liked it or not. The army had acclaimed Artorius and he thus had the real power. The one city that had rebelled, Venta Belgarum, was now occupied by that same army. The cities were not going to risk the same themselves. Perforce they all accepted that they now had an Emperor.

Artorius had decided, reluctantly, to retain the Council of Britannia. It had failed to defeat the Saxons. It had tried to emasculate Ambrosius' efforts. It had put self-interest before the common good. His instincts had been to abolish it but it was the only institution that represented all the cities. It should have a voice as to how the Diocese should be governed. What he would not give it was the power it had abused. It would become an advisory body.

The worst of his problems would be taxation. There was virtually no circulation of coin. The barbarian invasions of Gaul had cut Britannia off from any new issues of coin from the mint at Trier. What coin there was in Britannia was old and worth little. Almost all of it was in the hands of the landowners who had hoarded it. Many of them had buried their valuables to avoid tax. Trade was now based on barter, one commodity for another.

Taxes would have to be tithes of produce and the collection would require transport. Depots would have to be set up to store the produce and thence distribute it for consumption. The only agency that could do this was the army. His men would have to be tax-collectors too.

The problem of corruption was endemic. Magistrates and judges were drawn from the senatorial class. They knew all the great landowners as their friends. They could easily be persuaded that complaints against their friends were false or malicious. They could be bribed with gifts or offers of promotion. The senatorial class had always held the common folk in contempt. The magistracy had to be purged. This would not make him popular.

His hope was in the Combrogi. If they proved loyal to what he had defined as the true Britannia, they would begin the process of removing unjust magistrates, curbing the tax evasion of the rich and restoring Justice for the poor. When rich men learned the army could not be suborned, bought or corrupted, then there might be a chance that some morality might return in government.

Chapter 16: Theoderic.

While Artorius was on his progress round Britannia, events moved apace elsewhere. The Franks, who had taken most of northern Gaul, destroying Syagrius with it, had converted to Christianity. To their south lay the Visigothic Kingdom of Aquitaine. The Visigoths, too, were Christian but were deemed heretical by the Western Church. Clovis, King of the Franks, attacked them and defeated them so utterly that they fled Gaul for Hispania.

They had had a fleet based at Bordeaux whence it had patrolled to intercept Saxon raiders. Now it had no harbour. Its Admiral, Theoderic, determined to seek employment elsewhere. He had heard rumours of the wars of the British against the Saxons. He would take his fleet to Britannia.

He came into the Channel just when Artorius was visiting Venta Belgarum. Artorius was concerned when he had news from Cato's patrols that a fleet of fifteen ships was sailing towards Portsmouth. Was this yet another Saxon raid? He rushed to meet the threat. He had few troops immediately available, only his bodyguard and the infantry garrison of Venta. He had sent to Cato to rush him reinforcements and a similar directive had gone to Bedwyr in Londinium.

He drew his men up by the port and awaited events. They waited and then saw the fleet heading in. They were not Saxon ships. They had sails as well as oars. They were bigger, more like the old Roman warships. They came on into the harbour and anchored in open water. Only one ship came to the quayside. It was the largest and was filled with armed men.

As the ship was secured and a gangplank was lowered, a tall, bearded man walked ashore. His warriors followed, forming a mailed bodyguard around him, but they kept their swords sheathed. They walked towards

Artorius and his men. They formed no line. Artorius said to Vortipor, "Ride forward and ask them who they are and what they want here."

Vortipor trotted to meet them. At first it seemed there was a language barrier. These people did not speak the British tongue. Vortipor had more success with Latin. He came back, escorting Theoderic. "This is Theoderic, former admiral of the Visigothic King of Aquitaine. He seeks employment in Britannia. He has no British, but can speak in Latin."

Artorius rode forward to speak. "If you come in peace, you are welcome here. If you come to take land from my people you will be opposed. This is only a part of my army. More are on their way."

"We come in peace," said Theoderic. "We seek a strong Government that could use a fleet. We heard that you are at war with Saxons. We could help."

"But we have defeated the Saxons," replied Artorius. "We have them penned behind defended frontiers. They are no longer a major threat to us. We have other enemies with whom we are constantly at war. How could you help?"

"I have one hundred fighting men on each of my ships. I can take my ships anywhere along the coast quicker than any army can march. All I need to make a landing is a beach. Could you use such a force?" Theoderic was confident that his proposal would be attractive.

Artorius knew he could use such a force. It all depended what payment this Visigoth would want. He decided to be blunt and open. "I cannot promise you lands or payment other than what you can wrest from my enemies. I can offer supplies while you fight for me, but permanent gain will be what you can conquer, provided you swear that whatever you take will be added to my Empire under my authority."

"That is honest and fair," said Theoderic. "I will be equally honest with you. We will take only enough to support ourselves. Whatever else we take will be given to you to dispose as you wish. We are not greedy. We are mariners, not farmers, and seek harbours where we can safely keep our ships."

"Then you are welcome. I can use you. Our enemies lie to the west. They are heathen Irish who have long settled the extremities of our lands and raid across our borders. If you can raid their coasts, I can invade by land. Their strength will be divided and make our task easier. Your men may land here and camp near their ships. You will forgive me if I post men to watch them but we have been betrayed by federates before and have learned to be cautious."

Theoderic agreed. He knew how fickle could be foreign federates. The Franks who had conquered Aquitaine had once been allies of the Visigoths. He did not blame Artorius for not trusting him at once. In this fractured world it paid to trust no-one totally.

A plan had begun to form in Artorius' mind. The Irish of Demetia were the most powerful of the Irish settlements. Those of Dumnonia were split into tiny kingdoms that often fought each other. The two groups were separated by the Severn Sea but could, if threatened, reinforce each other. A fleet under his control could thwart such links. If Theoderic raided the southern shores of Demetia, Agricola and Marcellus could march from Deva along the old road into the heart of the Irish Kingdom.

With Demetia conquered, he could then turn on Dumnonia in the same way. Theoderic could attack the southern and northern coasts while Cato advanced overland. There was now a chance to expel the Irish or absorb them into the Roman Diocese under strict control. There would only remain the Irish of the Lleyn Peninsula. They would be more difficult since the only access was by narrow mountain routes and there were few harbours or beaches for Theoderic to use. He would need to think more about how to deal with them.

He invited Theoderic to come to Venta. There they could discuss the strategy more fully. He needed to understand how Theoderic could operate, where he could make his attacks and to give him some rules as to how to prosecute the war. This was to be a war of conquest. It was designed to eliminate the Irish Kings but not to massacre the people.

It was autumn. There would be no possibility of launching any attacks before spring other than minor raids. Perhaps Theoderic could keep the Irish in a state of alert through the autumn and winter. If they had to maintain a host through the autumn, there would be fewer men to plough and plant and this would reduce the supplies they might have in the spring and summer.

Theoderic had formed a good opinion of Artorius. He was obviously a competent general. He had a disciplined army. He had spelt out what he could offer with a refreshing honesty. He had made no extravagant promises. He had made it clear that if Theoderic wanted to help him it would be totally on Artorius' terms. Theoderic liked that. It was clear and simple. He could do business with this man.

They went to Venta, Artorius having left cavalry to watch the Visigothic camp. Once there, Theoderic was received with honour. Artorius reckoned that an admiral had to rank, in Roman terms, as a Prefect. That made him of equal status with any senator and so he was received. He was not a typical barbarian. The Visigoths had been within the Empire for some generations. They had absorbed much of the culture. They were Christian. They had learned the Latin tongue.

Theoderic was entertained by the Senate with the usual banquet and after adjourned to Artorius' quarters for talks. Winnifhoere found him refreshingly honest. He said that he was simply an admiral who had lost his base and needed employment for his ships and men. He had lost faith in his incompetent King who should have been able to defeat the Franks. His precipitate retreat into Hispania had been premature. Theoderic felt he had been abandoned and thus could withdraw his allegiance.

He had come to Britannia because it had a ruler who was competent and victorious. He could serve such a man. What would Artorius have him do?

Artorius explained his plan. Theoderic immediately saw the sense in it. He did not know the Severn Sea. He would have to find a secure harbour there from which to operate. Artorius suggested that at first he might wish to sail into the Severn as far as Glevum. There his ships would be out of range of Irish attacks. Later, when the war was fully under way, he could move to Cardiff where there was a good harbour closer to the Irish. He might wish to spend the autumn scouting the coast of Demetia for landing places and harbours through which raids could be launched.

Artorius stressed that he wanted the raids to be limited. They were to draw the Irish into guarding their coast. Women and children were to be spared. Only men in arms were to be attacked, and if they surrendered, they were to be given terms and left in peace. "I do not want to make the common folk my enemies," he said. "My war is against their King and their nobility who insist on raiding my lands for booty and slaves. Once they are defeated, the people will come under my rule and I would wish them to feel it better than that of their King. If they are full of resentment and seeking revenge, it will be difficult to win them over."

"So you want me to harass their coastal settlements, taking supplies and burning barns rather than totally destroying them," said Theoderic. He had quickly grasped what Artorius was about.

"Precisely. I do not wish to inherit a desert. A little hunger, a little deprivation, will cause the people to demand protection from their King. It will split his forces, and that is all we need."

Theoderic said he could accomplish that with ease. He could sail the coast and attack wherever there were no strong forces gathered against him. Wherever there were such, he could simply sail on, faster than they could march, strike elsewhere and be gone before they could reach him. "They will need their chiefs to stay near their homes," he said, "and not join a general muster against your army."

Artorius hoped that Theoderic would have sufficient control over his men. Most barbarian forces went wild in battle and afterwards degenerated into rampage and rape. He stressed he did not want that. Theoderic laughed. "My men obey me." he said. "They know I will tolerate no excesses. Blood-lust leads men into danger and I will not have it."

Artorius believed him. This was no village chief with dreams of conquest and a future Kingdom. He was as professional as any of Artorius' officers. He felt he could trust him.

Once strategy had been agreed they could relax. Winnifhoere asked him about his ships. They were bigger than Saxon vessels and had masts and sails. How did they operate? Theoderic explained that when the Visigoths came into Gaul they had found the Roman fleet based at Bordeaux. They had learned how to use it. "We row the ships when there is no wind or when it is against us. With the wind from anywhere astern we can sail. If we encounter enemy ships, we resort to the oars and ram them, or come alongside them, shattering their oars. Then we can board and take them.

"Saxon ships are smaller and more lightly built. If we ram them they tend to break and sink rapidly. If they lie alongside, we are higher and they cannot easily board us but we can leap down into them."

"But where do your men sleep? There cannot be much room on board."

"We tend to sleep ashore. It is not safe to navigate in the dark unless we are miles offshore. Then we sleep on the decks while a few men sail the ship."

"And how do you find your way if out of sight of land?"

"We use the stars at night, if we can see them. They tell us where is north. By day we can use the position of the sun. When we are in unfamiliar waters we keep men on lookout. Where there are reefs the sea breaks over them. We can see breakers even at night and so keep clear of danger. If we cannot see the stars or the sun, we can trail a sail behind us to slow us down or even stop us. If the sea is shallow, we can anchor."

"And how do you not collide with each other in the dark?" she asked.

"We hang lanterns at the stern of each ship. A light can be seen for miles at sea,"

"It seems a skilled business," said Winnifhoere.

"It is. A crew has to be disciplined. One man's error or lapse in his duty can endanger all and all know it. The sea is unforgiving and should never be treated other than with caution. Each captain is King on board his ship. He has power of life or death over the crew. That is why I can tell Artorius that my men will obey me."

Artorius was pleased at how Winnifhoere engaged with the tall Visigoth. She showed genuine interest in his work and drew him into conversation. It helped Artorius get to know his new ally better and he realised that that was Winnifhoere's intention. She seemed to have an instinctive grasp of how she could be of help.

Theoderic was impressed with Winnifhoere. She was intelligent and beautiful. She was obviously in love with Artorius and he with her. That was good. Their mutual trust would allow Artorius to prosecute his war with his entire concentration. He almost envied Artorius.

He spent the night as Artorius' guest and departed next day to take his fleet to Glevum. Artorius would meet him there and have Agricola and Marcellus come to plan the campaign in detail. After that, Artorius would go north where he had further business.

Chapter 17: Glevum and the Settlement of the North.

The meeting at Glevum was a success. Agricola, who was to command the invasion of Demetia, was impressed by Artorius' strategy and by Theoderic. He and Marcellus had soon warmed to the Visigothic Admiral and could see how useful his role could be.

They had discussed routes into Demetia. They could bring their forces down towards Glevum and advance along the coast road but this would allow the Irish to concentrate their forces, thus weakening Artorius' plan of campaign. Instead they would strike from Deva to Hay-on-Wye and take the old road from there. It would be a more difficult route but it would lead into the heart of Demetia while Theoderic tied down Irish forces along the coast.

Agricola pointed out that the road passed through narrow valleys in mountainous country. His cavalry would be of little use in battle there. The brunt of the fighting would fall on the infantry. The cavalry could scout ahead and discover where the Irish would try to block the way but the terrain would militate against their use in battle. Cavalry cannot charge down steep slopes and lose impetus if they charge uphill. It would be a hard slog all the way.

Only when they reached more open ground far to the west would the horsemen come into their own and it was there, in the heart of the Irish Kingdom, that they would likely fight the decisive battle.

Once details had been finalised, Artorius was free to deal with other matters. The City Prefect of Glevum was the chief magistrate. The other magistrates took their lead from him. All had the reputation of being somewhat corrupt, the City Prefect most of all. It was time to grasp this particular nettle. If corruption in Glevum was dealt with sternly, a message would go out to other magistrates in other cities to mend their ways.

To this end, Artorius called in the records of all court cases going back ten years. He had given no warning, so there was no time to doctor the record or 'lose' any documents. He spent a week going through the mounds of scrolls. Winnifhoere assisted. Her Latin was now as good as her British and she had learned to read and write.

"What are we seeking?" she asked.

"Any cases where the evidence is very strong and the verdict seems inexplicable or the sentence far too lenient. We only need a few examples. Then we can question witnesses as to how the trials were conducted. If we find evidence of partiality on the part of magistrates, we confront them. Those who cannot convince us of their probity we dismiss. The mere threat might lead some to incriminate others."

It took time, but soon they had a dozen cases where the verdict did not seem to match the evidence that had been presented and five where serious charges had resulted in verdicts of guilty but had received very lenient sentences.

Artorius had some of the witnesses brought to him and questioned them. Some of them were still aggrieved that their strong cases had been dismissed to their cost. One or two admitted paying for a favourable hearing and were furious when the case went against them, only being able to assume their opponent had paid more. It was enough.

Next Artorius called in one or two of the least senior magistrates to ask about perverse verdicts and sentences. They admitted that they seemed unfair but said they were under instructions from the City Prefect. He made them swear this in front of witnesses, Agricola and Marcellus. Now he could act. He gave Marcellus a warrant to arrest the City Prefect. He was to be held in solitary confinement until his trial.

The arrest caused quite a stir in the city. Many of the senators were affronted and others nervous. Who might be next? The commoner folk were rather pleased. They had no liking for the chief magistrate who had borne down hard on them, imposing heavy fines for minor offences and always giving credence to the rich and disbelieving the poor.

The trial was held before the Senate, Artorius presiding. He summarised the evidence he had. He had the sworn statements read out. He called the witnesses who had admitted paying the Prefect and then not getting the verdicts they had expected.

When the Prefect was asked to enter a defence, he said he was unable. He said he had only done what all magistrates did. He had supported his friends.

Artorius asked the Senate to vote their verdict. They looked at the stern visage of the Emperor, and condemned the Prefect. Artorius looked at him. "You were the highest representative of Roman Law in Glevum. You used your power to make the Law serve you and your fellows. You debased it. You abused it. You used it to make yourself richer. You took bribes.

"The Law demands punishment. I could impose the severest penalty for these crimes. I could demand your exile and the confiscation of all your property. Your family would be penniless and your sons without rank. In times past you would have been given the choice, disgrace or suicide. That option is not open to you.

"I am not one to punish the innocent with the guilty. Your family had no part in your crimes. I will let them have what is commensurate with their rank, just sufficient to live within that rank. You will be debarred from using your senatorial rank. You can no longer hold any public office. You can no longer attend meetings of the Senate nor tender any vote as to its proceedings. You will confine yourself to your estate and guards will be posted to keep you there for a period of five years. The ban on public office is for life. Your excess wealth is confiscated to the State.

"Now I will issue my first Imperial Decree. In future, any magistrate who is convicted of taking bribes or is proved to have presided over the trial of a friend and shown partiality, will face the death penalty. Any man convicted of offering a bribe will face the same. The Law is too important, too fundamental, to be bought and sold. Since the Law in Glevum has proved to be tainted by corruption, all cases heard over the last ten years will have to be tried again. If witnesses have died or gone away, the evidence in the court record will suffice. I will give the magistrates one year to put all to rights and I will return to scrutinise the records.

"My Government is based on Justice and Righteousness. I will not tolerate corruption of any kind. Wise officials will avoid receiving gifts from any outside their family. There will be some among you who think they might bribe my officers. Do not try. They are sworn to uphold the Law as am I. The attempt will be as suicide."

Artorius had shown a modicum of mercy. Amongst the senatorial class public humiliation was worse than death. At least he had spared the Prefect's family from total ruin. The sons might have a chance to redeem something of their family's former status and honour. Senatorial rank was based on land ownership and wealth and he had left them just sufficient to retain that rank. His sentence, his new Decree and his expressed attitude would be noised abroad as a warning to other Senates. His attention to detail would be noted. He had shown his hand and he would gain popular support.

Having made an indelible impression on Glevum, he left next day to go north. Agricola would remain in Glevum to supervise the re-hearing of old cases. Marcellus would return to Deva to train the army for the campaign. Artorius was going to settle the northern frontier in consultation with the Dux. He had another plan germinating in his mind.

First he went with Marcellus. It was time he introduced Winnifhoere to his mother in the convent by Deva. Winnifhoere was eager to meet her new mother-in-law, sensing that she must have been the main influence that had made Artorius the man he was. They stayed the first night in the praetorium of the fortress and then went, next day, to visit Helena at the convent. She was overjoyed to see Artorius again and took to Winnifhoere straight away. They spent much time together, shooing Artorius away so that they could chat one to one. Artorius wondered what his mother was telling Winnifhoere. Judging by her peals of laughter it could not have been very flattering! At last he was allowed back and had to accept a somewhat mocking obeisance from his mother who could not really accept that her 'little boy' was now Emperor of Britannia. "I used to have to change your nappies and wipe the snot from your nose,' she said, 'so don't put on any airs with me!"

His response was a simple embrace. "Whatever I am and whatever I have achieved is all down to you - and I think you know it." They dined together, courtesy of the nuns. Helena was happy in the convent. It took her away from the various men who might want to marry her for her property and latterly for her rank as the mother of an Emperor. Widows were fair game for powerful men. In the convent she was safe and free, protected by the Church.

The convent was an old villa that had been given to the nuns and whose tenant labourers still farmed the land. Helena acted as the factor for the estate in return for her keep and enjoyed the work.

Once they had ensured that Helena was indeed well and contented, they could set out for the north to meet with the Dux. They said their farewells, returned to the fortress and set off the next day.

They rode to Eboracum. It took a week and a half to get there and the Dux was waiting for them. He had received news of Artorius' acclamation by the army and had been relieved when Artorius had sent to him that he was minded to confirm him as Dux in command of the north. Now he would discover what manner of man was this new Emperor.

They met at the gate of the old Legion fortress. Vortipor and his cavalry had ridden up in perfect order. Artorius wore his full armour, the gilded helmet gleaming in the evening light and the great purple cloak draped over the hind-quarters of his horse. He was determined to impress. Behind came a horse-litter with purple curtains in which travelled Winnifhoere.

Eboracum was supposedly a city. In reality it was a huge military base with a small civilian settlement outside. There was no Senate, since there were no rich villas to supply the senatorial class. The few villas of the north were state-owned and were operated by tied labour to supply the army. Only towards the east were there a few private villas. The settlement was made up of traders and craftsmen whose business was to supply the needs of the troops. There were brew houses and bars, cobblers and smiths, clothiers, leather workers and even jewellers. Itinerant traders came and went to sell knick-knacks to the soldiers and, as always where there are troops, there were brothels and prostitutes. Eboracum was the capital of Britannia Secunda and, as such, ranked as a Colonia, a self-governing city for retired army veterans. It was not rich and lacked men who qualified for senatorial rank. It was something of an anomaly - a city without a Senate.

The Dux, Coelestius, led the way to his house within the fort alongside the principium. He kept few troops in the fort, he said. Most were on detached duty, guarding supply bases or patrolling the coasts. The garrisons on the Wall were too few in numbers and too rooted in their forts to risk moving them around. He lacked recruits. The majority of his people were the sons of old soldiers, 'born in the camp' and brought up to follow their fathers into the army. Some of the garrisons on the Wall had become rather like villages, growing much of their own food and looking to their own defence.

Artorius had not been overly impressed by the troops he had seen. They seemed sloppy. The sentries atop the gate had not known to salute when he arrived. The wide dispersal of Coelestius' troops must have made it difficult to maintain their training and efficiency.

What were the most pressing dangers, he asked, and was told it was the perennial problem of the Picts. They regularly probed as far south as the Wall. The Dux got little warning. The Votadini, north of the Wall, rarely informed him of such raiding parties. Then there were the Irish to the west. They had settled in Kintyre, north of the Clyde and kept the King of the Clyde busy repelling their raids. That left the western end of the Wall vulnerable. It was very exposed to raids from Ireland into the Solway Firth.

Artorius asked about the tribes north of the Wall. Had they not been given Romans as chiefs? Were they no longer reliable? Coelestius replied that King Dyfnwal of the Clyde had been so. Marianus, chief of the Votadini was less reliable. He gave no warning of small raiding parties, only of large incursions towards the Wall. He seemed unwilling to oppose the Picts himself.

"These Irish in the west, where are they from?" asked Artorius.

"They are Scotti, from the northeast corner of that accursed island. Their King there is beset by more powerful rivals and his people seek safety across the sea. Once here they cannot resist raiding their neighbours. King Dyfnwal finds them a menace. Thanks to you, I was able to lend him cavalry to push them back within their bounds. Your Gawain is a good commander. I wish I had officers as good."

So Gawain was in the west. That might be useful, Artorius thought. He would have opened a way to negotiate with the King of the Clyde. "I have a plan in my head. It is complicated. It will require the agreement of yourself, Marianus, Dyfnwal and the King of the Scotti. If I can get it, I might relieve the pressure on the Wall. You would be able to regroup your field army and train it. I could lend you officers to bring it back to full efficiency."

"I can contact Marianus and Dyfnwal easily enough," said Coelestius, "but Fergus of Dal Riada is a different matter. He is based across the sea and at war with his neighbours. You would have to send an embassy to him; he could not meet here."

Artorius thanked the Dux. At dinner that night he and Winnifhoere with Vortipor were introduced to Coelestius' wife. She was thrilled to meet Winnifhoere. She was the only woman in Eboracum of senatorial rank and her social life had been circumscribed. Now she was dining with an Empress! Coelestius spent much time asking about Artorius' battles against the Saxons. Artorius sensed he was probing to assess how good a general he really was, so let Vortipor answer most of the questions. Vortipor laid it on with a trowel. It was Artorius' planning that had brought victory. In battle it was his sense of timing that had proved decisive. He described the fight with Caradoc at Badon in detail. "That is why the army acclaimed him Emperor," he said. "He is a general who can fight!"

Coelestius was impressed. Artorius was a genuine soldier. He was not one of the jumped-up senators of the south who had tried to order his father about. He would understand the problems he faced and how under-resourced he was. He obviously had an acute, strategic mind. Whatever his plan was, it would merit hearing and real consideration.

Next day Artorius sent letters to Gawain and Dyfnwal. Vortipor was to take the despatches to Gawain and then take ship for Ireland and King Fergus. His embassy would take at least a month. The most important player in Artorius' plan was Marianus. His agreement was crucial. Everything else depended on it. While Vortipor was away, Artorius and Coelestius should meet with Marianus.

They left two days after Vortipor was gone. Winnifhoere remained in Eboracum with Coelestius' wife with whom she became a firm friend. Artorius and Coelestius went north with a full escort to pass through the Wall in search of the Chief of the Votadini. Eventually they found him, not at his Hall, but way to the north on a hunting trip. They knew when they were getting near when armed men challenged them. They were escorted to his hunting lodge.

Marianus was young. He had recently inherited from his father, son of the Cunedda who had gone to fight the Irish in northern Wales. Marianus regarded himself as an independent King even though he was, like all the chiefs immediately north of the Wall, of Roman descent. The tribes had been given Roman Prefects as chiefs by Count Theodosius after he had defeated one of the most devastating Pictish raids in the fourth century. However, Marianus was not part of the Empire of Britannia and need show no deference to Artorius.

Artorius sensed his arrogance. He would need all his tact to get this young man on his side. He began with flattery. Marianus' men had been most efficient and courteous. That spoke well of their Chief. He was impressed by their discipline. Some had been mounted, and had ridden well. He could see Marianus enjoying the praise of his men.

Then he came to the reason for his visit. The Picts had been proving a problem again. Now that he had a fleet at his disposal, he was minded to mount a major punitive expedition against them. He would bring his whole army north. It would of course involve his marching through Marianus' territory and the Picts might resent that Marianus had allowed it. It was only fair to tell him that he might face reprisals afterwards. The Dux would, of course, come to his aid if need be but was quite a distance away at Eboracum.

He could see the young Chief weighing up his options. If he refused transit, Artorius could treat him as hostile and march through anyway. If he gave permission, the Picts might well seek revenge on him.

"I have a proposal to put to you," said Artorius, "that might protect you and your people. The Picts are too numerous and fierce for you to face on your own. You have fewer people ever since Cunedda took half your folk into Britannia. I am willing to give you new lands far from the Picts and close to your cousins in Britannia. You and your people could all move and if you take extra lands from the Irish there, whom I wish to expel, I will give you that land too. True, you would be in my Empire but I would leave you be as long as you prove loyal. Think about it. Talk to your wise men. I think it is a fair offer. If you agree, I will be able to advance across empty lands and not have to regret the deaths of innocent people after I am gone."

Marianus was dubious but said that he would put what Artorius offered to his people. It would mean leaving their ancestral lands and that would be hard. It would be good not to have to watch his back all the time, having to turn a blind eye to Pictish raiders advancing on the Wall and hoping the Dux would not come against him in reprisal. His numbers were too small to risk any major war with more powerful neighbours and, when his land lay between two such neighbours who were at war, it put all his people in danger.

Artorius could hardly have put it better. "Say that to your people and they might well agree," he said.

Marianus bade them stay three days. That would be time enough for him to sound the minds of his leading people. Then he could give Artorius an answer.

He was as good as his word. After three days he told Artorius most of his people would accept the offer. They could not move before the spring but then they would go. Artorius promised him escorts and supplies for the journey and to maintain supplies for a year after their arrival until they could support themselves. "I would not have any of your people suffer want on the way, nor hunger after their arrival."

The first piece in his grand plan was in place. Now he would have to draw

Dyfnwal and Fergus into his scheme. They would be easier. First he would approach Dyfnwal. His letter to him had merely said that he had a proposal to put to him and would come to him to discuss it. They could ride across the north to Dyfnwal's great fort, the Dunbreaton (Dumbarton), the fort of the British, on its great rock beside the Clyde.

King Dyfnwal was a doughty warrior. He ruled from the Clyde to the Wall and had long maintained peace. He had met Artorius before when they had jointly expelled Irish raiders from the Solway region. He ruled a large population in rich lands. His only problem was the frequency of Irish raids that exasperated him. He greeted Artorius warmly. "Last time we met you were Dux Bellorum. Now you are Emperor!"

"Not by choice," Artorius laughed, "It was rather forced on me. Now I have to be a politician and a diplomat as well as a soldier. I think I might have a proposal that might interest you."

They went into Dyfnwal's Hall where Gawain waited. "This horseman of yours has proved invaluable," said the King. "He has forced the Irish back into Kintyre and kept them there."

"That's what I'd hoped he would do," said Artorius. "It is about the Irish that I have come. I've persuaded Marianus to leave his lands and go to Wales in his grandfather's footsteps. I can use him there to clear the Irish for me. That has solved one problem for me but it creates another here in the north. The Picts will have a clear run at the Wall. Someone needs to occupy and rule the lands that Marianus is leaving."

"And you thought of giving them to me."

"To you or one of your sons. You could have a Kingdom stretching right across the north from sea to sea. It is good land. Your people could grow there."

Dyfnwal looked dubious. "The idea is attractive but I need all my folk here to face the pestilent Irish. If I send people east, I reduce my host here. My kingdom is bigger, but I am weaker."

"What if I could persuade the Irish to leave your lands alone?"

"And how would you do that? They are settlers without any ruler. Each village chief leads his men on raids whenever they lack cattle. My land is the nearest and the raids all fall on me."

"They have a King, in Ireland," said Artorius. "He is hard-pressed by enemies. I have sent an embassy to him. I have invited him to come to Kintyre and fight the Picts. If he does that, the Picts will be busy defending their frontiers and will not attack south. Your new lands to the east would be safer and mine too. Coelestius here could regroup and strengthen his army. It could fight as an ally."

"An Irish King on my frontier! That makes things worse for me!"

"Not if he is sworn only to fight the Picts. The Picts have been the biggest threat to peace in the north for centuries. The northern kingdoms should unite against them. You and Coelestius could oppose them from the south while the Irish harass them from the west. The Picts are kept busy. The Irish are kept busy. We have peace."

Dyfnwal still looked dubious. He could see the merit of the plan, but all depended on the Irish King. What if he did not come? Even worse, what if he came but refused to fight only the Picts? The Kingdom of the Clyde could then face full war rather than just raids.

"We'll know more when Vortipor returns," said Artorius. "He knows the plan, and is a good diplomat. If he succeeds he will bring Fergus of Dal Riada with him to meet us. Then it will be up to us to persuade him." Artorius went on to point out that there were advantages for all if agreement could be reached. Dyfnwal would have a larger, more secure kingdom. Fergus would be safe from his Irish enemies. Coelestius would have less pressure on his forces. The Picts would be contained.

"When he comes, he needs to see a show of force." said Artorius. "If we assemble on the Clyde, your host and my army, he will think twice about taking us on. The Picts will seem easier. We muster as many as we can and let him know that this is only part of our force. The sight of trained professional soldiers and your great host should make enough of an impression."

Dyfnwal agreed that it might work. He would call out his host. Gawain's cavalry and Artorius' escort were impressive enough. If Coelestius could bring trained infantry it would be even better.

Coelestius rode back to the Wall to summon troops. Gawain fetched his cavalry back to Dunbreaton and Dyfnwal called a muster of his men. It would take two weeks to assemble all, and that would leave one more week before the expected return of Vortipor.

Dyfnwal and Artorius became firm friends. Dyfnwal liked the straight talking Briton who had risen so high so quickly. He was in awe of his strategic sense. Artorius liked the King. He was open to ideas. He could think things through. He was concerned for the safety of his folk and would do nothing rash.

They spent time hunting while their forces gathered. A great camp grew on the banks of the Clyde. Gawain's cavalry patrolled the coastal area. As time passed the tension rose. Would Fergus come?

A week passed after the muster was complete. Artorius organised parades and training exercises to keep his men busy. Coelestius drilled his infantry. Dyfnwal's men played rough sports. It is difficult to keep an army happy waiting in camp for any length of time.

At last came news. A ship was coming up the estuary. At its mast-head flew a red banner with a white boar worked on it. "It's Vortipor," said Artorius. "He's using the badge of the Ambrosiaci."

In short order the troops were turned out to form near the landing. Dyfnwal, Coelestius and Artorius waited in front of the army. Gawain waited with a turma of cavalry at the landing.

The ship came on slowly. Soon they could see armed men on board. As it came alongside the jetty these jumped ashore and formed a bodyguard around a short stocky man. Gawain added his men to the escort and they marched towards King Dyfnwal and his guests.

Fergus of Dal Riada was a noted warrior King in his own land. He ruled a small territory in northeast Ireland and his borders adjoined the great holdings of the Clan O'Neil. This family had supplied High Kings in Ireland and each branch sought to do so again. Its chiefs were constantly pressing against Fergus' borders and he was steadily losing territory to them despite fighting valiantly to keep what he could. He was isolated and could get no direct aid from allies further south. As his borders shrank, the population in his lands became denser and this was why many of his people had migrated across the sea to Kintyre.

He had talked with Vortipor and was intrigued by what Artorius proposed. He needed detail. As he landed, he had seen the great host drawn up to receive him. He noted the disciplined ranks of the Roman infantry, all uniformed and drawn up in centuries behind their standards. He saw the cavalry with their red plumes, oval shields and spears formed up in their turmae, each with its vexillum. He saw the great mass of Dyfnwal's men. This was a very powerful army. If he had a host like this he need have no fear of the O'Neils.

He walked with Vortipor towards the three mounted men at the head of the host. Dyfnwal sat his small horse like any Irish King. He was dressed in fine linen and wore much gold. Coelestius wore parade armour, all polished iron that gleamed silver in the sunlight. Red plumes decorated his helmet and a great red cloak draped over the quarters of his horse. The third man was the most impressive.

He sat his tall horse as though he was part of it. Gilded scale armour glittered below the great purple cloak and the gilded helmet shone below its white plumes. At his hip hung a splendid sword in a scabbard covered with gold plaques and its hilt was gilded and jewelled.

This must be Artorius, the famed Emperor of the British. These were powerful men with whom it would be wise to be friends. If he were to make foes of them, they might ally themselves with the O'Neils and he would face enemies on two fronts. The sea gave easy access to his lands from Britannia and he had heard that Artorius had a fleet. He determined to take care how he dealt with him.

As he approached, Artorius sprang down from his horse, doffed his helmet and walked to meet him. "Welcome," he said, smiling broadly. "I am glad you could come. It could not have been easy, nor convenient, to leave your land in difficult times."

"My sons hold my land for me. They are good warriors and I can trust them," replied Fergus. He needed to show self confidence in the face of this display of power. He must not appear to have come as a weak King seeking aid or refuge.

"How was the voyage?" asked Artorius, walking with him towards a great tent set up behind the lines. "The sea is not too kind in Autumn. I trust it was not too rough."

"It was lumpy and a bit uncomfortable but not too bad. It got better as soon as we entered the Clyde." If Artorius wanted small-talk, he would oblige. They would come to hard business later.

In the tent was set a table and five camp stools. Coelestius, Vortipor and Dyfnwal joined them and they sat. Artorius started the proceedings.

"We asked you here because we would like your help." That seemed odd. Why would such powerful men need help from a minor Irish King? "We face difficulties on our northern frontier that tie down too many of our forces. I would prefer to have my army concentrated further south against heathens who have settled in the west. The Picts of the northeast constantly threaten my frontier. I have to keep permanent patrols and garrisons to prevent their raids. I could do with someone powerful further to the north and friendly to me to distract them."

Fergus was flattered to be considered powerful by such a man as this. "How could I help? I have problems of my own at home. I too face raids across my borders." He would not admit to losing territory although he suspected that Artorius was quite aware of his real predicament in Ireland.

"King Dyfnwal has problems too." Artorius came to the nub of his proposal. "Your folk who have come to settle in Kintyre are doughty warriors and have taken to raiding his lands for cattle and slaves. He knows this is without your knowledge or sanction and would have peace with you. He does not wish to advance his host against your people but if the raids persist his hand will be forced and I have promised to aid him as my ally and friend. This is a problem you could solve. If you were to take residence among your people in Kintyre, you would be able to divert their raiding and direct it against the Picts. Your sons could continue to protect your lands in Ireland."

So this was the offer. He could move to Kintyre, well away from the O'Neils and live in comparative safety. He would be King on both sides of the sea. There was an implied threat that, if he did not agree, his people in Kintyre would be attacked in force and this great army would be more than enough to extinguish their settlements. He would have to come to their defence, exposing his Irish lands to invasion by the O'Neils. This Artorius was a clever devil. He had set him on the horns of a dilemma.

He thought for a while and then asked, "What conditions would you require of me? If I came, I could well make my people in Kintyre even stronger and threaten King Dyfnwal more." He sensed that this was Dyfnwal's fear and that the King of the Clyde had also been steam-rollered into a situation not of his making.

Artorius laughed. "No conditions save one. You and Dyfnwal swear to maintain peace on your borders. He will not attack you and you will not attack him. You will swear that all your military activity, if any, will be directed against the Picts. You will discipline any of your chiefs who break the agreement and raid into Dyfnwal's lands. Dyfnwal will swear that if the Picts come against you in force, he will aid you as an ally. I have offered him lands to the south of the Picts. If they attack you, he will invade their land from the south and force them to desist from any campaign against you. Together you can contain these heathens and maintain yourselves secure. Separately you will be vulnerable."

"So you wish us to be allies against the Picts?"

"Precisely. It makes sense. We Christians should be friends and allies against the heathen. We should not war amongst ourselves and give them opportunity to invade or raid."

This appeal to their mutual Christianity was powerful. Fergus was a recent convert. If his churchmen agreed with Artorius' assessment of Christian duty, he would perforce agree - and he knew they would.

"Very well. I accept. I can see sense in it. In the spring I will move my seat to Kintyre. I will swear the necessary oath if Dyfnwal will swear his." He well knew that the greatest beneficiary of all this would be Artorius.

He would have his borders secured by northern allies. He need swear no oaths. He had the major power.

Agreement reached, they adjourned for a celebratory banquet. Dyfnwal and Fergus sat together and soon became friends. Artorius, Coelestius and Gawain helped the process with talk of their battles against heathen enemies.

Thus was settled the northern frontier of Britannia. Dyfnwal and Fergus would contain the Picts. Marianus and the Votadini would move to Wales and expel the Irish from the Lleyn Peninsula. Artorius would be free to tackle the Irish in Demetia and Dumnonia. Coelestius would be able once more to concentrate his field army and improve its training. It was a triumph of diplomacy.

Chapter 18: The Demetia Campaign.

The following spring, Artorius could launch his campaign against Demetia. Theoderic's fleet would cruise the southern coast and land where possible to harass the Irish settlements. This should be sufficient to require the local chiefs to stay near home and not join any general muster against the real attack. This would be a thrust via Hay-on-Wye into the heart of Demetia. Agricola and Marcellus would march first to Brecon. This might seem just a raid to the Irish King and he would leave the defence to his local chief. Once past Brecon, the attack would seem more serious and he would have to gather strong forces to oppose it.

The advance would become more difficult, and Theoderic's coastal raids more important. He would need to raid much further west to tie down forces that would otherwise confront Agricola. Artorius spelled all this out before the troops marched. He told Marcellus to avoid unnecessary casualties. He should rely on Agricola's cavalry to report where enemy forces were concentrating and use just sufficient men to force passage. Steady pressure was what was needed and the avoidance of major ambushes in the mountains. As soon as Agricola reached Brecon, Theoderic was to move his base to Cardiff.

Artorius would remain at Glevum with sufficient reserves to advance along the coastal route if Agricola was halted or slowed too much. He might even advance as far as Isca Silurum (Caerleon) himself to keep the Irish King guessing which was the real attack.

Winnifhoere would accompany him. He had decided that she had been apart from him too much. He needed her company and her support and he valued her advice. She had a wealth of common sense. Besides, he loved her and could not bear to parted from her for long.

To the north, Marianus would come to take lands on the west coast of Wales. From there he would advance north against the Irish in the Lleyn Peninsula and seek to expel them. His cousins in what was now called Gwynedd (the land of Cunedda) would move west to the same end.

Thus two campaigns would be launched simultaneously against the Irish in Wales. Artorius had called a meeting of the Council of Britannia to explain his strategy. They applauded his settlement of the north, although many senators would have preferred to have been consulted first. They applauded his intention of solving the Irish problem to the west. Glevum was particularly pleased with this as it was the nearest great city to the Irish in Demetia. They were wary about allowing Marianus to settle. Was he not just another barbarian federate?

Artorius was aware that they had learned and understood little about his role as Emperor. They still saw themselves as the Government of Britannia and not as his advisors whom he could consult or not as he wished. To make a point, he sent some of his officers to inspect the court and tax records of several cities with a view to removing corrupt magistrates and officials.

Roman bureaucracy was complex and all-pervading. Everything was written down. It was easy to use this bureaucracy to discover abuses. It would, of course seek to protect itself but Artorius' inspectors would arrive without warning with his warrant to inspect all. Discrepancies would have to be accounted for and his officers were diligent and incorruptible. City Senates learned to fear their arrival.

Gawain had been left at Eboracum. He was to select and train men from Coelestius' forces as cavalry. Once they were proficient and could take over the training role, he was to return to Glevum with his men. Coelestius' new cavalry would recruit and train the remnants of the Votadini as a mobile frontier force between the Picts and the wall.

Once Marianus and his people had come south and were established on the west coast, the campaign could begin. Agricola and Marcellus marched from Deva. The cavalry scouted far ahead on a broad front and found no opposition until they came near Brecon. There forces were gathered against them in open land. The battle was easy. The Irish charged Marcellus' infantry and were held. Agricola's cavalry took them in flank and routed them. Their chief, Brychan, was captured and many of his warriors killed. He was given a choice. Go west in disgrace to tell his King he had lost his lands to the Romans, or stay and rule the remnants of his people under the Law of Rome.

He chose the latter. Among the Irish, a chief who was utterly defeated in battle lost status. He was too proud to grovel to his King. He had seen the power of the Emperor of Britannia. He had been at the sharp end of it and had lost. Better to rule under Artorius' protection than go west to be defeated again.

Despatches were sent to Artorius and Theoderic moved his base. His ships roamed westwards probing the coast. Wherever there was an undefended beach or anchorage, his men landed and raided nearby settlements. They killed any warriors who opposed them and killed many cattle. They spared the houses and the women and children and the elderly. Where strong forces were gathered against them, they sailed on and landed at least a day's march away.

Artorius, with his bodyguards and five turmae of cavalry went to Isca Silurum. This was one of only two Roman cities in southern Wales. To its east were rich villa lands, still occupied and functioning. They went via the Usk valley and had to fight a skirmish against Irish fugitives from Brecon near Venta Silurum (Caerwent) before reaching Isca. The battle had been easy but Artorius had been conscious of the risk of defeat and the consequent danger for Winnifhoere. It was, after all, not good to have her nearby when he was fighting. Artorius was welcomed warmly in Isca Silurum. The villa owners feared the Irish to the west. They had appealed in vain for help from Glevum. Now they had an Emperor who was willing to make them safe.

Isca was, like most Roman cities in Britannia, a settlement that had grown around a former fortress. It was also near the port at Cardiff and still had sea-borne trade, although much reduced now that Gaul had fallen to the barbarians. Now its trade came mainly via Hispania (Spain). Good wine came in and olive oil as well as metals from that ore-rich Diocese. Coin came too and this was the last part of Britannia that had something of a money economy.

The Senate made a great fuss of Artorius and Winnifhoere. They were feted at banquet after banquet, both public and private. The troops camped in the old fort, long disused. Theoderic came with regular reports on his progress and messengers kept contact with Agricola and Marcellus. They were advancing steadily. The Irish were trying to halt them by holding the passes where the road crossed between mountains but Agricola's cavalry gave prior warning of each ambush site and Marcellus' infantry forced through. Where the ground militated against cavalry charges the horsemen supported the infantry with archery and javelins from close behind the lines. The Irish had few archers and no throwing spears, so they had no counter to this tactic. Once an Irish line was broken, the cavalry could pursue and prevent any regrouping. They had to fight a minor battle every twenty to thirty miles along the road.

The advance was far from easy. The road was merely a track and had not been maintained. It was impossible to use wagons so the men had to carry their supplies. It rained incessantly and they marched through thick mud that caked their boots and often tore them off their feet. When they climbed to a pass they were often in cloud and could see very little. Most of their battles were fought in these conditions. Their discipline gave them victory but every skirmish was difficult, fighting uphill against opponents they could barely see.

At length they came down towards Porth Mawr. They had marched clean through Demetia and here the Irish King made his last stand. His host far outnumbered Agricola's force but the ground was more open and allowed cavalry to play a proper part in the fighting. Even so it was a hard battle until Theoderic's ships came into the harbour. With enemy troops landing to his rear, the King surrendered.

In the battle he had lost two sons and many warriors. Agricola gave him choices. He and what was left of his dynasty along with his surviving chiefs and their families could return to Ireland or they could go as prisoners to Camulodunum, far away from Demetia, where they could live as Artorius' 'guests'. They were never to return to Demetia. They chose Ireland and were ferried there by Theoderic's ships. Agricola left a strong garrison to hold the territory where the people had no stomach to continue the fight and marched back to Isca Silurum.

Artorius was happy. His strategy had worked. Demetia was under Roman control once more. He decreed a Triumph for Agricola, Marcellus and Theoderic to be celebrated in Glevum. It was time the lukewarm Senate there was overawed by his real power. He summoned a meeting of the Council of Britannia to Glevum and at the same time called a meeting of the Combrogi.

Marianus had begun the expulsion of the Irish from the Lleyn Peninsula. Cato and the Cornovii were already advancing in Dumnonia. Theoderic was now free to aid that campaign. Artorius was on the verge of re-establishing Roman control over all the west. He had to begin to think as to how he should govern after the wars.

Agricola's army marched to Glevum and camped outside the city. Artorius waited for the Council and the Combrogi to assemble and then decreed the day of the Triumph. Agricola's forces assembled in full parade order outside the walls. Traditionally the victorious general should drive a chariot at the head of his army but chariots had long gone out of use. Agricola would ride into Glevum. The Councillors and the Senate of Glevum gathered at the Senate House with Artorius and Winnifhoere enthroned on the steps. The Combrogi sat on one side facing the senators. Cato's infantry escort lined the forum where the citizens gathered to watch.

Agricola ordered his men to march. They entered the city in perfect order, marching six abreast with Agricola in the midst of his cavalry. They were a splendid sight. Marcellus rode at the head of the infantry. Theoderic marched at the head of his seamen.

They marched through the city, cheered by the citizens, and halted in ordered ranks in the Forum. The Senators looked in awe at the disciplined, uniformed troops: they had not seen such for many years. For the first time they saw and understood the real power of the Emperor. Agricola, Marcellus and Theoderic went to the Senate House where Artorius stood to greet them.

"Welcome, Agricola and Marcellus, and Theoderic," he said. "You have done well. You have defeated the most powerful of our enemies. You marched through difficult country. You fought five battles before you could bring the enemy to bay. Theoderic harassed the enemy coasts to distract and weaken the defence of the Irish King. All was done well. The King and all his dynasty have been expelled and their people brought under my rule.

"A Triumph is the State's reward to a victorious army. The spoils of war are granted by the State to be divided among the victors. You have earned them. It is only just that those who bore the brunt of the fighting should have some tangible reward.

"Agricola was my choice to command this enterprise. He has vindicated my decision. The nature of the terrain meant that the hardest fighting fell on the infantry. Marcellus should be praised for the dogged courage of his men, their discipline and conduct in battle. They were always outnumbered. They had to fight on ground the enemy had chosen. That is never easy.

"Theoderic played a most important role. His ships cruised dangerous and unfamiliar coasts to land where they could and damage the enemy. He and his captains showed remarkable seamanship. They lost not one ship in dangerous waters. Without their work, Agricola would have had a much harder time of it.

"All deserve the highest praise. They have served Britannia supremely well. The Irish of Demetia are quelled. Their King is expelled. The people are subdued. Our western frontiers are now more secure.

"Now it falls to me to determine how best to keep them secure. Agricola is to be my Dux in Demetia. He will rule it for me. He will keep it safe from further Irish incursions. He will be the guardian of the west. Theoderic and Marcellus have other tasks. They will transfer to Cato's command against the Irish in Dumnonia. There they will earn more laurels in the rebuilding of Britannia.

"Normally it is the commanding General who receives the laurel crown. In this case it is only just that three are awarded. Come forward, Agricola, Marcellus and Theoderic and receive your crowns."

They approached to the foot of the steps and Winnifhoere came down with three gilded coronets in the form of laurel leaves which she placed on their heads. All applauded.

The three commanders went back to rejoin their men. Artorius rose and, standing on the steps of the Senate House, addressed the troops.

"You are the strong right arm of Britannia. You have proved yourselves in its defence. You have fought hard battles against powerful and more numerous foes. You won them all. I am proud to have such troops.

"Your commanders have been given laurel crowns. They are symbolic. They decorate not only them but all the troops who served them so successfully. The booty from this campaign, and it is substantial, will be divided between you all. Those who did outstanding deeds will be rewarded further.

"You will now march back to your camp where you will be dismissed. I decree three days leave for each of you. You have earned a respite from your duties. You will be free to come and go as you will within the city. I am sure you will receive heroes' welcomes, for heroes you are, all of you."

With that the troops marched back out of the city, once more cheered all the way. They were dismissed and then streamed back to sample the taverns and shops, where many were served free of any charge. Glevum was in festival mood.

Next day the Council of Britannia met and approved what Artorius had done. One or two senators complained about Agricola's appointment as Dux in Demetia. The area, they said, should be governed by a civilian rector, someone from the senatorial class. Artorius patiently explained that there were no cities in Demetia where a rector could be based. He had not the means to build one and the economy could not sustain one. Demetia was like the north and was best ruled as a military region.

He saw yet again that the senators and landowners had still not grasped realities. They sought advancement and wanted posts in government to be reserved for them. Their class was status-hungry. They wanted titles and positions. They would compete for them. They would lobby him for them. They would seek to do down their rivals. He knew that if he gave them position and rank they would be lethargic in their duties and spend time plotting and intriguing against each other and himself. It was in their nature and they would not be able to resist.

The meeting of the Combrogi was more to his liking. Its membership comprised most of the senior officers. They were all known to him. He knew their worth. They were more than his subordinate officers, they were his brothers-in-arms.

They gathered in their circle, each laying his sword on the table in front of him. They told the tales of what they had done and how. They congratulated Agricola and Marcellus. They in turn congratulated Artorius. It was his plan, his strategy, that had won them the campaign. When all had finished, Artorius spoke.

"The wars are nearly over. The Council of Britannia will want me to demobilise most of the army. Their class would, they think, have less to pay in taxes. I intend to resist their demands. We all know how fickle they are, how self-serving and arrogant. Few put Britannia before themselves. Few have any care for the common folk.

"When I re-order the government, they will have their place. Some of them might become rectores, governing regions in my name. I will want the Combrogi to watch them carefully. You will check any corruption or partiality in their rule. It is sad that it has to be thus but they have proved unreliable and unable to shake off their past misgoverning. It will take years before the governance of Britannia can be fully entrusted to civilians once more.

"I have to rule through men I trust. You are they. Your oath to uphold

Justice and Righteousness is my guarantee that you will serve faithfully and well and that my rule will be seen by the common folk as fair. I care nothing as to what reputation I have among the rich. They will complain and plot but, while I have you and my army, they will not prevail.

"Once Dumnonia is ours again, and I trust we still have time this year to win it, we shall meet again. We should augment our numbers. This will be up to you. Each can nominate men they believe worthy and you will elect or refuse any such nominations. Do not flatter me by choosing all I nominate; I am as capable of error as any of you.

"Now we have work to do. Cato and Marcellus must meet with Theoderic to plan a campaign into Dumnonia. It must commence very soon. Agricola must leave to rule Demetia. Gawain must finish his work with Coelestius in Eboracum. Bedwyr has pressing duties in Londinium. The rest of you must join your commanders too. We will have two days relaxation here and then all must move."

With that the meeting broke up after a renewal of their pledge. Artorius went to his lodging. Business had kept him too long from Winnifhoere. Even at Isca, he had been preoccupied and unable to relax with her. She deserved better of him. He determined that that night they would dine in private.

Chapter 19 : Dumnonia.

Dumnonia was a difficult region. The easiest access was along the coasts. Inland high moors were obstacles, the roads, where there were any, difficult. These would have to be patrolled else the enemy could retire into the empty wastes and vanish, only to reappear and harass the rear of any army passing by the coast.

There were few places where cavalry could have ease of action. This would be a largely infantry operation. Cato had advanced as far as Isca Dumnorum (Exeter). A third of the territory had been recovered. Further west the country became even more difficult. There were no proper roads to make marching quicker and easier.

Theoderic suggested that his ships could act as transports. The army could advance and confront the enemy while he sailed further west to put men ashore behind their foes. The Irish here were divided into separate Kingships. They would not unite. It should be possible to conquer them piecemeal.

Cato was certain he would need some cavalry. His army must have its eyes and ears scouting ahead and on the flanks. In battle he would need them on either wing to prevent his close order infantry being overlapped by the enemy line. He put his concern to Artorius who gave him eight turmae for the job. He borrowed them from Gawain's men and, on his advice, appointed a young Tribune, Medraut, to command.

When not involved in transporting troops to the rear of the enemy, Theoderic would send ships to harry the coasts, much as he had done in Demetia. This time he would harass them far to the west to make it less likely that the western Kings could come to the aid of those facing Cato.

It was a good plan. Artorius could think of no better, and said so. His generals were learning strategy.

On the eve of their departure, Marcellus came to speak with Artorius. He had a grievance. In the Demetia campaign his men had done almost all the fighting and it had been hard fighting all the way. Afterwards Agricola had been given Demetia to rule. It did not seem fair.

Artorius heard him out. He agreed it did not, on the face of it, seem fair but he had reasons for his decision. "The rule over Demetia is not a reward. It is a heavy duty. I thought long and hard what I should do with regard to its government. I could have annexed it and made it subordinate to Isca Silurum with a civilian rector. I deemed that that would be too much for a senator. He would need troops anyway to hold it. Better to give it to a professional soldier like yourself or Agricola.

"Your father has made himself a King in Armorica. When your father dies, you will inherit and have to fight the heirs of the previous King, Maxentius and Budic. You could not be, at one and the same time, a ruler in Armorica and Governor of Demetia. I would have to replace you. On balance it was more in Britannia's interest to give it to Agricola who will be permanent."

Marcellus could not fault the logic and left. He still felt somewhat aggrieved but did not blame Artorius for the decision. He was, however, jealous of Agricola.

Theoderic too came. He wanted lands for his men. They were mariners but eventually would get too old to go seafaring. Some land would be as a pension for them. Artorius thought this request reasonable. He gave instructions to Cato that lands in Dumnonia were to be made over to Theoderic to apportion among his crews. Ideally they should be near good harbours.

He liked the fact that Theoderic had asked nothing for himself. His concerns were for his crews. Perhaps Theoderic would make a good member of the Combrogi.

Next day the Combrogi dispersed to their various stations and soon after the Dumnonia campaign began. Cato divided his forces. Dumnonia is a great peninsula with highlands along its centre. Cato would advance to the south of these while Marcellus took the northern coastal route. Theoderic would open hostilities by attacking the settlements in the far west. He too would divide his fleet, some attacking along the south coast, the rest to the north. Medraut would provide a scouting service to both infantry armies and give flanking support in any actions.

The campaign went well. Cato advanced first and as soon as he drew opposition and was slowed, Marcellus would advance to the north. They leap-frogged their way along the length of the peninsula. In this way the various Irish Kings could not co-operate. Each was too busy looking to his home defence to aid a neighbour.

Desperate pleas for help were sent to the westernmost Kings but they too faced problems. They could not anticipate where and when Theoderic would next strike. They mustered forces to guard their coasts but Theoderic could move faster than any host could march. They dared not march east to face Cato or Marcellus.

Like the Saxons, the Irish of Dumnonia had never faced professional Roman armies. They had no counter to close-order infantry and had never faced any cavalry. When they did stand to fight they were quickly thrust aside, broken and relentlessly pursued.

The campaign became almost a direct march to the west. King after King surrendered, each being too weak to fight alone. As in Demetia, the royal families were expelled. The people could remain under Roman government or return to Ireland as they wished. Most chose to stay.

Theoderic soon had new harbours that he could use and made Falmouth his main base. This was the best harbour on the south coast of Dumnonia and had ample resources of timber for ship repairs.

Medraut's cavalry had played an important role. They had had little fighting to do but they had criss-crossed from north to south and back again carrying despatches. They rode ahead of the armies spying out ambush sites. They patrolled the roads in conquered territory. Medraut himself had led the way and became quite popular with the officers. Cato formed a high opinion of him as a promising cavalry commander.

The end came in the far west. Five small Irish Kingdoms were all that was left under Irish control and they at last combined to face the Roman threat. Marcellus and Cato joined forces and advanced into the narrow end of Dumnonia. The Irish combined host advanced to meet them.

The Irish fought on foot. In the past they had used chariots but these had long passed into oblivion. Their host was drawn up as five blocks of infantry. Like the Saxons, each man needed space to wield his weapon, either the short stabbing spear or the long sword. They had never faced close order infantry advancing like an iron wall. They had no counter to cavalry riding on either flank. As the cavalry threat loomed large, the Irish bunched into a denser mass and became hampered by their own numbers.

The battle was comparatively short. The Irish tried, and failed, to break the Roman line. A slogging match ensued until Medraut drove in against the flanks. Men at the rear of the Irish line began to waver. Then from behind they were attacked by Theoderic who had landed further to the west and marched swiftly to join the fray. The Irish broke and hundreds fell to the pursuit.

After the battle, five Kings were found among the dead. Dumnonia was

Roman once again.

Cato sent Medraut to take the news to Artorius. His despatch praised the competence of the young Tribune. He commended Marcellus for his co-operation in the long advance and Theoderic for his timely raids that had so helped the campaign.

Artorius received Medraut at Glevum. He had already had news that the Irish were gone from the Lleyn Peninsula. He had given the land, as promised, to Marianus and his people. His western strategy was complete. The Irish threat was no more.

He invited Medraut to share dinner with him and Winnifhoere. The young Tribune was flattered. Artorius asked him about the campaign. Medraut told him all he had done. He told him of riding across bleak wind-swept moors in mist and rain carrying despatches. He told him of skirmishes with enemy scouts. He described the final battle.

"It was touch and go when they charged but once I launched my cavalry on the flanks they began to break. I think the battle was won before Theoderic arrived. His coming merely speeded up the rout." Artorius had learned little of the role of the infantry, how hard they had fought, how dogged had been their resistance, how disciplined their conduct. It had all been Medraut and his horsemen. Of course, he was a cavalryman and had the horseman's bias as to who won battles. Even so, not once had he said what Cato or Marcellus had done.

Artorius asked him how the campaign was controlled. "I kept Cato and Marcellus informed as to where the other was and whether an advance by one was necessary to reduce the pressure on the other. They relied on me to give them information, so I had scouts riding ahead to find the enemy. By the time the infantry came up, the enemy either fled or came forward to surrender."

Afterwards Winnifhoere said, "That is a young man with a very high opinion of himself. From what he says, we should credit him with winning all the battles and masterminding the whole campaign."

"He is young," laughed Artorius. "He thinks cavalry alone win battles. He played a vital role but under orders from Cato and Marcellus. He just seeks recognition and overstates his case."

Cato and Marcellus soon arrived with their versions of the war. Cato was full of praise for his men who had marched doggedly and fought hard. Marcellus likewise gave credit to his soldiers. "They often had to fight after a ten mile march carrying all their gear. There were no roads suitable for wagons, so everything was carried by the men. They never complained. They just got on with the job."

Cato once again commended Medraut but with one proviso. "He did not wait my signal to launch his attack in the final battle. I wanted to give Theoderic time to arrive first. It didn't matter but he could have lost men by going in too soon."

Artorius felt this confirmed his view of the young Tribune. He was competent but lacked discretion. He was the sort of officer who could inspire his men with personal courage, but would be inclined to be rash. He was too hungry for glory and might get it at his men's expense.

He kept Marcellus back after Cato was gone. He wanted to reassure him that his service was valued and would be rewarded. "I know you felt hard done by after the Demetia campaign. I explained my decision and you accepted it but I think you felt you had earned some public status such as I gave Agricola.

"Now that the Irish have been dealt with, I must turn to re-ordering the government of Britannia. This will not be easy. I will offend many senators who have been used to office. I will need men I can trust and I do not trust many in the senatorial class. They criticised my appointment of Agricola. They will criticise any appointment they think should go to them.

"Somehow I must teach them that times are different. I will have to rely heavily on my officers to keep the Senates in check. Britannia was divided into five provinces. Each used to have a Vicarius appointed by the Emperor as its civil Governor. I am minded to make you one of my Vicarii. I do not yet know where but you will get your due reward."

Marcellus stammered his thanks. This was a great promotion. The Vicarius stood for the Emperor in his province. He oversaw all legal cases, all tax collection, the maintenance of roads and bridges and had troops to act as his police. In terms of political status, a Vicarius was second only to the Emperor himself.

Chapter 20: The Government of Britain.

Artorius was under no illusions. Britannia after the Saxon wars was a very different place. The fall of Gaul to the Franks had cut any hope of a renewed supply of coin from the Imperial mint at Trier. There had been little coin in circulation for years. Britannia had little source of gold or silver from which to mint its own coin. What coin there was in Britannia was in the hands of the rich.

They were very rich. They held lands that they had accrued over many generations. They had invested heavily in industrial enterprises, smithies, potteries, tanneries, quarries and mines. They had held shares in import/export businesses, financing voyages for a large share of the profits. Before the Saxons came they had had huge cash incomes. They had stored their coin in strong boxes.

Once the barbarian raids had become a nuisance and tax demands became heavier, they had hidden large parts of their bullion and coin, burying it in their land to avoid it being found by tax collectors. With coinage scarce and of little intrinsic value, property taxes were often collected as bullion, so the landowners had even buried their silver plate to avoid it being demanded. Now that coin no longer circulated and industry had ceased for lack of it, their coin reserves were of little value. Only the oldest gold and silver coins had any intrinsic value. The most recent were worthless, being made of copper and merely washed with silver or gold.

They remained rich through their huge landholdings. The largest villas could boast a thousand tenants, all paying rent in kind. Off this the landowners lived very well.

Artorius' government would have to collect tax in kind. There was no available coin. Public works would have to be constructed in wood, the quarries having closed and the skills of brick making and tile making having died. Even the lucrative import revenues had gone. The Diocese used to gain much in customs dues from traders. Now they were very few. The fall of Gaul compelled traders to navigate around Hispania. It was a long and risky voyage and only the occasional ship came as far as Britannia.

Artorius knew he could not turn back the clock. The cities were slowly dying. They had existed as cash markets and craft centres. The lack of coin was killing them. Some had already died. When he had marched to Badon, he had passed the ruins of what had been Cunetio, abandoned some fifty years before.

What he could restore was the rule of Law. Roman Law was comprehensive and most of it was written. If he could snatch much of its administration out of the hands of the senators, he could enforce real justice in the land. He would need new and trustworthy magistrates and judges. He would also have to have honest tax collectors. Too often in the past the erogatores had been open to bribery by the super-rich.

The roads were overdue for maintenance, particularly in the east where the barbarian incursions had hit hardest. The way stations along the major roads would have to be restored and staffed so that despatches could travel rapidly and travellers could have safe lodging overnight. If travel became safer and easier a modicum of trade could begin to flow from city to city.

He put these thoughts to Winnifhoere. She was quick to grasp the essentials of the problems. "You will have to use the army for much of what you want to do," she said. "The army can make the roads safe. Use cavalry patrols. They will become your police. The army can repair the roads where they are damaged."

On the matter of the Law, the problem was more difficult. Senators had always been the senior magistrates. They would expect new appointments to be made from among them and, indeed, that was the Law. Many of the less wealthy senators had sought to avoid magistracies since the rank carried obligations as to public works and entertainments that they could ill afford. Winnifhoere suggested that there must be some honest senators he could appoint. Surely not all were corrupt. Ambrosius Aurelianus had been honest and there must be some more like him.

Artorius admitted that this was likely, but he did not know them well enough to decide who was honest and who not. "Then put some of your Combrogi to oversee the workings of the courts," said Winnifhoere. "If each city has a small garrison of your troops, they can keep the senators in line. You could claim the troops are there to help defend the cities if troubles come again, so the Senates could hardly object."

Artorius saw sense in this. He had been made Emperor by the army and now he would have to rule through it. He would appoint his own Vicarii to govern the provinces. They would almost all be drawn from the Officer Corps, and particularly from the Combrogi. He could promote them to senatorial rank. Each would retain troops under command. Cato would retain Dumnonia and also Venta Belgarum. The newly conquered land in western Dumnonia would be named Cornwall after the Cornovii who had taken it. Dumnonia would in essence become a new province under military government. Coelestius would remain as Dux at Eboracum, ruling Britannia Secunda. Gawain would be given Valentia with his capital at Luguvalum (Carlisle). Lindum, the capital of the province of Flavia Caesariensis would go to Bedwyr. Britannia Prima, once ruled from Corinium would go to Marcellus based in Glevum. Agricola would keep Demetia. He would have to find someone who could supervise the Votadini in North Wales. Britannia Superior which had always been ruled from Londinium would be the Imperial Province ruled directly by Artorius with its capital at Camulodunum. The City Prefect would be the Vicarius to maintain the administration whenever Artorius was away.

This would provide that the city Senates would not be able to over-awe the Vicarii as they had always done in the past. He himself would base his rule in Camulodunum. The Senate there had proved loyal and it was strategically placed to watch over the ceded lands held by the Saxons. He doubted the men of Cantium would try anything while he was nearby.

The problem of the magistracy would take time. He would have to tour Britannia from city to city to find the right men for the job. If he ended the financial obligations that magistrates had had in the past, more might be prepared to take the posts and might prove more honest than those super-rich who saw the magistracy as simply another way to accrue wealth. Then he would appoint, from his junior officers and whichever senators proved honest and competent, rectores to supervise the administration of each city and town and its environs. Government would be shared between civil and military officials but the military would hold the whip hand.

Having thus sorted out in his mind the mechanics of his new government, he next had to put it into effect. This would require some diplomacy, some arm-twisting and, if need be, some force. The first step had to be a meeting of the Council of Britannia. There he would outline what he proposed. Let the senators fight among themselves for the crumbs of power he might offer. Their mutual intrigues would keep them busy and diverted from plotting against him.

Next he could install the Vicarii and rectores. He would take them personally to each province in turn, introduce them to the various Senates and at the same time select magistrates and judges. This part of the task would not make him popular. The richest and, almost by definition, most corrupt senators would want these posts as of right. He would deny them. He would proclaim that the qualification for the posts would not be wealth but integrity.

Men passed over would be resentful. That could not be helped. If they sought to cause any trouble, he could trust his Vicarii to squash them. If a few very rich senators were placed under the Ban of the Empire, it might teach the rest to fear if not respect him.

He called the Council meeting to convene at Camulodunum in mid December. They would not like travelling in winter but they could celebrate Christmas together. This would be one way of getting to know some of the leading senators better. They were invited to bring their wives too. Artorius was sure they would come. Their wives would want to socialise with Winnifhoere.

Winnifhoere laughed when he told her. "You are a wily fox," she said. "You know full well the women will be eager to come, more than their husbands."

"I want them all here," said Artorius. "If I can swing a vote of confidence in what I propose, the various cities will have to comply even when they dislike the detail later."

All the Council came. They came in groups with wives, sons and daughters.

The City Prefect of Camulodunum was hard pressed to find suitable accommodation for them. There were plenty of vacant houses but not all were sufficiently well-appointed for the super-rich. Much repair work and decoration had had to be done to make them ready. Huge stocks of firewood were gathered to fire the furnaces that heated the houses. Streets were repaired and cleaned. Artorius was amused at the effort the Prefect put in to make his city seem prosperous and well maintained. The Prefect wanted the Councillors to see Camulodunum as a real Capital.

When the meeting convened in the Senate House Artorius was last to arrive. He was escorted by Vortipor and his cavalry bodyguard. He was determined to fully act the part of an Emperor. He dressed in white tunic and trews and donned the purple cloak. The gilded laurel wreath crown and the gold belt and his sword completed his attire.

He strode into the Senate House and straight to the praesidium. The senators all stood as he entered and only sat when he did. He declared the session open and settled back to hear the flattering speeches. They came. He was lauded as another Vespasian, a Suetonius Paulinus who had defeated Boudicca, as another Agricola who had conquered the north. He was compared with the Emperors Titus, Trajan and Theodosius. He let them have their say. When they had finished he stood to speak.

"I thank you for the praise you have offered me. Most of that is due my officers and men. They fought the battles. Without them I would have achieved little. Now that our enemies are beaten and contained I have a new task as your Emperor. I have to restore what I can of Britannia. These wars have damaged us much. Trade is severely diminished. Much of the east has been ravaged and many of its people killed or forced to flee. Industries have perished. We no longer have potteries or brick works. The quarries have closed. Glass is no longer made.

"These things will take a long time to re-establish. In the meantime Britannia has to be governed. Britannia has five provinces. Each needs its proper government. Britannia Secunda, based on Eboracum, can be left, as always, to the Dux. Coelestius is a good man who will rule it well. The rest lack normal government.

"I intend to appoint Vicarii to administer each province. The Emperor always appointed such in the past. It is time to do so again. Their regions will be somewhat different. Cato, my Magister Militum, will retain control over Dumnonia and the rebel city of Venta Belgarum as the Count of Dumnonia. This will be a military province like Britannia Secunda.

"So too will be Demetia, under Agricola. These newly reconquered lands need a strong military presence and strong Governors. They lack cities to accommodate a civilian administration so it is best they are left to the army.

"In addition the cities and towns should have rectores, administering not only the cities but the lands dependent on them. Since Honorius cut Britannia loose from his direct control, we have had none such. I think it time to restore these posts.

"The foundation of our way of life, our civilisation, is Law. This has fallen into disrepute. Many of our magistrates and judges have proved partial and corrupt. I intend to progress around Britannia. On my arrival at each city, the magistrates and judges will resign their posts pending re-appointment or replacement.

"These posts have always been reserved to senators and I see no reason to alter that. I will, however, require total probity from them. Magistrates and judges proved to have taken bribes or shown partiality to friends will in future face death. In future no man will face trial in his own city. Witnesses and magistrates all know each other too well and this is what breeds corruption and partiality. To make the magistracy less of a burden, magistrates will no longer be obliged to maintain roads and bridges at their own expense: these tasks will fall to the army. Equally they will no longer have to finance public entertainments.

"My government will be based on Justice and Righteousness. My officials will have to swear to the same high standards. My army officers have already sworn thus. I see no reason why civil officials should not do likewise.

"Times are uncertain. We have stemmed the incursions of barbarians for now but they might come again. Each city needs to have adequate defence. I will station small garrisons in each city to help train the citizens how best to defend their walls. When folk feel secure they have the incentive to prosper.

"The army will undertake to repair the roads and patrol them. If the roads are made safe, trade might improve and that is to the benefit of all. We lack coin. That is a problem I cannot solve. The Imperial mint in Gaul is no more. We have insufficient bullion to mint coins. Taxation will be in kind, cattle or grain. We have no alternative.

"These proposals are based on present realties. We cannot hanker after the past. We have to build a new Britannia on the ruins of the old. Our foundations are our values and our means are what we now have.

"I put my proposals to you as the Council of Britannia. If you see any flaw in them, speak out. I ask your advice and will consider all objections. In this Council you are free to say what you will without fear. I shall not count any man my enemy simply because he disagrees with me. I would rather know what you think and whether you have better solutions."

He sat and let them speak. Most were in favour. He had expected that. They sought to curry favour and many had half an eye towards becoming a Vicar or rector or to gaining a magistracy. Some expressed reservations. He listened to them attentively. Most of these were wary of having troops in their cities: would they not over-awe the civil administration?

When all had had their say, he called a vote. It was overwhelmingly in favour. He noted those who had voted against. These were men he would need to get to know. Some were automatically hostile to any central government but he sensed most were thinking, honest men whom he could trust. It was from amongst these that he would choose his magistrates.

At the end of the meeting he invited them to a banquet that night in the basilica. He had wanted to use his house but had realised it would be too small. The citizens of Camulodunum were already referring to it as his palace but it was in reality just a large town-house. It did not compare to the rich villas of the west and held far fewer riches. He could guarantee all the senators would attend: they wanted preferment and influence.

That night the basilica was crowded. The Councillors were joined by the whole Senate of Camulodunum and the bishop and by all the available ranking officers of the army. Wives came too. Winnifhoere played hostess to perfection and the cooks, Artorius having borrowed several from the senators, produced a feast. Afterwards he was able to circulate and chat to the company. He made a point of talking with those men who had expressed reservations as to his plans. By the end of the evening he had a clear view as to which were honest and which just hostile towards him.

When all were gone and the servants were clearing the debris, he retired home with Winnifhoere. "I am glad that is over," Artorius said. "I am wearied of flattery and insincerity."

"They seek advancement," said Winnifhoere, "and you are now the only source of that. They will flatter and dissemble until they get what they want. After that they will try to thwart you."

"That is why I will promote from among those who disagreed with me. They at least are honest. The flatterers are too hard to read."

It had in reality gone rather well. The senators were hopeful of positions in government. They would have the judiciary. They could hope for rectorships and the Vicariate but Artorius had not told them that he intended most of these posts for the army. He had got the vote of confidence he wanted and could now set things in motion.

Christmas was celebrated in the great church of Camulodunum and the bishop, at Artorius' prompting, gave a sermon on good governance. The Christ child was King of Kings but let himself be born in poverty. He was Emperor of the Universe, yet was humble. He judged fairly with regard to the woman taken in adultery and lambasted the hypocritical Pharisees who made petty laws they did not keep themselves. His judgements were based on the spirit rather than the letter of the Law. Rulers, whether Emperors or Imperial officials, should follow His example. Government should be based on morality and not just on the letter of ancient laws.

When all was over and the Councillors had gone home, Artorius held a meeting of the Combrogi. New members were admitted, notably Theoderic, Medraut and Coelestius. The oath was renewed. Afterwards Artorius told them of his intended appointments. Vortipor was to go to north Wales, into the lands of the Votadini to supervise their rule. Medraut would go with him with a detachment of cavalry to police the roads. Gawain, as a friend of both Dyfnwal and Coelestius would be Vicar of Valentia. Bedwyr, now a good friend of King Icel, would have Flavia Caesariensis with its capital at Lindum. Marcellus would base himself in Glevum as Vicar of Britannia Prima. Numerous Tribunes were appointed to become rectores. Theoderic would be the Admiral of the Classis Britannica, the British Fleet.

Cato, whose position was unchanged, gave Theoderic lands in Dumnonia beside Falmouth and Fowey and above Padstow and a villa near St. Ives. Each had a harbour for Theoderic's ships and Theoderic was charged with patrolling the coasts to prevent raiders coming from Ireland. At Tintagel Theoderic established one of his captains with the task of patrolling the Severn Sea to protect traders coming from Hispania. He had a hall built on the headland for him. Theoderic was officially accorded the rank of Prefect with pleased him inordinately.

It took several years to place all these appointees but it gave Artorius the chance of visiting every city and town in Britannia. He had to preside over many court cases, and particularly those where a defendant had appealed to the Emperor. His judgements were acclaimed far and wide. The common people began to trust the Law again and the rich to respect it.

Artorius was still not popular with the senatorial class. They had got few posts as Vicarii and few as rectores and they deemed these theirs as of right. Many of the richest had been passed over for magistracies. They sensed that Artorius did not fully trust them. They disliked the ubiquity of the army. They disliked the erogatores who could not be bribed to take less tax than was due. To them Artorius was a tyrant getting his way by force. In the past they had accepted the Emperors because they were very far away and almost never came to Britannia. Now they had an Emperor close at hand and backed by an omnipresent army. They were uncomfortable and chaffed at the restrictions that prevented them from living as they had in the past, able to ignore Imperial Decrees or circumvent them. Their aristocratic status cut no ice with Artorius or his officers and their wealth could not buy them immunity from his laws.

Chapter 21: The years of Peace.

Once all was in place a semblance of normality returned. The land had good government. Law was enforced without fear or favour. Taxes were collected, the burden falling more on the rich than the poor and none paying what he could not afford. The roads were repaired apace, the army moving along them to put all in order. The inns, too, were restored and staffed by soldiers whose role was to police the roads and keep spare horses for Imperial messengers.

In the cities small garrisons trained the civilian militias to defend their walls and operate outside them too. Places like Calleva could extend their cultivation well beyond the walls now that it was safe to go out into the countryside. A new spirit of optimism prevailed. In Viroconium (Wroxeter) half ruined houses were torn down and replaced with new timber houses and shops. Trade was reviving a little. More ships ventured to Britannia now that Theoderic guarded the seas. They brought the luxuries that Britannia lacked, wines, olive oil, fine pottery, silks and ornaments and jewellery. These were bartered for corn, hides and fleeces.

Britannia was, indeed, the last remnant of the Roman Empire of the West. Here the Romans had held their own. They had beaten back the barbarians or absorbed them. They maintained their government. They kept their Law.

The capital was now Camulodunum. For much of the year Artorius based himself there. Its access to the sea enabled some trade to come to it once traders realised they were not too close to Saxon Cantium. It was still necessary to watch the Saxons in Cantium and it was conveniently near King Icel's East Anglian lands. King Icel was now very old and Winnifhoere often visited him. Artorius liked to go too when he could. He admired the old warrior King and they had become firm friends. He liked Icel's sons too and felt certain the treaty would hold long after Icel's death.

Nevertheless, he had to move around Britannia too. The taxes stored in the west and the north had to be used and what was collected in the east was not enough to sustain an Imperial court for a whole year. Besides, he needed to maintain regular contact with his Vicarii, so nearly half the year was spent travelling from provincial capital to provincial capital, hearing appeals and appointing new judges where necessary but, above all, renewing friendships.

When he went to Valentia to see Gawain he made a point of meeting King Dyfnwal to check that Fergus was keeping his bargain. Coelestius reported that Pictish raids had virtually ceased. His field army was now concentrated around Eboracum and was better trained. He now had cavalry too, thanks to Gawain who had loaned him instructors. The northern borders seemed secure.

Only in the west were there problems. Marcellus reported that the Senate of Glevum had a grievance against Cato as to exactly where Cato's Dumnonia bordered Britannia Prima. They had not liked Dumnonia being enlarged and 'given away' and wanted as much of the good land to remain with Britannia Prima as they could get. The land of the Durotriges (modern Dorsetshire) was a particular bone of contention even though most of its villa estates had been Imperial lands. Artorius had to go to Glevum, listen to turgid speeches as to how the city was losing revenue since taxes in Dumnonia went to the army, and then get Cato's side of the argument. It was as he had suspected. Some of the richest senators still held lands in Dumnonia. Cato was very experienced in finding hidden produce and taking from it the due tithe. He was hurting their pockets.

Artorius travelled the bounds of the two provinces with Cato and half the Senate of Glevum. He placed markers to show where the border should be and told Cato to make a permanent, visible border around his lands. Cato set his men to work and they dug a huge dyke backed by a bank along all the disputed bounds.

It was while he was at Glevum that Artorius was warned that some of the Senate, egged on by the deposed City Prefect, were plotting his assassination. Marcellus had been warned and set men to closely guard Artorius. He told some of his junior officers to investigate, telling them to seem to be disaffected so as to gain the confidence of the conspirators. Very soon he had evidence as to which senators were involved and how and when they intended to act. The would-be assassin was arrested in the Senate House and was found to be carrying two daggers. Ever since the time of Julius Caesar it had been a capital offence for any civilian to carry weapons in public. Interrogation obtained the names of five senators involved and they too were arrested. Artorius had to impose the death sentence on the knife-man and exiled the guilty senators.

There were problems in Wales too. The Votadini were restless among themselves. Vortipor reported that the descendents of those who had come with Cunedda were resentful that Marianus had gained most of the Lleyn peninsula. The grandsons of Cunedda were likely to fall out and fight a civil war among themselves. Artorius had to go to sort out the fracas. He again marked a frontier. Medraut was promoted to oversee Marianus and based himself at Dinas Emrys. Artorius could not afford the Votadini to indulge in civil war. It would encourage the Irish to renew their raids. Instead he recruited a joint force from both territories to invade and occupy Mona (Anglesey). There were still Irish there. It gave the Votadini something to do together. Vortipor was in command with Medraut as his deputy. Theoderic too was involved and refurbished the old naval depot at what is now Holyhead to prevent the Irish getting reinforcements from Ireland.

Thereafter things calmed down. Peace settled over Britannia. People felt safer in their daily work. A modicum of prosperity returned. Travel became easier now that the roads were regularly patrolled. Merchants could get produce to the ports and bring back luxuries. Of course trade was still slow. There were few ships from Gaul and industry could not thrive without coin. Most manufactures were locally made out of what came to hand. People got used to using wooden platters instead of pottery and everywhere timber had replaced stone and brick for building.

At last Artorius and Winnifhoere could have something of a normal life. He had been preoccupied with campaigning. The wars had taken him away from home and away from Winnifhoere. She had been patient and long-suffering. When he apologised for his many absences she said, "I married a warrior who had a war to fight. If you had not gone away, I would not be Empress. You are what you are, and I would not have it otherwise." Even so he felt guilty as though he had neglected her.

They had had no children. It was a sorrow to them both. She felt she had failed to give Artorius an heir and he that he had denied her motherhood.

Maybe the years of war, the fact that he was too often away, often overburdened by cares of government and was much older than her had had something to do with it. There was sorrow too that Icel had died. Despite their Christianity, they had gone to his funeral. He was buried within a funeral ship with his weapons and furnishings for the afterlife and a great mound was raised over the tomb. His two surviving sons divided the lands between them and renewed the treaty with Artorius. The division would prove to be permanent with the North Folk and South Folk adhering to new dynasties.

Thousands of Saxons left Britannia for the Rhinelands. They feared to expand westwards and the old Frankish territories were now vacant. What had been the land of the Franks was now becoming Saxony. Artorius was glad. The pressure on the eastern frontier was diminishing.

Saxons also went to Gaul. They settled around the mouth of the Seine and in what would become Normandy. There they were opposed by the British of Armorica who retained a visceral hatred of Saxons. War was constant. The Frankish king, Clovis, let them fight. While they were at each other's throats, he could consolidate his power over all of what was becoming France. He offered support to one side or the other to ensure that neither could win an outright victory.

Among the British in Armorica there were frequent civil wars. Kingdom vied with Kingdom and when a King died his sons divided the land and then fought for the crown. Often they came to Britannia seeking aid in ousting a usurper. Artorius treated them with respect but steadfastly refused to get involved in their squabbles. Britannia had just recovered from years of war at home. It was not time to join in foreign wars.

It was about this time that Helena died. She had contracted a fever one winter and, like Ambrosius Aurelianus, succumbed to pneumonia. The nuns notified Artorius and he and Winnifhoere went to the funeral. It was a very simple affair and she was buried in the nuns' cemetery. The prioress told Artorius that that was what she had wanted. "She had become like one of us. She joined in all the hours of prayer and lived simply. Most of her personal wealth she gave to the poor. She was a better Christian than many a professed nun and we will miss her. Do not mourn her dying:

she has gone to God and we will pray that she will intercede for us all in heaven."

The Combrogi grew steadily. It was harder to judge men in time of peace. The first Combrogi had all been veterans of the Saxon War, men who had distinguished themselves in command or in battle. Now many were men who had risen in the army in times of peace and it is harder to judge a man's worth when he has faced no crises. Even so, the Combrogi, meeting annually, always had nominations for membership and most were accepted on the word of their sponsors.

Winnifhoere counselled caution. "Many of these new men you do not know," she said. "Some see the Combrogi as a means to advancement. They seek to join as though it is just some sort of club. Their oaths might be just as lightly taken as were the oaths of senators in the past. Ambition is a corrosive thing."

Artorius knew she was right, but he had given the Combrogi the right to nominate new members and the right to vote to accept or reject them. He did not feel he could now change the rules. He had to trust the membership. Even so, he sensed the ideals were becoming somewhat diluted as the Combrogi grew.

It had taken time to reform the magistracy. Among the senatorial class old habits were hard to change. He had had to remove some magistrates who had proved partial towards friends. One or two had taken bribes. Reluctantly he had had to impose death sentences where clear proof showed guilt. This did not make him popular with the rich. "They seem to think that wealth puts them above the Law," he complained to Winnifhoere.

"They always will," she replied. "Wealth is power. It buys the poorer. These men will always think that wealth gives them rights above the commoner folk. They resent the fact that they are ruled by a man who has less than they and whom they cannot buy. They believe that each man has a price, and you affront them because you do not."

"They are not fit to have power," he said. "They would use it to bolster their own kind at the expense of all others. They applaud when I enforce the Law over ordinary folk but resent it when I force them to comply. The petty crimes that I punish are as nothing to the injustices they indulge in every day. They even presume to use the Law for their own enrichment, forcing men who cannot read to sign contracts that they could never fulfil and then prosecuting them in the courts to take from them what little they own. Most of the civil cases in the courts are brought by the rich against the poor."

"That will ever be so," said Winnifhoere. "The rich can use lawyers: the poor cannot. The rich know the Law: the poor do not. You must use discretion in deciding such cases. How fair was the contract? Justice is more than the letter of the Law. It should be based on what is morally right."

Discretion was a difficult option. Roman Law was a written compendium of past Imperial decrees and judgements. It was complex. It was based on statutes, Imperial Decrees and precedents and many of these did not suit the new world in which Britannia lived. It was however the only Law and it was what acted as a cement holding all together. Artorius knew he could not sweep it all away and replace it with his own. He would have to set new precedents.

He regularly called the magistrates together to explain how he wanted the Law to be interpreted and enforced. He insisted that witnesses be closely questioned and evidence sieved. He set as a principle that 'evidence' brought by men of power should be particularly closely examined. It was not the number of witnesses a man could call but the quality of their evidence that mattered. Witnesses could be bought.

He insisted that, where there was any doubt, cases should be referred to him. It gave him much to do but, as the highest court of appeal, his judgements would become precedents. Among the common folk he was seen as their champion against the greed and power of the rich. Among the rich he was resented as a power they could not suborn. His Vicarii followed the same line as he and, in the minds of the rich, the army was equated with Artorius.

There were many plots against his rule. Senators with grievances sought to persuade others to stand against the Emperor. Many tried to persuade Artorius' officers to lead revolts against him but all failed. The Combrogi remained loyal.

When he visited the various Senates in their cities he was still feted as the saviour of Britannia. He still had to listen to flattering speeches. He knew them for what they were. Senators would outwardly praise his government whilst actively seeking to undermine it to their own benefit. Very few actually saw his rule as good. The majority were frustrated and angry and hated him.

Gawain and Coelestius could not understand his situation. They had no rich senators in their provinces. They were the Law in their lands. Cato too, once he had purged the Senate of Venta Belgarum of the supporters of Caradoc, had few problems. In Artorius' name he had expelled the sons of Caradoc and confiscated Caradoc's estates. He kept a strong garrison in Venta to remind the remaining senators as to where the real power lay.

Bedwyr and Marcellus knew what Artorius was up against. They had cities in their lands with power-hungry senators who were ever ready to complain about their administration. They too were often flattered by men who wanted favours or sought to worm their way into friendship so as to seem innocent of wrong-doing.

Artorius had learned that wealth was corrupting. It led men to go to exceptional lengths to acquire and protect it. They rarely used it for the good of others. Even their very public gifts to the Church were merely an attempt to buy favour of God. He told the bishops to beware of men who thought they could bribe their way into Heaven. He saw churchmen getting richer from gifts to the Church, marking out the lands they had been given and jealously guarding them, and this saddened him. Some of the civil cases referred to him were disputes between a rich man's heirs and the churches to which lands had been given. If he judged for the heirs he was condemned by the Church: if he favoured the Church he was the more hated by the rich.

He tried to steer a middle course but knew that in every civil judgement the loser became another enemy. He tried to rule well. He based his rule on the principles he had set for the Combrogi, Justice and Righteousness. His Christianity was simple but deep-rooted. He based his life, his rule and his judgements on it. He said to Winnifhoere, "They may hate me as

Emperor but I trust none will be able to say I am an evil man."

She was his mainstay. She happily accepted to live simply despite her rank. She had soon seen through the posturing of senators' wives. She disliked their malicious gossip, their determination to upstage each other by ostentatious display and their contempt for any poorer than them. "I can talk more easily to the servants," she said. "They have more common sense. They are forgiving of each other and generous with what little they have."

Eight years after Badon, Marcellus' father died. Marcellus was heir to his father's throne in Armorica. Artorius counselled him to leave the inheritance to the sons of the former King whom Marcellus' father had usurped. "You are an important man here. Your province, which you rule in my name, is bigger than the tiny Kingdom you will have in Armorica. If you go there you will become embroiled in wars. Better, I think, to let others have the Kingdom. They will be more secure and you will be safe here."

Marcellus, however, was adamant. He was to be a King, even if only a very minor one. He would go to claim his birthright in Armorica. He saw that he could not remain a Vicar under Artorius at the same time, so resigned his office. Artorius was sad that he went. He wondered what Kingship might do to Marcellus. He had been a good soldier and general but Kingship required a lot more than that.

That left Britannia Prima without a Vicar. It was the most difficult province, the one with the most cities filled with dissatisfied senators. Artorius transferred Gawain to be its Vicar and promoted Donatus, one of his cavalry Tribunes to be a Prefect and Vicar of Valentia. He needed Gawain further to the south. He was someone he could trust implicitly, a talented commander and a sound diplomat. Marcellus had regularly upset the senators, sometimes needlessly, and a more diplomatic Vicar might mollify them somewhat. Also he needed someone to aid Vortipor in north Wales. The sons and grandsons of Cunedda were a quarrelsome lot who required much watching lest civil war break out among them. Gawain was told to put a strong garrison in Deva as an ever-present threat to any who broke the peace.

The land enjoyed the peace of Artorius by giving him none. Winnifhoere told him that that was only right. The ruler gave peace by taking all the stresses on himself. He should not worry that he was not loved: it was better that he was feared. "Popular Kings are usually weak," she said. "Among my people the truly great Kings were always those the people feared. They became loved and honoured only after they died. You have all the power. For that you are resented. It cannot be helped: it is the nature of power. After we are gone folk will look back on your rule as being a good time in Britannia. They will remember that you were just and did right. That is all you can hope for."

Chapter 22: Camlann

The year 515 was a turning point. It was some twenty years since the battle of Badon. Artorius was now old. He was still supremely fit. He could still ride his horse and wield his sword but he was conscious that time was not on his side. He tired more quickly and took longer to recover. The cares and years of rule had greyed his hair. The same was true of the first Combrogi. They were all men in their late prime. The younger men had not known war as they had. They were all good officers and competent on exercise but none had faced the trauma of real action. Some hankered after it. Coelestius had died at Eboracum and was followed by his son, Eleutherius, as Dux.

The New Year was marked by a meeting of the Combrogi at Camulodunum. Artorius sensed that the younger men were somewhat discontented. They had had little advancement. In peacetime it is hard for an officer to shine and catch a general's eye to earn promotion. There were factions among them, little sub-groups gathering around charismatic fellows. Medraut, with his tales of derring-do among the Votadini, told with his usual self-flattery, was particularly popular. He was also a malcontent. When Marcellus left for Armorica he had expected the Vicariate of Britannia Prima almost as of right. He would have settled for Valentia, but that had gone to Donatus.

He said nothing openly, but grumbled steadily with his friends. He said that Artorius was getting old. Gawain, Cato and Bedwyr had too much influence over him. He was losing his grip.

They held their meeting and renewed their oaths and went back to their postings. Artorius held Gawain back. "I am worried," he said. "I fear Medraut is not happy."

"That little upstart!" exclaimed Gawain. "I'm sorry I ever proposed him for the Combrogi. He is all bombast. He talks as though he kicked the Irish out of Mona all on his own. It was Vortipor's men who did most of the work. Vortipor can't stand him. He tells me that in all that campaign Medraut never bloodied his sword. He launched his cavalry in charges and carefully rode behind them. Now he talks down Vortipor's role. The younger men are all convinced he commanded the enterprise and sing his praises. It isn't right."

"Right or wrong, he is unhappy. He wants advancement and has received none. If what you say is true, he deserves none." Artorius pondered a while. "He is far away in western Wales. He can cause little trouble there but his faction among the Combrogi is a worry. He is infecting many of them with his discontent. Marianus sings his praises. Medraut should be watched. He is the sort of man who ends up believing what he claims of himself and then holds grudges."

Gawain was perturbed. He had never known Artorius to hold suspicions about any of the Combrogi. If he felt thus about Medraut, something was amiss. "Have you talked with Cato and Bedwyr? They might have ideas as to how to cure the rot."

"Cato is his normal no-nonsense self. He says, 'Sack him. Get him out of Britain where he can do no harm,' but I cannot sack him for no crime. All I have are suspicions."

"And Bedwyr?"

"Much the same. He sees him as dangerous to the unity of the Combrogi. He does not trust him."

"They are probably right. They are canny judges of character. There is one way you could get rid of him, for a time. Send him away as an ambassador. Invent some mission for him that will take him abroad. It will make him feel important. He might even take it as a promotion."

"True, but it would have to be a real mission. He would soon see through a charade. He is a fool but an intelligent one."

"You could negotiate a treaty with King Clovis of the Franks."

"That would not wash. We have no need of such a treaty. The Franks have never threatened us, nor we them. He would see that as an unimportant matter designed to get him out of the way. I'll sleep on it and see what I can concoct for him. I would rather tell him to his face that I no longer trust him but that would split the Combrogi down the middle. I cannot risk that."

He talked with Winnifhoere about it. She too had sensed a threat around the brooding Medraut. She had noticed how he curried popularity among the newer Combrogi. She saw him as a cancer that was growing. "Whenever I meet him he makes my flesh creep," she said. "His eyes are always watchful, calculating. They never smile. He keeps his real nature hidden deep away. Everything about him is artificial: what he says, how he behaves - all is contrived."

"But what to do about him is another matter," said Artorius. "I cannot do what barbarian Kings would do. I cannot send assassins to remove him. I cannot set up false witnesses to condemn him. I am bound by my Combrogi oath and he knows that, even if he takes his lightly."

"Send him to Ireland. Open talks with the High King, Muirchetach Mac Erca, with a view to ending forever the Irish raids. Then send him on to the rest of the O'Neils to negotiate peace between them and Fergus. We know he will be likely to fail: the High King has little power outside his own lands and the O'Neils see Fergus' Irish lands as weak and know there is little we could do to help him there. It would keep Medraut there for most of the year. He might even find opportunities for his ambition there, like Marcellus in Armorica, and stay."

It was an attractive idea. An Embassy from the Emperor of Britannia would flatter the High King even if he could not promise any real change. It might seem important enough to satisfy Medraut's vanity. Artorius waited a week and then sent for him. He would sense some urgency if he was summoned back just after arriving in north Wales.

It was another week before he arrived in Camulodunum. He was taken straight to Artorius who greeted him warmly. "Welcome, Medraut. I must apologise for dragging you back across the country but I have a delicate task that needs someone I can trust. You have fought the Irish in the Lleyn Peninsula and on Mona. You know something of their ways. I am minded to use you as my ambassador to the High King in Ireland. For now we have expelled or absorbed the Irish that were here, but raids continue. We guard against them and they do little damage.

"I would have an agreement with King Muirchetach. I would have him prevent his folk from raiding our coasts. You, as conqueror of Mona, have status among the Irish as a general. That makes you eminently suitable to act in this for me. You know where and whence the raiders come: you are based in the west. You can speak from experience. You have fought them and won: you can speak from strength.

"Also I would wish for peace between the O'Neils and King Fergus, my ally in Kintyre. It will not be possible to negotiate that with the High King. The other O'Neils covet the High Kingship for themselves and will not brook his interference in their domestic affairs. I would have you talk direct with them.

"How say you? Will you act for Britannia and me in this?"

Medraut was flattered. He saw this as his chance for permanent advancement. When he succeeded, Artorius would owe him a lot. He might even supplant Bedwyr as Comes Britanniarum!

"I will be honoured to serve as your ambassador," he said.

"I am glad," said Artorius. "You will have to stay here awhile until we have worked out exactly what we want and what we can offer in return. I will not send you on a fool's errand, asking much and giving little. You must be given every chance to succeed."

Medraut was happy enough to stay at Camulodunum while a draft treaty was drawn up in Latin. It took about a week and in that time he confided his new mission to his friends. He was going to be the peacemaker between

Ireland and Britannia. It was a most important and difficult task. Artorius had turned to him as the only person he could trust for the job.

At last he left. Artorius and Winnifhoere breathed a sigh of relief. The insufferable egotist was gone. Winnifhoere admitted hoping a great storm would sink his ship before he got to Ireland.

Artorius wondered what his mother would have advised. She had been very like Winnifhoere, full of common sense and intuition. He missed her letters which were always full of anecdotes and good ideas. He mourned the fact that he had rarely had time to visit her. What would she have thought of Medraut?

Life returned to normality. In the spring Artorius set out as usual to tour the country with Winnifhoere. Bedwyr came too. His province was secure and it was time he, as Comes Britanniarum, inspected the rest of the army. They visited the Senates of Ratae and Lindum and then went north to Eboracum. It was there that Winnifhoere fell ill. Eleutherius summoned his surgeons to tend her and for a while their potions seemed to work. They told Artorius that she was not fit to travel, even in a litter. Better to leave her at Eboracum and continue his tour without her. When she was better, Eleutherius would have her escorted back to Camulodunum.

Artorius was for staying with her until she was better but Winnifhoere insisted he go on. "You have a job to do," she said. "I am in good hands here and will meet you in Camulodunum when you get back." Reluctantly he went. He and Bedwyr travelled slowly along the Wall, inspecting the garrisons and finally reached Luguvalum. Thence they went south to Deva.

At Deva they got news from Ireland. A messenger had come from King Muirchetach. Medraut had been to him a month before with Artorius' proposals. The King was willing to enter into friendly relations but could not coerce the other Kings without fighting them and he had no wish to go to war with them. Medraut had been sent on to the O'Neils. As a postscript the High King had added that Artorius' ambassador seemed a little inexperienced and somewhat arrogant. He would not be welcome as an ambassador at Muirchetach's court again.

So Medraut had failed, not through any fault in his instructions but in how he had conducted himself. It was almost as Artorius had expected. He wondered what the O'Neils would make of him.

They continued southwards to Glevum where Cato was to meet them with Gawain. Here they had news from Eboracum. Winnifhoere was still too ill to travel but was making progress. Artorius offered prayers of thanks. Bedwyr had noticed how on edge he had been since they left Eboracum.

They had the usual fractious meeting of the Senate, with all the normal complaints about the level of taxation, the demands of the military, the lack of suitable posts for the senatorial class and the lack of adequate imports of wine and silks. Artorius let it wash over him. He had heard it all before. He had explained it all before. These people would never learn.

They were about to leave for Venta Belgarum when a messenger came post haste from Donatus at Luguvalum. A large fleet of ships from Ireland had put in on the Cumbrian coast. Some three thousand men had landed and marched inland.

This was no raid. This was an invasion. Gawain rushed north to Deva to call out his cavalry. Artorius had to discover where the Irish were and where they were headed. Cato galloped south to gather infantry for the long march north. Messengers went to Vortipor to muster the Votadini. The army was to gather at Deva. A warning was sent to Eleutherius at Eboracum. He was to guard all the passes over the Pennines.

Artorius and Bedwyr, with the whole garrison of Glevum, went to Deva. Bedwyr wondered at the timing of the invasion. If it had the sanction of the High King, he was duplicitous. If not, it had to be the O'Neils. Fergus' folk were too hard pressed to launch such an enterprise but the O'Neils were powerful and had ports on their north coast whence the fleet might have come.

Artorius agreed that the O'Neils were the likely source of the invasion. "But why strike inland into the mountains?" he asked. "Why not advance south into richer, more cultivable lands?" In his heart he already knew the answer. In the mountains his cavalry would be less of a threat. Someone had told the O'Neils to avoid fighting in too open ground. That someone could only be Medraut.

What had Medraut done? Had he bragged of his prowess as a cavalryman? Had he allowed himself to be made drunk and then been pumped for information as to how the British fought? Where was he? By now he should have returned.

He put his fears to Bedwyr. "I'll bet Medraut is back: with the Irish," Bedwyr said. "He failed in his mission. He will have lost credibility with his friends. I heard him bragging as to how only he could negotiate peace with Ireland. Having failed, he would be too embarrassed to come back with his tail between his legs. He's come back to carve a Kingdom for himself where we will find it hard to dislodge him."

"We don't know that," said Artorius. "I hope it is not so. If it is, what of his oath?"

"An oath means little to a man with huge ambition," said Bedwyr. "He wanted a Vicariate but just for starters. He would only be happy with the purple."

When they reached Deva, a grim-faced Gawain met them. "The Irish are in the hills," he said. "They have only moved some ten miles inland. They are led by Medraut." He almost spat the name.

Artorius felt a wave of almost grief pass over him. One of the Combrogi, one of his 'brothers-in-arms', was a traitor. Medraut had broken his oath.

Gawain had more. The entire Irish force was armed with spears. They were practising close order fighting. Medraut was going to train them to fight in the same way as the British. "He is going to make it hard for us. He'll limit our cavalry if he can and make it an infantry fight. Cato had better be prepared for a slogging match."

"We must move fast," said Artorius. "As soon as Cato gets here, we march. We must move faster than even Medraut might think possible. We must force him to fight before he is fully prepared."

Cato soon came. He had brought the best part of his infantry with him by forced marches. They continued as fast as possible north. Gawain's horsemen rode ahead to scout the enemy positions. "Tell me the lie of the land," Artorius had said and they ranged the hills to find where Medraut was.

The news was not good. Medraut was camped at the head of a narrow valley between steep hills. The valley slowly opened out below his camp and then hooked left around the flank of a hill. Below this bend the land was much more open. "He'll try to force us to attack around the bend and into the narrows," said Bedwyr. "There we could not have room to use cavalry on the flanks and his infantry could fill the width of the valley."

"Then we must draw him down into the more open ground," said Artorius. "He has about three thousand men in a narrow place ringed by steep hills. We get control of the hilltops and close the valley where it bends. He will be bottled in. We wait. He cannot have much in the way of supplies. In time he must fight his way out. We let him attack. We give ground. The Irish will think they are winning and will come on into the wider valley where we can launch our cavalry at them. If we get round their flanks, they are lost."

They were joined by Donatus and the garrison of Luguvalum. He had sent scouts to keep an eye on Medraut's force and could guide the army to the valley where they were camped.

They marched to the mouth of the valley. It was called Camlann, the crooked glen. Cavalry were sent to climb the hills. Once on the tops they could ride over the treeless moors. Artorius told them to make sure they were visible from Medraut's camp. He wanted Medraut to know he was being watched. He wanted the Irish to know there was no escape up the hillsides.

They advanced along the valley towards the bend. They camped about half a mile below the bend and posted picquets forward. Medraut was bottled in. Several times parties of the Irish sallied out around the bend to attack the picquets. They were chased back by cavalry but not pursued beyond the corner. As days passed these sorties became larger. Artorius told Bedwyr that Medraut was trying to draw a major pursuit into the narrows. "He's getting a bit worried," he said. "We're not playing his game. His Irish are getting hungry. In a few days we will be seeing deserters breaking up the hillsides."

He was right. Men began slipping out of the Irish camp and climbing the steep hills to escape. Those who went in daylight were soon spotted and ridden down by horsemen as they reached the tops. Those who escaped by night were let go. There would be fewer to fight when it came to battle.

There was dissension in the Irish camp. The Irish followed war leaders proven in battle. They gave their loyalty to heroes. These men had followed a self-proclaimed 'hero' who was now proving to be anything but. He had led them into a trap. He seemed unwilling to launch an attack on the Romans, even though he outnumbered them. Finally they called his bluff. They formed a battle line and advanced to the bend.

The picquets sounded the alarm and Cato's men took their positions. Two lines of three ranks of infantry formed to face the Irish. Behind were the cavalry in two divisions, Gawain commanding the left and Artorius the right. Bedwyr and Cato took position close behind the infantry. They marched slowly forward.

The Irish filled the width of the valley where they stood, but seeing the Romans advancing, they broke into a charge, running pell-mell forwards into the wider space. They crashed against Cato's centre, halting its advance, but his flanks pushed forwards channelling the Irish in towards the middle. Cato rode behind his line watching and waiting. He ordered his centre to give more ground, pulling the Irish after them. His wings began to wrap around the extremities of the Irish.

Artorius watched as open ground appeared. He drew his sword and led his men at a canter through the gap and behind the Irish. Gawain did likewise on the left as soon as open space permitted. Then they charged. The effect was instant. As horsemen smashed into their rear the Irish broke.

Some threw down their weapons and ran for the hillsides. Few reached safety that way. Others formed small compact groups to fight their way back into the narrows. These made better progress but renewed cavalry charges broke them up. Cato's infantry began to hack their way into the remaining mass of the enemy, who gave ground rapidly.

Artorius had led three charges into the rear of the Irish. He had seen the tight knots of men trying to escape and had recalled men and directed charges to break these groups up. Then he saw Medraut. He was at the centre of a large compact group of Irish making for the narrows. Artorius gathered some thirty men, formed them in a line and charged. He led the way, his eyes fixed on Medraut.

As he thundered down on the group he saw Medraut see him. The man blanched. Artorius' horse skittled six men aside and Artorius' sword laid four more low as he cut through the group towards the traitor. He did not see the man who thrust a spear at him. He did not feel its impact. The man went down under his horse's hooves and then he was on his quarry. He leapt from his horse and bore down on Medraut.

Medraut looked about in terror. His group was scattered. Artorius' horsemen had followed in Artorius' wake and the close knit band was now split and fractured and fleeing. He made a wild lunge with his sword. As he did so he saw the Sword of Britannia sweeping from his side. It was the last thing he saw. It sliced through his neck and his head fell some six feet from his body.

Artorius looked down on the corpse. It was then that pain hit him. He sensed blood running down his side. He felt dizzy and sick. He sank to his knees and then pitched forwards unconscious.

He came to in his tent. He had been stripped of his armour and bandaged. He felt weak but had no pain. Bedwyr, Cato and Gawain were there and the surgeon. "The battle?" he asked.

"Won," said Cato, "with little loss. Your plan worked."

"I killed Medraut."

"We know. He deserved no better. If he had lived and been captured, you would have had to execute him."

Bedwyr said, "We are clearing the field now. About two thousand Irish dead. We lost a hundred and fifty. It is a great victory. The rest of the Irish have been rounded up. We've patched their wounds and they are under escort back to their ships. We thought it best to send them home."

The surgeon intervened. "Let him rest. He has a bad wound. I've packed and dressed it but he will need much rest if he is to recover. He must have regular draughts of poppy juice to kill the pain and he will sleep much of the time. We need to get him somewhere with a solid roof and no draughts. A tent does not make a good sick-room."

Next morning they lifted his bed onto a litter and began to carry him back to Deva. It fell to Cato's men to carry him and they did it gently and almost reverently. The march was slow and took several days. Bedwyr and Gawain were concerned. They had spoken to the surgeon and he had been frank.

"I have seen many wounds in my time," he said. "This one is bad. He took a spear in his side as he charged. The spear head broke and remained in the wound. Thanks be to God he was unconscious as I removed it: the shock could have killed him. He is old and he has lost a lot of blood. How he struck the blow that felled Medraut I shall never know. The effort opened the wound wider and that is why he fainted."

"What are his chances?" asked Gawain.

"Not very good. If the wound is kept clean and there is no fatal internal damage, he might recover. Men of his age heal slowly. If the wound festers, I would put his chances at fifty-fifty. If the spear has ruptured an intestine or the kidney, than he will die, unless I can find the damage and repair it. Even so, the operation would be very dangerous and the shock might kill him."

"We need him to live," said Bedwyr. "He has no heir and he is the only person who unites this Diocese. If he dies there will be much jockeying for power. We will appear weakened. The barbarians will come again."

"I can only do my best," said the surgeon. "You had better start praying. His fate rests more with God than with me."

They reached Deva and commandeered a house as a hospital. Artorius slept much. When he was awake he was alert. He asked questions as to the care of the other wounded, as to the on-going business of government and above all as to any news of Winnifhoere.

What news there was, was not good. Winnifhoere had suffered a relapse and was still not fit to travel. Bedwyr forbore to tell Artorius this. Time enough when he was well on the road to recovery, he thought.

Artorius lay on his bed. His mind wandered back and forth over his times. He remembered Winnifhoere on her first coming to Camulodunum with King Icel, how fragile and perfect she had seemed and how he felt protective of her. He remembered his march from Deva to Sorbiodunum when he was a raw young Tribune. How fast and how far he had risen! He recalled incidents from his battles, the waiting while Cato fought in the Medway ford until the right moment to charge and end the battle, the desperate fighting on the Black Water where all had turned on the discipline of the infantry and the three days at Badon, waiting for Oesc to break out into open ground.

He remembered people. Ambrosius Aurelianus, Caradoc and Gerontius, Marcellus and Theoderic, Vortipor, Agricola, Coelestius and, of course, good dependable Bedwyr, the charismatic Gawain and the common-sensical Cato: all men who had helped shape his life. He remembered his mother who had been the major force in moulding his character.

He had fought to make Britannia safe. He had tried to give it just government. Now he knew, deep down, that he was dying. His career had come full circle. It had started here in Deva all those years ago and here it would end. The surgeon could do no more. His mind moved to the future. Only the Combrogi could keep Britannia safe. Their oath to uphold Justice and Righteousness was all that stood between order and chaos. There must be no more Emperors. He had seen what the Imperium could do. It had filled Medraut with ambition and treason. It had alienated the Senates. Any new Emperor would face the same jealousies, the same opposition and even civil war.

He called Bedwyr to him. "My sword," he said, "Where is it?"

"Why, here of course. It is on the table by the door. I'll get it." Bedwyr lifted it and drew it from its scabbard. "I had it cleaned for you. It was caked with Medraut's blood." He held it for Artorius to see. It glittered in the light. The great ruby in the pommel flashed. It was a thing of great beauty.

"It must be hidden," said Artorius. "When I am gone, it will become something that men will covet. They will fight for it. The days of Empire are over. The Combrogi must take my place and not any one of them. If any man has that sword he will aspire to be Emperor and the rest will oppose him. Take it to the lake at Avalon by Glastonbury. Throw it far out into the water where none can find it."

Bedwyr went to Glastonbury. He was loath to throw such a valuable thing away. He took it from its scabbard and marvelled how the light flickered along the textured blade. He traced the intricate patterning on the hilt with its rich enamelling and the garnets glittering in their settings. He balanced it in his hand.

He took it to the abbot of the small monastery at Glastonbury and told him what Artorius had said. "I do not know that I should obey him in this," he said. "This is too valuable, too important, to be thrown away."

"It is a symbol of power," said the abbot. "Artorius is right. Wherever you put it, men will seek it, not for what it is but for what it represents. They will use it to make themselves tyrants. Artorius was an Emperor, and a good one too. Lesser men will seek his power, and that sword would give them leave to claim it. It must disappear. Do as he says. Throw it into the lake."

Bedwyr went to do so with a heavy heart. That sword, in Artorius' hand, had been the security of Britannia. He was momentarily tempted to keep it for himself. As Comes Britanniarum he could claim supreme power as superior over all the other officers but he knew many of them would resent that and would oppose him. He swung his arm and the sword flew in a glittering arc out over the water. As it splashed into the lake he felt his world shift. Certainties were no more. The future seemed unsure, more challenging and less safe. He rode back gloomily. No-one but himself and Gawain knew what had been done. Both sensed that Artorius knew he was dying. Both feared for the future.

Artorius died of his wound three weeks after the battle. He never knew that Winnifhoere had also died. Her coffin was sent to Deva and placed beside his. Bedwyr had decided that they should be buried at Glastonbury. Artorius had supported the new monasteries, and Glastonbury had been among the first in Britannia. Bedwyr, Cato and Gawain had all agreed that Artorius' death be kept secret for a time. They did not want the inevitable power-struggle between the Council of Britannia and the army to begin until they were ready for it. Artorius had entrusted the rule of Britannia to the Combrogi. They would need to meet to decide how they should rule without him.

The bodies were taken quietly to Glastonbury. The abbot said the funeral Mass and officiated as they were lowered into one grave, side by side in the cemetery alongside the church. There was to be no great monument raised over the grave, only a plain stone cross stating that here lay Artorius. As Gawain said, "Britannia is his monument. He saved it. He built it as it is. He needs no other monument."

Chapter 23: The aftermath.

The peace that Artorius had won continued after his death. The Combrogi, in their various postings continued his rule. They did not announce his death and kept secret his burial at Glastonbury. He had gone into semi-retirement to recover from his wound, they said, and wanted the Combrogi to rule in his name. The Council of Britannia was thwarted in its attempts to garner power to the senatorial class. Gawain, Bedwyr and Cato, the senior members of the brotherhood, kept all as it was while they lived. Bedwyr, as Comes Britanniarum, kept the army united. The Saxons remained cowed and quiescent.

Marcellus, in Armorica, fought the brothers, Budic and Maxentius, and was killed by them. Maxentius then expelled his brother, Budic, to rule the Kingdom alone. Budic fled to Demetia seeking justice where Agricola sympathised and sent him to Theoderic. Theoderic gave him ships and men and went with him to restore him to his rightful throne. Maxentius had been unjust. In the ensuing campaign Maxentius was defeated and Budic regained his half of the Kingdom.

Cato groomed his son, Marcus, also named as Connomorus, to succeed him. He nominated him as a member of the Combrogi. He took delight when Marcus gave him a grandson, Drustan. Now that there was no

Emperor, military command would devolve from father to son. It was a tendency that had started before the time of Artorius and now it became the norm. Eleutherius 'of the great army' at Eboracum would be followed by his son, Peredur. Military commanders were becoming more like petty kings.

On the death of Cato, Mark Connomorus made himself a King in Armorica and ruled Dumnonia in the same way. Each military command was headed by an officer who was de facto King in his own domain. However, while the Combrogi remained as a society and met annually, things went well. Gradually the name came to symbolise all the British. It was what they called themselves in distinction to the barbarians. The memory of Rome was fading fast.

The cities faded faster. The lack of trade and luxuries sapped their strength. People left them to farm homesteads outside. The markets declined. Calleva was abandoned. Men found they could live without great cities. Many senators gathered their wealth and migrated with their tenants to Armorica.

When a commander died having several sons, they divided his territorial and military command between them. Inevitably they competed to gain control of the whole. This was particularly true of north Wales in the lands of the Votadini, now named Gwynedd after Cunedda. Dynastic warfare became the norm there until a younger son of the dynasty, Maelgwyn, murdered his way to the throne.

The land was split into petty kingdoms based on subdivisions of Artorius' military settlement. Some remained powerful, Eboracum, Gwynedd, Dumnonia and Reged, the renamed Valentia. Others were small or too sparsely populated to be strong.

The armies still needed supplies and recruits. The fabric of Roman administration survived and the erogatores toured around to extract the tithes from a now unwilling civilian population. There were still magistrates and judges, but increasingly they were seen as tools of the kings and tyrants who now ruled. People began to look back at Artorius' rule as a golden age when things were done fairly and justly in contrast to how things had become.

For seventy five years the peace of Badon held. When it finally broke, the revolt was led not by the Angles of East Anglia, nor by the Saxons of Cantium, nor even by the South Saxons. It came from the federates stationed around Londinium, by Cambridge and on the isle of Vectis who struck into the midlands in 571. It is possible they rose against the exactions of the tax gatherers. They were of the few Saxons who dwelt within the Empire of Artorius and were thus liable to tax. The society of Britannia was rotting from within and weakened by plague which affected the Britons and not the Saxons and this new Saxon invasion plucked down one petty kingdom after another until it reached the borders of Wales. Truth to tell, the 'kings' were but leaders of war bands who could extort obedience from the civilians at the point of the sword but who lost all power and the ability to recruit as soon as they suffered even a slight defeat.

The plague hit the British hardest because they lived in tight communities and still traded with the continent. The disease came via Spain and Gaul to south Wales and then spread along the roman roads from city to city, possibly carried by the cavalry patrols. The Saxons, with no foreign trade and isolated within their respective territories, were effectively quarantined and had no harm from the plague that decimated the British. They saw the weakened state of the British armies, resented the rule of rapacious generals and broke out into the midlands.

Even so, the legacy of Artorius endured. In the west it became fashionable to name children 'Arthur' and the tradition continued among the later 'kings' of Glamorgan The Saxon conquerors themselves remembered an Empire of Britannia with one Law. They set out to copy it. The greatest of their Kings were considered great because of their law-giving. Eventually they made a land called England. To the north was another called Scotland and to the west, Wales. Dumnonia survived, reduced to just Cornwall, until the tenth century as an independent state ruled by the descendants of Count Cato.

The new England was populated by a minority of Saxons. The Britons remained as quiescent tillers of the land under Saxon lords. They were tired of the demands of professional war bands and felt better off and more secure under their new masters whose culture and language they rapidly adopted.

The memory of a just central government based on Law survived. That was the real achievement of Artorius. That was at the root of the epic poems sung by bards in Wales and Brittany on which the later legend of King Arthur was built. In defending Britannia and defeating the barbarians, he had laid the foundations of the future. His Empire could not endure because it lacked the economic base to support it. He had restored the forms of the old Imperial Government and the rule of law but, by the time of his death, it was clear that there was little of substance to the Empire of Britannia. Its strength lay with one old and famous man. However, England, Scotland and Wales came to be because of what he did. He preserved enough of Roman Civilisation long enough for it to influence the successor States and for that he fully deserves to be remembered, not as a mystical magic figure dressed in all the mediaeval trappings of Romance, but as a real historical ruler, the last Roman Emperor of the West - even if all that was left of it was the Diocese of Britannia.

Glossary and Notes.

Chapter 1.

Deva: Deva (Chester) had been the depot of the 2nd Legion from the 2nd century until it was moved to York and later to Richborough, probably in the 4th. Designed to accommodate six thousand men, by the 5th century it was far too large. It remained a military base, for much time unoccupied, with space for a greatly reduced garrison.

Vortigern: Vortigern is not a name but a title meaning 'great king', 'overlord' or simply 'Governor'. His real name may have been Vitalinus or Vitalis and he probably came from the Gloucester region. He would have had to have been elected by the Council of the Cities of Britain to whom Honorius had granted the right to organise their own defence.

Saxons: The word 'Saxon' is simply the Celtic word for foreigner. The Saxons did not call themselves such until at least the ninth century. 'Welsh' is the Saxon word for foreigner and, in Britain, was applied by the Saxons to all the Britons. The Saxons who came to Britain in the fifth century were of diverse origins coming from Denmark, the Netherlands, the Friesian islands and the banks of the river Elbe. There were some Franks among them too. Many had come earlier as settlers permitted to enter Britain. Hengest and Horsa were the first to be recruited as federates.

Principium: The headquarters of a military base or camp. In it were kept the standards and the image of the Emperor. It was the religious focus of the army unit as well as the administrative centre. It invariably stood at the centre of the camp facing the main gate.

Praetorium: The commander's quarters in a Roman fort usually positioned beside or immediately behind the principium.

Sarmatian Cavalry: The Roman army had always drawn its cavalry from subject peoples or from outside the Empire. The Sarmatians were originally horsemen from well beyond the frontiers of the Eastern Empire. They were heavy cavalry and used armoured horses. They were probably posted to Britain in the early 3rd century when Septimius Severus had brought a field army into Britain to restore order after a combined raid by the Irish, Picts and Saxons. Thereafter they replenished their ranks with local recruits so that by the 5th century they were totally British. Like any regiment anywhere, they maintained ancient traditions inherited from their foundation.

Decurion: The commander of a turma of cavalry. A turma was a company of thirty two men plus a standard bearer. The decurion was the cavalry equivalent of an infantry centurion.

Dux: The title, 'Dux', originally simply meant 'leader' and in military terms 'General'. In the Late Roman Empire it was used to describe the Commander-in-Chief of the frontier troops of a military Province. The Dux Britanniarum was the supreme commander of all the troops stationed in Britannia Secunda and Valentia which was basically the whole of north Britain to the north of the River Trent in the east and from Chester northwards in the west. He had one legion at York and numerous scattered detachments of auxiliaries at his disposal most of them stationed along Hadrian's Wall. Most of these auxiliaries were permanently based in their forts and did not move any distance from them. The theory that the Wall garrisons were no more than a civilian militia is inaccurate. They were still professional, trained troops and were as competent as any others but lacked numbers and resources.

Armour: Late roman cavalry wore long-sleeved tunics, trousers and chain mail armour that covered all the upper body and the upper arms. Their legs were unarmoured and this accounts for the scars that most cavalrymen had on their thighs. Their helmets were similar to those of the infantry except that the cheek guards also covered the ears. They were pierced with small holes to enable hearing. In a cavalry melee a man could expect to be attacked from the side and needed adequate protection. Also the neck guard was more vertical. If it protruded too far at the back and a man fell from his horse in such a helmet, it could break the neck. Heavy cavalry also armoured their horses with chain mail and leather chamfrons over the head. These were covered in bronze decorations and had domed eye guards. It is an error to assume that cavalry could not charge home without stirrups: the Celtic saddle gave a very secure seat and a cavalryman could strike an opponent at full gallop with confidence.

Glevum: Glevum (Gloucester) had started its history as a legion fortress.

When the frontier had moved northwards the fortress remained to become a city. It might have been designated as a Colonia, a city for retired veterans from the army. Its position on the Severn made it an attractive port and it had wharves and warehouses and much industry. It was surrounded by rich agricultural lands with many very large villas. When the third and fourth century barbarian incursions fatally weakened the economy of Gaul, Britain had experienced an economic boom and Glevum became one of the richest cities in the Western Empire. The villas of the west country were often huge and palatial, some of them being equal in size to Blenheim Palace, and reflected the vast wealth of their owners.

Sorbiodunum: Modern Old Sarum, the origin of Salisbury. It stood on the road from Winchester to Bath and Gloucester. It became a small Roman village but was strategically important, dominating the great Salisbury Plain.

Tribune: Originally a political rank in Rome as an elected representative of the common people, the rank of Tribune had become a military rank. A Tribune was an officer attached to a legion and at the disposal of its commander for virtually any duty. The legion's second in command was a tribune of senatorial rank. In addition there were five equestrian tribunes. Often they were used to command auxiliary units, such as cavalry detachments. A full cavalry wing of some thousand horsemen, would be commanded by a Prefect, but there were no units of such a size in Britain by the 5th century.

Optio: Second in command of a century of infantry (80 men). In battle the centurion stood in front of the century and the optio behind. The optio had a long staff with which he kept the rear rank of the century in line. When armies broke in battle, they almost always broke from the rear. The optio was there to steady the men and prevent any from fleeing.

Chapter 2.

Mail armour: By the 5th century the standard Roman armour was of chain mail doubled over the shoulders. The old segmented armour of the first century had proved too expensive to manufacture and too difficult to maintain. Its bronze hooks and buckles caused electrolytic corrosion of the iron and often fell off. Scale armour was also used, particularly by standard bearers and cavalry since it took a high polish and made them look more impressive. Scale armour was easier to make but more difficult to maintain since scales often fell off. Most of the barbarian enemies of the Western Roman Empire used very little armour, relying on padded leather jerkins instead. Only chiefs could afford mail armour and they often used captured Roman armour.

Pilum: The pilum was a throwing spear. It had a wooden shaft some four feet long topped by a spear head of some two to three feet in length. This consisted of a thin, soft iron shaft with a tiny pyramidal point. When thrown, these spears could penetrate armour and shields. The thin iron was designed to bend if it hit the ground or impaled a shield thus preventing the pilum being thrown back by the enemy. In the late Roman Army the pilum had often been replaced by short, heavy darts that were carried clipped into the back of the shield but the pilum was still retained as a basic infantry weapon. To increase their hitting power, pila were often given lead weights on the base of the iron shaft. Most legionaries also had lighter javelins available.

Diocese: Britain was originally a Province of the Diocese of Gaul. In the later Empire it became a separate Diocese divided into five smaller Provinces. The Emperors thought that by dividing administrative areas into smaller units there would be less chance of local officials gaining enough power to challenge for the Imperium. This too probably explains the division of the army into small field units and static frontier forces. Emperors were more afraid of coups and usurpers than of external enemies.

Chapter 3.

Vexillum: Infantry century standards were poles with a hand or an ornamental spear-head at the top and discs attached below. A legion would have an eagle standard too. Cavalry used simpler standards that could be borne by a rider. These were banners in the form of a rectangular cloth suspended from a cross-bar near the top of a pole. The foot of the pole was tapered to an iron-shod point so that it could be stuck in the ground in camp and, possibly, serve as a weapon in battle. The top of the pole often had a decorative spearhead. The cavalry also used the dragon standard in the same way as a legion used the eagle.

Ravenna: Since just before the sack of Rome in 410 AD, the Emperors of the West had made Ravenna, near Venice, their capital. It was secure in the midst of marshes and was conveniently placed to be near the Alpine frontiers. The Emperors were now more concerned with defending Italy than the rest of the Western Empire.

Caradoc: The later Saxon Kings of Wessex traced their lineage back to Cerdic. 'Cerdic' is not a Saxon name. It is a corruption of the British, 'Caradoc'. He had to have been a man of power and importance in late Roman Britain and must have been based in Venta Belgarum (Winchester). The fact that he was adopted as the ancestor of the Wessex Saxon Kings and was killed at Badon shows him to have been a British rebel. The choice of Winchester as the Wessex Capital is probably due to Caradoc having ruled there.

Calleva: Calleva (Silchester) was a small Roman city. It had been fortified in the third century. It is likely that it was never fully occupied or had most of its buildings made of wood leaving little trace for archaeology. The revolt of Hengest had reached as far as Calleva but the city had survived. Archaeological evidence shows that in the fifth century it was in decline. Corn-drying kilns had been set up inside the city, showing that the citizens felt insecure outside the walls. It survived well into the sixth century but was abandoned later.

Armorica: Brittany. This part of the Roman Diocese of Gaul had been very much damaged by the peasant revolt of the late third century. On the defeat of the usurper, Magnus Maximus, his British troops had been given Armorica in return for keeping order there. The Saxon revolt in Britain had led many of the landowners to migrate to their cousins in Armorica where they established small kingdoms. Brittany still bears names showing their origins - Cornuaille and Dumnonie, for example.

Ballistae: Roman catapults in the form of large crossbows mounted on a swivel. Unlike a crossbow where the energy is gained by flexing the arms, the ballista derived its force from twisted cords of sinew that tightened as the two separate arms were drawn back by a rack and pinion. In good condition they were extremely powerful, firing iron bolts and/or stones. In poor condition they could endanger their operators if the cords snapped and the arms flew backwards.

Chapter 4.

The River Medway: The Medway is the largest of the rivers that flow into the Thames estuary from Kent. It is a wide river and thus forms a good natural frontier. Although the road from Canterbury to London crossed it by a bridge, the river is often shallow enough to ford.

Saxon war gear: The Saxons all fought in much the same way as the other Germanic peoples. They favoured long, heavy spears and battle-axes. Only the richest men could afford swords. These were long and heavy with a rounded end to the blade which made them not very apt for thrusting. They were intended as cutting weapons, and, being some three feet in length, required space for the swordsman to swing the weapon. Few Saxons used armour other than simple helmets. They relied primarily on the heavy, round shield for protection. This was made of solid wood and had a protruding iron boss over the hand-grip which could also serve as a weapon.

Saxon standards: Like most Germanic peoples, the Saxons fought as war-bands raised by kings and chiefs from among their tenants. They tried to copy the Romans whose armies had always seemed invincible. The Romans used military standards as rallying points in battle. The Saxons developed their own to indicate where a chief stood in the battle line.

Chapter 5.

Londinium: Londinium (London) was in a uniquely strategic position. It occupied the north bank of the Thames at the lowest crossing point on that river. It had been where the first century Roman invasion had forced a crossing before advancing to Camulodunum (Colchester). For a long time it had been the administrative Capital. Its prime importance was as a port receiving practically all the trade from Gaul and the Rhinelands. The advent of the Saxons and their rebellion had severed its links with the continent and had impoverished it but its strategic position between the Kentish and East Anglian Saxon settlements made it a vitally important city.

Federates: The late Roman Empire often recruited barbarian war-bands to help defend the frontiers. These were not auxiliaries who were fully part of the army and served under Roman officers. These were tribal groups who served under their own chiefs and fought in their own ways. They were always stationed well away from their homelands. The forces of Hengest and Horsa had been recruited as federates by Vortigern. Federates were always a risky investment, requiring land and supplies in return for their loyalty.

The line of villages near the crest of the downs to the south and north of London show where these new Saxon federates were placed. Archaeology has shown them to have been a different people to those of Kent and also of those of most of East Anglia, having very different ornament. There seems never to have been any intermingling of these Saxons with the Anglians or the Kentish Saxons until the later sixth century. They maintained themselves separate, and possibly hostile.

Chapter 6.

The Sword in the stone: This would have been a standard cavalry sword called a 'spatha'. Its blade would have been between 70 centimetres and 90 centimetres in length, some 5 centimetres wide and tapered some 10 centimetres from the end of the blade to a sharp point. A short cross-guard could protect the hand and a large round pommel helped balance the blade. Such swords were good as both slashing and stabbing weapons and their length was such that a mounted man could strike down at an opponent on foot. In the late Empire the spatha had become the standard infantry sword too, replacing the shorter gladius.

Forged: Most weapons were made of iron. They blunted quickly in action, sometimes bent and occasionally broke. Forging iron was a complicated process involving heating, beating and then cooling it over and over again. The iron was heated in white hot charcoal and some of this carbon was beaten into it on the anvil. Quenching the hot iron before re-heating it tempered the metal. The result was carbonised steel which took a sharper, harder edge and was resistant to bending or breaking. The best swords were made from several bars of iron beaten and twisted together as a sort of laminate. Steel is lighter than iron as well as being stronger.

Chapter 7:

Small garrisons: Scattered across Britain in all the places where Saxons, Irish and British faced each other in the fifth century are places with names such as 'Amberley' and 'Ambrosden'. The root of these names is neither Saxon nor British. There are seven such place names between London and Cambridge, spaced on and beside the Ermine Street. One stands near the Medway. Three overlook the lands of the South Saxons. There are three more north of the confluence of the Avon and the Severn and one in the Thames gap. The root seems to be Latin and derived from the name, 'Ambrosius'. If Ambrosius had raised a new army, and he must have done since the army of the north was unavailable, it would have been called the Ambrosiaci. It would have given its name to its garrisons. It is significant that several of these names are associated with earthworks.

Camulodunum: Colchester had been the first city established in Britain by the Romans. It was a Colonia, a city provided for veterans of the legions who had first conquered Britain under Claudius in the 1st century. It had easy access to the sea. It had been destroyed by Boudicca but after her defeat was rebuilt. It is the only credible place which could have been the Camelot of the Arthurian legends. All other Arthurian 'residences' are associated with cities, so his capital must have been one too. Tintagel has absolutely no Arthurian connection. Camulodunum is the only place with a name that could be bowdlerised into 'Camelot'. Its walls and bastions could well have given rise to the 'many towered' Camelot of the legend. Its strategic position would make it a logical choice for the Capital of the Diocese once Kent had been ceded to the Saxons, London being relatively unhealthy, notorious for fevers and too close to Kent.

Chapter 8:

Tribunal: The lectern from which speeches were delivered in Senate meetings. It normally stood in the centre of the Senate House below the praesidium.

Praesidium: The raised platform at the end of a Senate House with a seat from which the Emperor, or in a city, the City Prefect, presided over meetings.

Buried bullion: Many roman archaeological sites have reports of coin hoards. These are often explained as the panic burial of wealth too heavy to carry when fleeing barbarian raids. This is unlikely since many such hoards have been found in places where there is no evidence of such raids. Another explanation is as offerings to the gods. It is strange how readily archaeologists explain anything they cannot immediately understand as being 'ritual'. Many such hoards are in the form of large pots sunk into the ground and filled with coins and jewellery. The coins are often of many different dates implying either regular depositing or long-term saving of monies. Usually the rim of the pot is close to the surface and a stone slab was placed to seal the pot and then covered with turves. Many such hoards have been discovered by later deep ploughing smashing the pots and then turning up the coins. In the later Roman Empire tax evasion was the normal habit of the rich. Since the erogatores (tax-gatherers) had right of entry and search, it is possible that many such coin hoards were actually buried to avoid an accurate assessment of wealth being made and thus less tax being demanded.

Chapter 9.

South Cadbury: South Cadbury hill fort was refortified in the late fifth century. Some people have thought of it as Camelot, King Arthur's capital, but this is totally unrealistic. It is not in any strategic place. It is too small. Its name does not match. It was given reinforced ramparts and strong wooden gates. It possibly had wooden buildings inside. It is more likely to have been some sort of military depot and its position between Salisbury Plain and the Cotswolds where horses were bred and much grain grown may well explain its function. Several other hill-forts show signs of re-occupation at this time and may also have been military depots or bases for small detachments of troops. Once taxation began to be in kind rather than in coin there would have been a need for defended depots.

Dinas Emrys: Dinas Emrys lies at what was the border between Gwynedd and the Lleyn Peninsula. Excavation of the site proved it to have been occupied in the late fifth and early sixth centuries. Emrys is the later Welsh form of the name Ambrosius. Its strategic siting and its name bespeak of a garrison watching out for Irish raids from their settlements to the west.

Chapter 10.

Black Water: We have one historical source that tells us that Arthur fought four battles on the River Dubglas. This translates as Black Water. The source tells us that it lay in the lands about Lincoln. There are many rivers hereabouts and any one of them might have been called the Black Water; it was a very common river name. It might have been the River Witham or the Glen or the Welland. Its location tells us the strategy. A victory hereabouts would secure Lincoln and the road to the north. Whether there were four separate battles or just one of such importance that it merited four verses in an epic poem we cannot know.

Saxon withdrawal: Throughout much of Lincolnshire and Northamptonshire there are many very early Saxon cemeteries. They are fairly easily dated by their burial and cremation customs and by their grave goods. In the late fifth century most go out of use. Later Saxon cemeteries commence use some seventy five years later and some actually cut into the earlier cemeteries showing that the people who used them were ignorant of the earlier ones. The only explanation for this occurrence is that the earlier Saxons had abandoned their lands. Such a wholesale withdrawal had to have been either through massive defeat or as a result of a diplomatic settlement, and possibly both. The only person who could have enforced such a withdrawal was Arthur or someone very like him.

Not all the Saxons withdrew, but those who remained were very few and very isolated and thus of no threat.

Chapter 11.

Winnifhoere: In the legends of King Arthur his wife is named as Guinivere. This name comes down to us through the French versions of the tale which themselves derive from Breton originals. Translating this back into English, the GUI becomes WI, hence Winnifhoere. (The Welsh 'Guinivere' came into the Welsh language via the French romances.) It is not at all improbable that Arthur would have a Saxon wife. Treaties were often sealed with marriages. Vortigern had married Hengest's daughter and it is perfectly possible that Arthur was involved in a similar treaty relationship. If so, it is most likely that the treaty was with King Icel and Winnifhoere was his daughter.

Forks: Forks had come into use among the Roman upper classes in the late Empire starting in Byzantium. Roman forks had just two prongs. Every diner would have their own personal knife for cutting meat from the joints. Spoons were normal for sauces and soups. Forks were the fashionable dining settings of the rich. The poor still used fingers. Bread was used for cleaning knives and forks between courses and for wiping plates.

Chapter 12.

Death of Gerontius: Gerontius, Geraint in Welsh, has his own legends. The name is common among the Cornovii. He died in battle at a place called Llongborth. This translates as 'the port of the warships'. The most logical place for this is Portsmouth (Portus Adurnis) which had been the westernmost base of the Classis Britannica, the British fleet of the 3rd and 4th centuries. The occupation of the Isle of Wight by Jutes from Kent and their attempt to gain Portsmouth gives the context of the battle.

Oesc: Oesc had been the chief of the tiny Saxon settlement near Bamburgh. This little colony had been planted by Hengest and Vortigern to prevent Picts sailing round the end of Hadrian's Wall. It had joined in the Saxon revolt, but was too small to withstand the field army of York. On Hengest's death, Oesc saw a chance of greater glory and power in Kent. Some traditions make him a son or nephew of Hengest.

Aelle: The South Saxons had occupied the coastal strip of Sussex between Beachy Head and the River Arun. They had been contained there. Aelle was their king. Several times he had tried to expand his isolated territory but was penned back. Ambrosius had placed three garrisons atop the downs to watch over the Saxons. The Devil's Dyke above Brighton may have been a frontier marker.

Fords over the Tamesis: The logical meeting place for armies coming together from Sussex, Kent and Winchester and aiming to strike westwards towards Bath and Gloucester would be around Reading or Hungerford, close to the Thames gap. Thence there were three possible routes to the west. They could pass via Hungerford and Wallingford through the gap and strike down westwards directly towards Gloucester. They could ascend the hills and use the Icknield Way and its extension, the old ridgeway, or they could move through the Kennet valley, both routes going towards Bath.

Chapter 13.

Badon: Historians have tried for years to identify the site of the Battle of Badon. All we know is that it involved a three day siege and that Arthur was the victor, killing 960 enemies. We know it was the decisive battle in which both Oesc and Caradoc were killed. Many historians place the battle on the ridgeway but this is unlikely: the open down-land would have been too favourable to cavalry and the Saxons would not have risked going that way. Others place it at Batheaston, near Bath. This strikes me as far too far to the west. No competent Roman general with strong cavalry forces, and thus good intelligence of enemy concentrations, would have allowed a large Saxon host to penetrate so far into the heartland of Roman Britain. If he had, he would have been seen as incompetent.

The logical site is Great Bedwyn in the Kennet valley. It fits the context of the campaign and the name Bedwyn, which could have been Badwn in the British tongue, could well have been Badon in Latin. It could well have been the name of one of the two villas in the valley. The topography and the old hill fort at Chisbury Manor, which could have been named Mons Badonicus, also suit what we know of the warfare of the time. It is inconceivable that Arthur and his cavalry were the besieged, since his greater mobility would have ensured that the Saxons could not entrap him. We know the 'siege' lasted three days, and that is significant. An army cooped up on a hill without water must, perforce, break out after three days.

Horse burials: Near the hill fort at Chisbury Manor, between it and the spur of the Savernake forest, are two tumuli. They are assumed to be bronze-age burials but they are not in a typical place. Bronze-age tumuli are invariably sited to appear on the horizon above a route-way such as a river. These are not. They are half way down the hillside just below its steeper gradient. Roman cavalrymen would bury their dead horses after a battle. Horses and riders had an affinity one for the other and the men would not accept that their dead horses should be left as carrion for the wolves.

The chapel: The hill fort above Great Bedwyn has a thirteenth century chapel built on its eastern side in a breach of the original rampart. The chancel is lower than the nave. Its siting is distinctly odd. It has to have been built in its present form as a replacement of an earlier religious building which must have had some significant reason for its position. The breaching of the rampart to accommodate the chapel proves it to be post Roman conquest and it is not where a pagan Roman temple might have been. It seems logical that it was made in the late, and therefore Christian, Roman Empire. It is not where an early Saxon church would have been and its siting makes the chancel lower than the nave. It never served as a parish church. If it was a totally new foundation in the thirteenth century it would have been built on a much easier site. Its dedication to St. Martin is also significant: such dedications were most popular in the fifth century among the monastic reformers who took their inspiration from St Martin of Tours. If Bedwyn was indeed the site of Badon and the hill fort had played a major role in the battle, the slighting of the defences would make sense. So too would be the erection of a shrine. Arthur had fought wearing a cloak with the image of the cross - his victory might well have been commemorated with a religious building. It is also possible that the circuit of ramparts might have made an excellent site for a monastery - all early monasteries were surrounded by earth banks delineating the sacred area from the outside world.

Chapter 14:

Count of Dumnonia: The title of Comes, Count, came into use in the late 3rd century. It signified an independent command for a specific purpose. There had been a Count of the Saxon Shore in Britain, with a chain of forts from East Anglia to Portsmouth, garrisons and a fleet. The commander of the field army was given the title too (Comes Britanniarum). Someone given the task of driving the Irish out of Devon and Cornwall and keeping them out, might well qualify for this rank. The inclusion of Hampshire and Dorset (the lands of the Belgae centred on Winchester) in an enlarged Dumnonia is the logical result of the rebellion and defeat of Caradoc.

Chapter 15.

Atrium: The entrance hall of a Roman house. This was used as a reception room for visitors, only trusted friends being permitted any further access to the more private quarters.

Circular setting: The 'Knights of the Round Table' is very much a 13th century ideal, interpolated into the Arthurian Legend. However, there was a long tradition of officer societies in the Roman army. These were often religious, the worship of Mithras for example, and acted rather like masonic lodges. It would not be anything odd if Arthur had instituted something of the same sort among his senior officers. The name, Combrogi (later Cymru), became what the British kingdoms of the sixth and seventh centuries called themselves. It might well have originated in the time of Arthur.

Caliburn: The origin of the name 'Excalibur'. It is unclear whether the sword was so named in Arthur's lifetime but it was so named in Breton record soon after his death. Legends grew up as to its origin, its magical properties and those of its scabbard. Swords were often named, sometimes by their owners and often by those who followed their owners. A successful warrior chief was often credited with having magical weapons - possibly to excuse those whom he defeated. Some legends give Arthur two swords, the one he took from the stone and one he was given by the Lady of the Lake. It would be unlikely that a warrior would use two swords, so I have stuck to the more traditional story.

Chapter 16.

Theoderic: The name Theoderic is well attested in Welsh record and also in Brittany. It is a specifically Visigothic name in the late 5th and early 6th centuries. Three places in Devon and Cornwall are said to have become his estates and he is known to have intervened in Brittany. All his estates are above harbours which would argue that he had ships. The Visigothic Kingdom of Aquitaine had maintained a fleet at Bordeaux to prevent Saxon sea-borne raids. The expulsion of the Visigoths from Gaul by the Franks might well have led a Visigothic Admiral who had lost his base to seek employment elsewhere.

Saxon and Roman ships: The Saxons were good seamen but used only large open boats with oars. Their ships were purely for transport of people and goods. They were built generally of pine and were relatively fragile. Roman ships were bigger and heavier with sails as well as oars. There were distinct classes of ships. Merchant ships were broad and had few oars. Warships were longer and narrower with rams and many oars. All could sail before the wind or with the wind on either beam but could not tack into the wind. Adverse winds would force the crew to resort to the oars or to heave to until the wind changed.

Chapter 17.

Coelestius: At the time of Vortigern the Dux Britanniarum at York had been Coelius, later called 'Old King Cole'. Most of the later dynasties north of Hadrian's Wall claimed descent from him. Some of the later dynasties of northern Britain claimed the same. The genealogies are confusing. Most of them probably refer to Roman Prefects appointed by the Dux to supervise the northern tribes and the north British dynasties probably derive from Roman officers who established hereditary rights in their commands but all deriving their power originally from the Dux. We do not know who was Dux under Arthur but he was likely the son or grandson of Coelius who was almost certainly the last officially appointed Dux Britanniarum under the Emperor Honorius.

Votadini: The Votadini were a Celtic tribe who occupied the land between Hadrian's Wall and Edinburgh. At the time of Vortigern their chief had been Cunedda who had taken half his tribe into north Wales to confront the Irish who were colonising the Lleyn Peninsula. Later, probably in the time of Arthur, their new chief, Marianus also moved to Wales. Cunedda gave his name to Gwynedd and Marianus names Merioneth. The remnants of the tribe in their original lands became the Goddodin who were famed in later history for their prowess as cavalry. This they had had to learn: both Gwynedd and Merioneth did not use horsemen. Arthur's wars had proved the value of cavalry that eventually became the most important branch of the sixth century British forces.

Chapter 18.

Demetia: The Pembrokeshire peninsula was only ever nominally Roman. Most of Wales was sparsely populated and too mountainous to sustain Roman agriculture based on villas. The only fully Romanised part of Wales was the land of the Silures around Caerleon where the land was good and there were easy communications eastwards. Here there were Roman villas and direct trade with the continent. To the west Roman rule was enforced by scattered garrisons in small forts. From the 3rd century onwards the Irish had begun to colonise and by the end of the 5th century had developed a single Kingdom of Demetia.

Lleyn Peninsula: The name, Lleyn, denotes the 'men of Leinster' which was the origin of the Irish colonists who had settled there. The Irish of Demetia seem to have come from Munster. The Irish had also made large inroads in Mona, the Isle of Anglesey.

Chapter 19.

Erogatores: Roman tax collectors. These were part of the civilian bureaucracy and were backed by troops. They toured their tax areas to assess what each tax-payer should pay. They had a fixed quota to collect. As low-ranking civilians they had been open to bribery by the rich and had had to make up their quotas by over-taxing the poor. This is what had caused the peasant rebellion in Brittany. If they were recruited from the officer corps of the army they would be less likely to be over-awed by rich, aristocratic senators.

Vicarii: The Roman Empire was divided into dioceses and provinces. Britain had originally been a province within the diocese of Gaul. Later it had become a diocese itself and been split into two and later four and then, finally, into five smaller provinces. Each provincial civil government was headed by a Vicar reporting direct to Rome. These men had been professional bureaucrats and ranked lower in the social scale than senators but had real power as long as there was an effective Emperor backing them. The last Province, Valentia, was probably a division of Britannia Secunda comprising the western side of the Pennines. It was set up after the great joint raid by Saxons, Picts and Irish and was probably designed to strengthen the western defences against the Irish. Britannia Secunda had always been a military province and Valentia is likely to have been too. Its military units are listed separately in late Roman records implying a degree of separation from the command at York. After Arthur's time it probably became the Kingdom of Reged.

Rectores: Roman provinces had a variety of population centres. The most important were the cities, usually founded on old tribal capitals. There were also towns, often at road junctions, and villages, often alongside the wayside posting houses of the Imperial post service. Only the cities and the largest towns had Senates since only such places had men rich enough to gain that rank. Local government was based on the cities and towns and each of these had a Rector heading the administration of the town and its surrounding area. In the military provinces local rule was maintained by detached non-commissioned officers called beneficiarii, rather like the district officers in colonial Africa and India.

Chapter 20.

Cunetio: Cunetio (Mildenhall) had been a small Roman market town at the head of the Vale of Pewsey. It had probably begun as a small settlement around a mansio, an inn, on the road from Silchester to Bath. It probably acted as a tax centre where the corn tax could be gathered. It had been important enough to get walls in the third century but was very small. By the fifth century it was struggling and was later abandoned.

Magistrates: Magistrates were more than just local judges. They were responsible for public works and festivals too. These they paid for out of their own pockets and only the senatorial class were wealthy enough to perform the role. Some less wealthy senators tried to avoid election so as to save themselves the costs. They could do this by getting aristocratic promotion or by taking church orders. Others succumbed to the temptation of bribes so as to finance their duties. Corruption was endemic in the later Roman Empire.

Chapter 21.

Dyke: The Wansdyke is a long ditch and bank that encloses what would have been Dumnonia and the lands of Winchester. It follows the bounds of Dorset and Hampshire. It is not continuous. Some historians have interpreted it as a series of works to channel prey for the hunt but this seems fanciful; it is too vast a work. It certainly was not defensive: its gaps would allow any defence to be outflanked and its length would have required a huge army to man it. Like most dykes, it seems to have been a frontier marker. The name 'Wansdyke' was what the 7th century Saxons called it - 'Woden's Dyke', showing that they did not know who had built it or why, and implying its existence before their arrival.

Chapter 22.

Eleutherius: 'Eleutherius of the Great Army' is attested as ruling York in the years following Arthur's death. The 'great army' could only be the descendant of the Field army of the Dux Britanniarum, the remnants of the Sixth Legion and the auxiliaries along Hadrian's Wall, and Eleutherius' Roman name implies descent from the Roman administration of the north. Whether he was the son of the Dux or simply an officer who took power for himself we cannot know, but throughout the post-Roman world the hereditary principle was taking hold.

Camlann: The name means 'crooked glen'. A glen is a valley and implies hill country. We have no evidence at all as to where the battle was. It is pointless trying to guess. There are crooked glens in every hilly region of Britain and any of them could have had the name. All we know is that in such a place there was a battle where Arthur and Medraut fell. Tradition has it that Medraut was Arthur's opponent in the battle but we cannot be certain even of this. I have followed the tradition since it seems the most probable.

Avalon: The name 'Avalon' is prosaic and common. It means 'Apple Town'. Tradition names Glastonbury Tor as Avalon and it used to be part of an island in a great marshy lake. Glastonbury nearby was one of the first monasteries in Britain. Monasticism was a new phenomenon in the Western Christian Church and was spreading rapidly. It took many forms. Some monasteries were set up in the great villas whose owners had taken monastic vows, like that of St. Illtud in South Wales. Others were groups of hermits who banded together in the wilderness to pray and fast. All had different rules. Dissatisfaction with the corrupt civil government and the increasing demands of war-bands led many to enter the monastic life. The greatest expansion of monasticism happened after the death of Arthur, when civil war and dynastic conflict broke the unity of Britain but the first monasteries began in his lifetime.

Glastonbury Abbey: Possibly the oldest monastic site in England, Glastonbury is steeped in mythology. The legend of Joseph of Arimathea and the Christ Child is one of these. The tradition that Arthur was buried there with Guinivere is very old. The ruins of the present abbey lie somewhat beyond the original church which was almost certainly a simple wattle and daub building. The late twelfth century discovery of the grave of Arthur and Guinivere might be genuine or simply an attempt by the Abbey to gain prestige and become a pilgrimage centre. This is somewhat unlikely since abbeys wanted Saints rather than legendary heroes to attract pilgrims. Glastonbury claimed to be the burial place of St Patrick. The lead tablet from the original grave seems to have borne writing in early tenth century script which might have been difficult for a late twelfth century monk to forge. This tablet might have been placed in the grave when the original tomb was buried by the raising of the surface of the cemetery in the time of St. Dunstan, in the tenth century, and the memorial cross and inscription being removed. That there was a real grave that contained the bodies of a tall man and a blonde haired woman and its position close to the bounds of the original church is not contested. Whether they were the remains of Arthur and Guinivere we cannot know but equally the possibility that they were must be admitted. In 1190 the bodies were exhumed and later reburied in the nave of the rebuilt abbey church. Excavation has identified the site of the original grave.

Chapter 23.

The break-up of Britain: It was the lack of any strong central authority that led to the fragmentation of the old Roman Diocese. Each commander held his own area with his own troops. They gathered their own supplies. Inevitably the army became unpopular with the civilians from whom they took corn and horses. Over time each military command became a petty kingdom ruled by a military elite. The war-bands could force obedience but if they were defeated the allegiance of the common folk would be withheld. It is notable that the longest surviving British Kingdoms were in the north and far west, the most long-lived outside Wales being that of the Cornovii in Cornwall.

War bands exist to fight. When there was no obvious enemy it was inevitable that they would eventually fight each other. This is amply recorded among the kingdoms of northern Britain. The division of Kingdoms among the sons of a king led inevitably to dynastic warfare. It was constant civil war and dynastic violence that weakened the kingdoms and lost them the support of the common people and the remnants of the wealthy landowners. It was this above all else that led thousands to take to the monastic life.

Most of the British Kingdoms relied over heavily, or even exclusively, on cavalry with the exception of the Kingdom of Gwynedd. This was a change from Roman practice. The Roman army had always been a mix of infantry and cavalry and usually had greater numbers of the former. The Saxon wars, where cavalry had proved the most effective means of defeating the Saxons, had tilted the balance away from infantry. Cavalry are expensive to maintain and hence the armies became very small. When the Saxons finally broke out into the midlands they overwhelmed the weaker kingdoms with ease. Rivalries among the British war-bands prevented concerted action. The Saxons had learned to fight in closer order behind their shield-wall and could thus face down cavalry attacks. When British Kingdoms fell there was usually quite a long time before Saxon colonists moved in.

The British civilian population simply transferred obedience to the new authorities. They soon adopted Saxon dress, culture and even language. Where Christianity had never been strong, as was the case in the countryside, it was easy to adopt the religion of the conquerors. There are many places such as 'Walton' and 'Comberton' which show where Britons continued to live under Saxon rule. It is a gross error to imagine that all the Britons fled west to become the Welsh. Saxon Britain had a majority of Britons and a minority of Saxons. Even as late as the eighth century, some Saxon Kingdoms were ruled by men with British names and Saxon law made provision for 'Welsh' freemen and bondsmen right up to the time of the Norman Conquest of 1066. Some of the former served Saxon Kings as royal officials.

What is noteworthy is that the later Saxon Kingdoms mainly followed established Roman boundaries. Northumbria eventually comprised all of Britannia Secunda plus the lands of the Votadini north of Hadrian's Wall. Mercia comprised the majority of Britannia Prima excluding its Welsh lands. Wessex occupied most of Maxima Caesariensis except for the small enclaves of Kent and Essex and the independent Saxon Kingdoms of East Anglia which followed the old civitas borders. Wessex also absorbed Dumnonia which had been split from Britannia Prima in the late fifth or early sixth century. Valentia remained in British hands as the Kingdom of Reged until it was absorbed into the larger Kingdom of Strathclyde and thus became part of Scotland until the reign of William Rufus. Only Flavia Caesariensis did not become a separate Saxon Kingdom but was partitioned and fought over until finally becoming part of Mercia.

The Saxons named most of their own settlements but Roman town and city sites retained their Roman names even if somewhat altered. Any walled town received the ending, 'cester', 'chester' or 'caster' as a matter of course. Lindum Colonia was shortened to Lincoln. Glevum had Cester tagged onto it and became Gloucester. Rivers and hills retained their Romano-British names. The names survived because the majority of the people knew these places by these names from before the arrival of their new Saxon rulers.

Acknowledgements

I am indebted to many writers for the historical content of this book. In particular I am indebted to John Morris' 'The Age of Arthur'. His book, though much maligned by some academics and archaeologists, is the only comprehensive and scholarly book about fifth and sixth century Britain which brings together what we know of Britain, Ireland, Scotland, Brittany and France. It contains much insight and makes more sense than many of the alternative interpretations of the period. Much of the adverse criticism of the work seems to me to be more academic pique than genuine critique. Archaeologists are poorly placed to criticise history: their discipline is the interpretation of 'finds' and contributes to historical understanding but, when taken beyond the evidence in the ground, often leads to fanciful and sometimes ludicrous conclusions when divorced from the wider historical picture.

I am also indebted to Adrian Goldsworthy for his 'The Complete Roman Army', particularly for its analysis of the later Roman Army in its dispositions and equipment. 'The Quest for Arthur's Britain' edited by Geoffrey Ashe which gives comprehensive accounts of important archaeological investigations of 'Dark Age' sites purported to be 'Arthurian' was also a useful source, if only to eliminate most of the legendary Arthurian sites.

I must thank my long-suffering wife who put up with my long periods monopolising the computer and my friend, Tim Wander, to whom I gave the onerous task of proof-reading the text.

My ultimate thanks must go to the series of talented History teachers who gave me my abiding interest in History in the days when teachers were permitted to inspire their pupils rather than merely force them through the examination sausage machine. I was lucky that I attended a school that chose to study Mediaeval European History rather than Modern History at 'A Level', a choice no longer open to most schools.

In writing this book I have been struck by the remarkable similarities of our own times and those of Arthur. The increasing gap between the rich and the poor, the evasion of tax by the rich, either individually or corporately, the attempt by the wealthy and by corporations to dominate government to their own advantage and their blindness as to the increasing dangers in the modern world are all symptomatic of a declining civilisation. The decline in religious belief and the concomitant decline in moral standards, the strident claiming of 'rights' without responsibilities and the demand that governments undertake more and more of what should be the role of moral individuals in society reinforces this. We live with the barbarians at our gates if not already amongst us. If this book leads any to question how things are going today and leads to reform and long term positive change it will have been worth the writing.

The Author

Peter Monaghan was born in Surrey in 1945. Educated at the John Fisher School, he commenced training for the African missions with the White Fathers and then as a teacher at St. Mary's College, Strawberry Hill, studying History and English. His special interests were mediaeval history and military history and he developed a growing fascination with the so-called Dark Ages, the period between the fall of the Western Roman Empire and the emergence of the mediaeval successor states.

He taught in London and Coventry, History, English and Religious Education, and then transferred into supporting pupils whose first language was not English. He worked across the curriculum helping these pupils develop competence in English and advising other teachers as to how to make their lessons easier of access for such pupils. He was horrified by the many inaccuracies and often downright errors in most text books and the over-reliance many teachers placed on them.

Disenchanted with the stultifying effects of the National Curriculum, he took early retirement and went to live in Spain to paint and write. This book is the result of much reading and reflection and is intended as an antidote to the modern fashion of reworking the legend of King Arthur with extra magic, aliens, anachronistic events and anything else that can be filched from history or fantasy to make 'good' television. This book does not claim to be an accurate history, but rather a balanced account of what might have been within the limits of what we know.